Overspill

Kay Inckle

SRL PUBLISHING

SRL Publishing Ltd
London

www.srlpublishing.co.uk

First published worldwide by SRL Publishing in 2025
This paperback edition first published in 2026

SRL PUBLISHING
THINKING DIFFERENTLY, DELIVERING CHANGE

Text copyright © Kay Inckle, 2025

Hardback ISBN: 978-1915-073-52-5
Paperback ISBN: 978-1915-073-53-2

1 3 5 7 9 10 8 6 4 2

A CIP catalogue record for this book is available from the British Library

SRL Publishing is a climate positive publisher offsetting more carbon emissions than it emits.

Chapter 1

Megan opened the balcony door and angled herself towards the street. The clapping had started, she had four and a half minutes. Turning back inside, she bolted the door behind her and wheeled quickly across the flat to the front door. She checked it was on the latch. Then she checked again, and again. It was eating into her precious time but she couldn't afford to take any risks. Jay hadn't given her keys and she had to be able to get back inside.

Taking a steadying breath she exited into the wide hallway. It felt vast as she moved towards the lift, but at least there weren't any security cameras. She pushed her fingers against the call button, ears alert for the sound of a door opening behind her, eyes pinned to the light slowly ticking off each floor as the lift crept upwards. Gripping her wheelrims, she readied herself to bolt back into Jay's flat if the lift arrived already occupied. Eventually, the doors slid open to reveal a vacant silver oblong. Hands shaking, Megan wheeled herself inside and pressed the button for the roof garden.

Jay leant back into the doorway and steadied himself

against his churning stomach. He could see most of the length of Bold Street sloping away from him and people milling about. There were one or two people he recognised a little further down the street, but otherwise it looked normal. Too normal for what they were about to do. His legs threatened to buckle beneath him and he pushed his hands against the boarded-up door to keep himself upright. How could he have thought he was brave enough for this? That any of them were? The grief and rage that had carried him along had evaporated like whisps of cloud leaving nothing but a bleak horizon of doubt and fear; fear of the police; fear of his parents if they ever found out about this; fear for his future; doubt about everything. They all had so much to lose. A couple of them worked for The Committee and there were other post-grads too, albeit not on security listed courses like him. But even the retail staff might never work again after this.

Would the journalist show up and was she scared, too? It was a huge risk for her if it was obvious she had been tipped off and hadn't informed the police. She said she would take a late lunch so she could "just happen" to be in one of the cafés when it kicked off. Now, he hoped more than anything they all would lose their nerve, that they would bail out and he could quietly slip away and go home.

Then the clapping started and it was too late, he no longer had a choice.

It felt like an age until the doors opened again. Megan shrugged off her cardigan, rolled it into a tube and jammed it in the door. She couldn't allow the lift to get called away or risk people re-entering the building before she was back inside Jay's flat. Scanning her surroundings, her heart sunk, this was her only possible escape route and hiding place, but all it offered was some faded ratan sofas and a few large containers with wind-weathered plants, nothing that would provide any cover. The lift shaft was the only thing that would conceal her from view, and even then not for long. Still, if there was no sign of her ever having been in Jay's flat then the police would have no reason to look for her, no reason to even suspect she was alive – unless, of course, Jay told them.

Jay glanced at the display on the comms tower, it was 14:00. As always, the clapping had started right on cue. People were lining the pavements and the police helicopter was buzzing into view to check everyone was doing their civic duty. It looked like every other Friday afternoon. Then, above the applause, he heard them. It was happening, they were really doing it.

'These lives matter! These lives matter!'

A group had peeled themselves away from the clapping throng and were marching down the middle of the road. They were punching their fists in the air and unfurling home-made banners adorned with names and pictures as they chanted. Jay looked directly across the street and saw two people he recognised. They caught his eye as they moved towards the middle of the road. Taking a deep breath, he stepped forward to join them.

Megan prized the lift doors open, bundling her cardigan onto her lap and pressed the button for level four. The doors shuddered but didn't move, she pushed the button again.

'Please no,' she whispered. 'Don't let it have broken.'

She pressed it again and then tried the button marked *close door.* There was a long pause followed by a dull beep. The door remained open and tears of panic flooded her eyes. She jabbed both of the buttons again, stealing herself for the worst, inwardly pleading she had not just made things a million times worse than they already were.

'These lives matter! These lives matter!'

Images of the dead bobbed ahead of him as Jay marched down the street, still too afraid to do any more than silently mouth the words the others chanted. He recognised a lot of the faces on the pictures. There was Cathy, one of the oldest residents, the head shot making her Downs Syndrome unmistakable. She was one of the last generation of Downs babies to be born; all affected foetuses were now terminated. He thought of Cathy, cold, wet, and terrified as the filthy water rose around her, it must have been the worst death. They would have all known they were going to drown and there was no way out with the security barriers in place. Even Cathy must have known that. What had those few last gasps of breath felt like before she went under? And what about Navida, Megan's roommate? She had been training to be a nurse until a spinal injury had left her in a wheelchair and condemned to a life in Bootle Cares. He wondered what it had been like for her. Had she floated out of her chair with the rising water until she was crushed against the ceiling, her lungs filling with dirty sea water, sewage, and oil? And Pavel, who had always seemed so wise and calm, how had he faced his death? Would it have been more or less terrifying not to be able to see what was happening? He shuddered, sometimes he could imagine it as clearly as if he had been trapped inside with the residents and the water pouring in all around them.

Megan should have been there. If he hadn't taken her out for Silvie's funeral she would have died with the rest of them: two sisters gone in less than a fortnight. He swallowed, the pain of losing Silvie rasped in his throat. It was still too raw to be real most days. At the same time, he couldn't stop thinking about how the death of one sister had kept the other alive. He would have swapped them in a heartbeat if he could. Every time Megan met his gaze it was like a knife in his heart. Neon blue eyes, paper white skin, a shroud of dark red hair: it was like he was looking at Silvie – even though they were physically different in every other way. Silvie was tall, athletic, and strong-featured in contrast to Megan's oval face and petite frame and, of course, her disability. But still, those eyes, and the way she had looked at him that morning when he had told her about the demo. He wasn't even sure what it was: fear, concern, shock, but it cut him to the core. He hadn't waited for her to translate whatever she was thinking into words, he had simply closed the door and walked away. He felt his heart breaking for Silvie every time he looked at Megan – if only it had been the other way round.

'These lives matter! These lives matter!'

Clearing tears from his throat, he joined the chanting to divert his mind from the fact he was wishing death on the person whose life he was protesting for.

Megan pressed her fingers against the button and closed her eyes, had she really done this to herself? The lift shuddered and she held her breath. An age passed and then finally the doors closed and the lift skimmed downwards just like it had done a thousand times before. She didn't breathe properly again until she was back inside Jay's flat with the door locked behind her.

Steadying herself, she checked the flat one more time to be absolutely certain she had removed every trace of her existence. Her bag was packed and waiting by the door. If Jay was not back by late afternoon she would assume the worst and get ready to make her escape upwards. She could only hope the police would arrive with sirens blaring or make enough noise getting through the front door to give her time to get to the roof. It was a fragile plan, but she had to do something. Jay clearly hadn't considered the implications of what he was doing: that they might arrest him and come and search his flat and if they found her there, that would be the end for both of them. Or perhaps he didn't care anymore? Perhaps nothing mattered to him now that Silvie was dead. She could see the pain in his eyes every time he looked at her and she could only guess what he must be feeling. So she kept out of his way as much as possible, shrinking her presence to invisibility, as if she could squeeze the whole of her existence into the small black holdall she had brought with her the day of Silvie's funeral, and stash herself out of sight.

Jay looked around him. The demo was having quite an impact. Some people were trying to continue clapping as if nothing was happening, but most were staring open-mouthed, hands frozen mid-air. The police helicopter had moved directly overhead and there were sirens approaching. Was everyone as scared as him? Either way, it was working, people were noticing, they couldn't just pretend this wasn't happening the way they had with the flood. A surge of pride washed over him, they were doing something important, this meant something, just like their chant proclaimed. He raised his voice a little louder. All of those people mattered, and this rag-tag collective of their friends and relatives were risking everything to make it known.

'These lives matter! These lives matter!'

The words resonated in his chest. It was amazing they had made it happen at all. Until two weeks ago they had been on nothing more than nodding terms – shamed, rather than allied, by their association. They had only bonded when they were confronted with the horror of the flood. No-one had been informed, so everyone turned up for their weekly visit only to be confronted by a roadblock with water lapping around it. They each stopped in turn, stunned, staring at the water in front of them, imagining what must lie behind. That was when they started talking to each other: shocked, grief-stricken and enraged. People began discretely swapping contact details and one or two went back every day so they could connect with as many of the others as possible. They monitored themselves carefully, passing on the role of contact-person every couple of days and making sure at least one person always left the roadblock as soon as the tenth arrived so that there was never any reason for the police to intervene. The police watched them anyway, apparently oblivious that an illegal organisation was taking shape right in front of the roadblock.

But this was about Silvie, too, not just to say that her life mattered, but because if she was still alive she would have been here and she would have had no doubts about it. Silvie would have done it for Megan, so it was the least he could do. Besides, he promised Silvie he would look after Megan – although whether or not an illegal demo counted as "looking after" was debatable.

'These lives matter! These lives matter!'

He was committed now, there was no going back.

Chapter 2

Megan checked her bag one more time: twenty-two years of her life crumpled into one small holdall with room to spare. Except this was not all of her life or who she was. There was the laptop with the stories, poems, and articles she typed late into the night when Navida slipped into her drugged sleep, writing about the things Pavel told her and the worlds she imagined she didn't need to be able to walk anywhere to access. There were no limits to what she could do with her mind and, even now, after everything that had happened, a residue of the hope Pavel had kept alive in her was still there. Perhaps things really could change for the better, perhaps Jay would help her, perhaps he already knew what Silvie had started?

Could that be why he told her to bring an overnight bag when he had come to collect her for Silvie's funeral? It had taken her by surprise, and she worked hard not to let him see how uncertain she felt. She had never had the chance to stay somewhere overnight in the decade she had lived in Bootle Cares, and she didn't even have a bag of her own. In the end she had taken one of Navida's. Navida kept the bags that she had arrived with four years previously under her bed as if she might have the opportunity to pack up and leave any day – anything must feel better than facing the reality that she was stuck there forever and unlikely to see her husband or children again. Once, Megan thought she overheard one of the managers asking Navida to sign divorce papers her husband had sent in, but Navida never said anything about it, so Megan assumed she had simply complied in the same drugged haze that she did everything else. Pavel warned Megan against the meds they were constantly plied with and he taught her how to hide pills under her tongue rather than swallow them. But mostly she hadn't needed to, she maintained a quiet, passive demeanour and was barely noticed.

On the day of Silvie's funeral, Jay went to talk to the manager whilst Megan gathered together her meagre toiletries, pyjamas, underwear, and a change of clothes from her funeral outfit. She put them in the smallest holdall she could find but it was still half empty. She added the laptop Silvie had given her, she couldn't risk it being discovered in her absence. Residents weren't supposed to have access to technology other than what was provided in the day room and even then for no more than two hours per day. The laptop was too important for her to be separated from for even just one night. She added a couple of books Silvie had brought the last time she had visited. The bag still wasn't full, so she threw in another set of clothes, some more underwear and zipped it up. That was pretty much everything she owned in one small fabric bag.

Jay didn't say anything about the size or weight of the bag when he picked it up, so she must have managed to create a normal overnight bag. He had arrived in his red Tesla, a present from his parents for his twenty-fifth birthday the year before. He struggled to fold up her wheelchair and get it into the boot. It was heavy, not designed for easy transportation as why would she have anywhere to go? He cursed as the wheels grazed his suit. It was jet black, button-up with a short high collar and fitted around his body like it had been made for him. His glossy chestnut hair was pulled back in a knot at the back of his neck, but wavey strands were escaping. He was clean shaven for once, which softened his jaw and cheekbones. His eyes were red-rimmed and his skin was pale with grief, but he still looked good, he always looked good to Megan.

Jay's chest tightened, they were about half way down Bold Street now, beyond the boarded-up top end and at the section that was lined with brightly coloured store fronts. There were all the usual chains, recognisable by their brand logos in Chinese and English, but they had been dressed up to look like the small independents that Bold Street was once famed for. That was partly why the group had insisted on Bold Street, despite his protestations, they wanted to remind everyone of what it was like in the days before The New Governance. And not just the independent shops, but the basements pulsing with political activism and the vibrant alternative arts scene. Not that Jay knew much about that, it was barely within his lifetime. For him, Bold Street would always be the place Silvie had died and this was the first time he had been back. His legs were beginning to wobble, but he forced himself on. They had almost reached the point where it happened: where the car had careered into her.

When he heard the collision and the screaming he bolted out of the bar where he had been waiting for her, but it was too late. He told her he loved her and she told him to look after Megan.

He promised he would, hoping she would say something more, something for him, but she was gone. It was like it was happening to someone else, even as he felt the heat draining from her body.

The driver said Silvie had been cycling on the wrong side of the road and the police believed him without question. It didn't matter how many witnesses there were, the police believed the man driving the Committee car. Fury rose like bile at the injustice of it, it was nothing he had ever felt before – but then he had never experienced anything like this. It was inconceivable that someone could kill Silvie with absolutely no consequence. And then there had been the flood, more deaths and no-one held to account. It was all so wrong. Rage boiled inside him with a power that frightened him. Sometimes he thought he could destroy the whole of Liverpool with it. The heat of ire pulsed though his body and he began punching his fist in the air and chanting at the top of his voice.

'These lives matter! These lives matter!' he shouted,

not caring who saw him or what they thought; it was wrong and he would say so.

Someone grabbed his arm and yanked him onto the pavement. It was Marcia, the journalist from the *Liverpool Voice*. She had her phone in her hand and she was feigning she didn't know him.

'Can I ask you about the demo today?' she said, careful not to mention he was actually in it as she recorded their conversation.

'Yes,' he replied, a bolt of fear passing through him.

He swallowed and tried to sound more assured than he felt. 'It's about the deaths in Bootle Cares, the home for disabled people.'

'But surely that was just a terrible accident?'

'That's not what the people on the demo think,' he retorted, momentarily ashamed of his cowardice in not admitting he was one of them but, of course, he had Megan to look after now.

'Bootle Cares had flooded twice already,' he steadied his voice, 'And it was known to be in direct danger from the tidal surge. All the other buildings to the west of Derby Road were cleared out months ago, Bootle Cares was the only one that was still inhabited. There are no sea defences along that part of the waterfront and the new security barriers meant no-one could get out. The residents were abandoned, trapped inside and left to drown.'

'But people had been demanding proper security on disabled homes after all the attacks. They were there to protect people.'

Jay opened his mouth to ask Silvie's question: why was everyone was so accepting of attacks on disabled homes, how had that become a routine part of life in a civilised society? But a commotion further up the street stopped him. An armoured police van crashed through the barriers at the bottom of the road, driving directly into some of the protestors. Police were leaping out with batons and shields, beating those who had not already been hit by the van. Jay started to run towards the carnage, but Marcia grabbed his backpack, dragging him back onto the pavement.

'Don't,' she hissed, staring into his eyes and shaking her head.

She started slowly walking down the middle of the road, her press pass swinging and talking loudly into her phone until she was ushered back by a police officer. She made sure they knew she wanted to get their side of the story to make herself look legit.

Megan watched the minutes plod by on the clock in the bottom corner of the EBC news channel. She had muted the sound. The drone of reports on loop was worse torture than waiting in silence and imagining the worst. But at least there hadn't been any images from the demo. That meant nothing bad must have happened – yet. Although the EBC was hardly a reliable source of information. There had been nothing about the flooding or the deaths in Bootle Cares, nor the carnage that must have unfolded around the other undefended parts of the country on the night of the tidal surge.

That night, the night of Silvie's funeral, Jay had brought Megan back to the flat and told her she could sleep in his bed and he would sleep on the sofa. Oblivious to the horror that was unfolding just a few miles north, she had snuggled under the soft sheets and plump duvet, simultaneously enchanted and pained by the thought that Silvie – and Jay – slept there, too. She stayed there again when they came back from the road block the following day, and she must have lain there in the fug of shock for at least two more days after that, immobilised by what she had seen, slipping in and out of focus, desperate for the oblivion of sleep and the relief of waking up to discover it was all a hideous dream. It was the only time in her life she had yearned for Bootle Cares.

At some point Jay told her he had not been given permission for her to be away overnight. He argued with the manager when he only authorised a day pass and then decided, by himself, he would keep her out illegally and deal with the consequences the next day. A flash of anger at his presumption burned in her chest. Even though his actions had saved her life, his total lack of regard for the ramifications of her being out unauthorised made her head swim. Then it slowly dawned on her that no-one but Jay knew she was alive. Everyone thought she had drowned along with all the others, and her fate now lay entirely in Jay's hands.

Gradually, she had become aware of Jay lugging furniture around in the background and eventually he coaxed her out of his bed and presented her with a tiny bedroom he had created for her from his study. Her immediate thought was that she would have preferred him to get into his big bed with her still in it, but then she felt terrible. How could she still feel those things after everything that had happened?

Moving over to the balcony, she gazed at the park, the spring bloom was already well underway and so at odds with the dark swirl of guilt and shame inside her. Love at first sight was a stupid idea, she knew that. It was a ridiculous fantasy that would never have anything to do with her life. Yet her heart told a different story, since the very first time she met him, before that even, from the time Silvie had shown her his picture, back when he was the new guy she was dating. She and Silvie had giggled over him like he was an exotic species, rich and gorgeous, utterly alien to their lives. But underneath she felt something else, a knotting in her stomach that magnified into a fist-blow when she finally met him. He was the most beautiful man she had ever seen. Sometimes she caught herself just staring at him as he and Silvie chatted together in the small courtyard garden at Bootle Cares, often falling silent, intoxicated by the exquisite torture watching them together. Once or twice she thought they might forget she was there, but it was never like that. Silvie cared about her, and she thought Jay did too, even if only because of Silvie. Sometimes she fantasised about Silvie finishing with him and him still coming to visit her, imagining what it would be like to kiss him, to run her fingers through his luscious hair and have those beautiful brown eyes focus on her with all the intensity he directed at Silvie, dreaming what it would be like to be alone with him for a while. And now her dreams had come true, but as if granted by a cruel and vengeful god that made her pay for her aberrations with the lives of everyone she loved.

Chapter 3

Jay turned his back on the carnage in Bold Street and fled, his terror propelling him as far as Myrtle Street before he even noticed the incline pushing against his legs. He stopped and caught his breath, safe at last in the grounds of the university. Then he panicked, the way he was dressed was bound to get him picked up on the security cameras, he looked like a squatter. He sprinted across the road and then jogged towards the loop of backroads he knew from his morning runs would eventually lead him through Sefton Park and home, never more glad of his running shoes.

That morning, he had spent a ridiculous amount of time deliberating over what he should wear for the demo, channelling his anxiety into trying to figure out if there was some kind of dress code. There hadn't been a demo in living memory so he had no idea of the protocol. His instinct had been to wear a suit in honour of the dead and to demonstrate their respectability as protestors – that seemed especially important given they were unlikely to attract much public sympathy. Then, he wondered if something more every day, like the smart casual attire that was expected at university, was more appropriate. Finally, he decided it was probably wise to look as little like his usual self as possible, so he dug out an old sweatshirt that he ran in on cold mornings, jeans from a long past euro-grunge phase that had horrified his parents, and running shoes. Stuffing them into a seldom-used backpack he had walked to campus leaving his phone and everything except his Uni ID and keys at the flat – it felt like a lifetime ago already.

He lay down in the grass in the park and let the cold earth seep into his bones, he needed to be alone. His head was throbbing as if he had just sobered up from two weeks intoxication, driven temporarily mad by losing Silvie, only to find himself trapped under the fallout of his rampage. More than anything he needed it to be over, as if it had never happened. It was like he had been possessed by someone else, none of this was who he was, he was not the person who would recklessly gamble his future or throw away everything his parents had given him, and for what? To make a pointless statement about people who were already dead.

Except Megan, she wasn't dead. The chill settled deeper into his marrow, he had no idea what to do about her, but he desperately didn't want her in his flat any more. He didn't want to have to go home and see the enormity of what he had done reflected in her face or to look into those big blue eyes that mocked him with the life that had been stolen from Silvie. If only there was someone or somewhere he could take her to. There had to be an alternative to her being holed-up in his flat forever more. His mind wandered towards the night of the funeral and the stirring of the wish he barely allowed himself to formulate, the version of events where he had taken her straight back to Bootle Cares. That way it would definitely all be over by now and his life would have gone back to how it had been – well, minus Silvie.

Every time he thought of Silvie it hurt so much that he couldn't understand how his lungs continued to fill with air and blood kept circulating through his veins. The rise and fall of her breathing against his was so palpable it could surely not be possible she was gone forever, that vibrant, luscious creature transformed into nothing more than an empty, drubbing pain inside him. And now he could feel her repulsion at him wishing Megan dead, her eyes burning with hurt and anger. He wrapped his arms around his body as if to hold her tight enough that she could never leave him.

'You know I would never hurt Megan,' he whispered into the empty air. 'I won't let anything bad happen to her.'

But even as he said it, he knew the truth was that he didn't want to be responsible for her, either. Another stab of guilt penetrated his heart, Megan asked so little of him, nothing really, she spent most of her time tucked away mouse-like in her room. Yet the weight of her presence was inescapable, an anchor chaining him to a tumult of darkness that he needed to escape more than anything else on earth. Clouds began to gather over the sun and he watched the greying sky through the branches above him and shivered. There was nowhere else for him to go and he couldn't stay in the park all night. Slowly, he peeled his body from the ground and trudged the rest of the way home, backpack trailing from his hand.

Megan was silhouetted in front of the TV in the living room, holding a vigil for news, waiting for something more than the little that he had told her. At six PM there was a brief headline about a disturbance in Liverpool and he moved towards the screen, keeping the sofa width between them.

The newsreader looked sombre, *'Today in Liverpool there was a violent assault on police officers during the Clap for Our Heroes.'*

Jay started, that was not true! That was a lie!

'A number of unpatriotic miscreants turned our moment of civic gratitude into an opportunity for unprovoked violence against our protectors. The trouble started when a small group charged at a police van brandishing homemade weapons.'

Jay crumpled onto the sofa, all the breath forced out of his body.

'Police have confirmed that one of those who attacked the vehicle sustained fatal injuries and eight others are seriously injured. A further fifteen sustained minor injuries during face-to-face combat with the police and are currently being questioned.'

What had they done?

The report didn't mention the demo, Bootle Cares, the lives of the people they were protesting for. They had failed, worse than failed. They were being made into mindless criminals. It was not really credible, was it? That a group would rush at a police vehicle and attack it?

Surely it was too much even for the po-faced EBC journalist to believe?

Above the white noise of his panic Jay could just make out the continuing drone of the reporter, *Ten others who appeared to have been involved in the planned attack have been arrested and are being examined by forensic psychiatrists pending detention under the Mental Health Act.*'

He felt sick. That was most of the group, was he the only one who had escaped? And who had died? They didn't give a name. But then again, perhaps being dead was preferable to being detained under the Mental Health Act, perhaps death was preferable to all of this. He gripped the sofa, sinking his fingers into the heavy upholstery, he was losing his mind, he didn't know who he was or what he was doing anymore. If only there was a way to rewind time. A few weeks ago his life had been simple: he was working towards his final assignments for his MSc in Military Bio-engineering, he had been with Silvie for just over two years and facing into a future ripe with possibilities. The MSc would secure him a prestigious government job and he would not have to worry about the economy which seemed to be crumbling faster than the English coastline. He had fulfilled his parents' expectations and, whatever was in store, his future was safeguarded – Silvie's too if she wanted to be a part of it. And now it was all trashed. It was as if the tidal surge had crashed through his life and all he was left with was rubble. It was like the inside of his head was rubble. He didn't know what to think or feel anymore, he didn't understand anything. He had just risked his entire future to be part of something that had only resulted in more death, pain, and lies and had left him so far out of his depth he wasn't sure if he could survive. He had never been so afraid or uncertain in his life and there was no one he could turn to. Glancing at Megan, he could see her eyes were wet, he definitely couldn't cope her tears as well.

As if reading his thoughts, she turned and wheeled herself out of the living room and into the box room. With the single bed she could just fit her wheelchair into the room and close the door. Jay put his head in his hands and let his tears flow, he hadn't cried properly since the day Silvie died, he had been trying to keep it under control, but he couldn't anymore. There was just too much death and chaos and none of it made any sense.

Megan shifted from her chair to the firm, single mattress and lifted her legs onto the bed. She lay down and stared at the ceiling pretending she couldn't hear Jay crying in the next room. At least he was crying, though, getting it all out. Every time she looked at him she could see all the grief and confusion in his eyes and she longed to put her arms around him. But she didn't know how she should act with him now Silvie was gone. Silvie had been the rock that she and Jay had orbited around in companionable familiarity, but her death had tipped the axis and dislodged them both. If only she could reach out and connect with him somehow, but any thought of trying to bridge the void between them made her burn with shame – in the cold light of Silvie's death nothing could be more wrong than the constant churning of desire inside her.

Perhaps it would have been better all round if she had died in Bootle Cares? The pain in her chest pushed tears out of her eyes. Everyone she loved was gone: her beloved sister, Pavel, the man who had been like a father to her since the day she had been sent to live there, Navida, Cathy, and now all those people who had dared to say that their lives mattered. What was the point to her own life now? She sobbed. Silvie and Pavel were her lifelines to hope, her only gateway into believing that something better lay ahead. What did her future hold now? There was nothing.

A muffled cry from the other room pulled her back, there was still Jay, he was there and she was not entirely alone. Even if she did sometimes feel a little abandoned all alone in his flat, he was a good person, she was sure of that. She inhaled, stemming the flow of tears. Jay loved Silvie, and Silvie wouldn't have been with him if he wasn't a decent person and she would certainly never have brought him to Bootle Cares if he was like everyone else. Her heart swelled, Jay might even help her to get away, after all, he had already done the first part of Silvie's plan. And, although he most likely knew nothing more than she did herself about what Silvie had actually intended, he might still be able to do something. Her heart stirred again, he had done so much already, surely that was a sign he would help her? Afterall, he had thought of her even in the shock aftermath of Silvie's death.

The image of him, when showed up at Bootle Cares, tear-stained and dishevelled, was burnt into her mind. For the first time since she had known him, he had neglected his appearance, his shirt was crumpled and his hair unbrushed. He sat down beside her and took her hand. She knew of course, even as her mind fought against it and his words turned to a blur of sound behind the thudding of her heart. What other reason would there be for him to show up alone and in such a state?

It must have been so hard for him to go there on his own and tell her. He didn't have to, and no-one else would have done, certainly not her parents. Left to them she would never have known that Silvie had died, she would have just slowly come to the conclusion that Silvie had eventually abandoned her the same way the rest of the family had done.

She had been too shocked to feel anything beyond the sensation of his large, warm hand cradling hers. His skin was soft against her calloused palm, hardened by the years against her wheelrims.

'You have to go to the funeral,' he had told her. 'I know how much you loved each other,' his voice wavered on the past tense. He swallowed to steady himself, 'You have to be there.'

They must have sat like that, hand-in-hand, for a long time, the numb silence stretching into the infinity of Silvie's absence, it was dark when he left.

Chapter 4

She wore her knitted black dress and thick, black tights —
it was the best outfit she had, despite her old grey shoes,
and as soon as they had driven away from Bootle Cares,
she pulled her hair free from the braid that kept it looped
up and out of sight of the regulation cuts and let it
tumble to her waist in a thick, amber curtain.

She felt Jay's eyes on her. 'You look nice,' he smiled.

Her stomach flipped and then soured at her own
betrayal. How could she feel that of all days? But when
she met his eyes there was nothing more than paternal
affection for his girlfriend's disabled little sister and her
stomach knotted tighter.

Still, he had been kind to her all day, regardless of
how awful he must have been feeling or how angry her
parents were when he arrived at the crematorium with
her in tow. Her mother's eyes blazed with fury from the
moment they fell on her and she maintained a careful
distance the rest of the day, deliberately positioning
herself beyond steps or furniture that there was no
possibility of Megan traversing, so there was no chance
of her being contaminated by proximity to her disabled

daughter. Her father and the few other guests followed suit and most people didn't seem to know who Megan was despite her obvious resemblance to Silvie.

Jay must have been able to see what was going on, but he didn't let any of it perturb him. He behaved impeccably despite it all, he commiserated and comforted their parents, taking his place as Silvie's partner and managing the formalities of the service with his usual outer confidence. Only Megan could see him swallowing back his tears so discretely that no-one else would notice. She ached to comfort him, but every time he came near her he was impenetrable, brotherly and caring with his own pain locked away. He was attentive, offering to fetch her drinks when they moved into the hall for refreshments. She refused all but one, she didn't know how long they were going to stay and there weren't any toilets she could use.

The more she thought about that day, the more it seemed a little bit of Silvie was alive in him: the way he had done what he believed to be right regardless of what everyone else thought, that was just like her. Or perhaps he had always been more like Silvie than she had realised. After all, Silvie had chosen to be with him, so maybe all she needed to do was summon her courage and go and speak to him now. She pushed herself upright and picked her laptop, decision made, it was what Silvie would have wanted.

Jay pulled a cushion against his face to muffle his sobs. He wanted Silvie so much; he needed her. Only she had the strength to get him through this. She was his compass and he was rudderless without her, cut adrift, certain he could not live his life without her. He pressed his face into the fabric, inhaling as if there was some last trace of her he could draw from the fibres.

Up until the first time he had brought her there, he thought the flat was nothing special, a two-bedroomed apartment in Merebank Heights overlooking Sefton Park. It was not what he would have chosen for himself, but his parents were adamant that he must be as far away as possible from any of the danger zones while still in easy reach of campus. But when he saw it through Silvie's eyes, him just twenty-four and already five years in his own flat, he had felt a first twinge of self-consciousness about all the things he took for granted – all the things their course mates could never hope for in a lifetime. Silvie didn't say anything about it, certainly not that night anyway. It was one of the few things she did not challenge him on, maybe because she knew his brothers did enough of that, or perhaps because even she did not always know how to reconcile her life with his. But whatever Silvie thought about it, it did not stop her spending a lot of time there. He had sometimes wondered about asking her to move in with him properly, but he never had. He regretted that now with all his heart, if only he had known how precious every moment of their time together would be, he would never have hesitated.

He heard Megan moving around and got up. He couldn't stay here, not with his memories of Silvie swirling around him and Megan chaining him to his mistakes. He had to put an end to it once and for all, even if that meant telling his parents what he had done – well, some of it. He didn't have to tell them about the demo, but surely they would understand why he had taken Megan to the funeral, it wasn't that difficult to explain, they were sisters and it's what Silvie would have wanted. There was no need to tell them he hadn't got permission for Megan to stay out, it wasn't relevant now anyway. The main thing was that he had brought her to the funeral, and now, because of the flood and how upset Megan was, he didn't know what to do. That was pretty much the truth of it anyway, it wasn't as if he was completely lying, he just wasn't telling them all the details, either. And he didn't always tell them everything anyway, they had only met Silvie once. It was like they had reached an unspoken truce where they didn't ask and he didn't tell, and they were probably just waiting for him to move on to someone more suitable. Perhaps they would be glad to help him get rid of Megan – his last connection to an entanglement they never wanted him to have. Still, he hated the thought of disappointing them almost as much as he feared the consequences of what he had done. But there was no other way out, he needed them to make things right again, to get Megan out of his life and to end this nightmare once and for all.

Chapter 5

Jay slowed as the gravel crunched beneath the wheels and gently steered the Tesla around the arc of his parent's driveway. The parking bay in front of the house was almost empty, only his dad's and Chris's cars were there. He pulled in beside the old petrol engine Jag that hardly ever moved and flicked on the parking brake, the certainty that propelled him there already ebbing away. The intimate chat he envisaged with his mother and father was not going to happen now, and navigating Chris was the last thing he wanted. Somehow Chris had taken on the mantle of older brother even though he was actually the middle child – but the fourteen years that separated him from Jay made him difficult to dislodge regardless of the additional three years to Adam.

Why did it have to be Chris and not Adam? Adam was softer, he had married well so hadn't needed to bully his way to the top like Chris, although Chris had also eventually married into a powerful Chinese family, twice, averting the potential disaster of his divorce by quickly attaching himself to a woman from an even more weighty clan. She was older than him, her children almost the same age as Jay, so making any babies with Chris to rival their heirship was highly unlikely – unless, of course, their own family history was anything to go by.

Jay had been a surprise baby when his parents thought it was no longer possible, his dad in his early fifties and his mum her late forties. Their careers had been their central focus by then and had remained so despite Jay's unexpected arrival – a wise decision as events had unfolded. Their commitment meant they were quickly appointed to senior roles under The New Governance: his father the head of the Northwest Security and Protection Division and his mother Deputy Chief Administrator for the region. From then on, they had unquestioningly provided Jay with everything he ever needed. Before him, Chris and Adam were raised with an ethos of having to earn what they had, but by the time Jay came along their parents softened and simply indulged him. Well, that was how his brothers saw it, and Chris never missed an opportunity to remind Jay he was the cosseted favourite. Sometimes Jay wondered if his parents' generosity had been to placate their guilt that he was mostly raised by paid help. Even so, he didn't doubt they loved him, he knew they had wanted to give him the most advantageous start in life and they had done it the very best way they could.

He let his hand hover over the door, knowing how much they loved him didn't stop the doubts from crowding in, especially given what he had done to repay them. And he couldn't say anything in front of Chris. Chris would completely loose his shit about Megan. He had no empathy about Silvie, no ability to see what she had meant to him, so anything about Megan would only be fuel to the fire. Was there any point in going in at all? Except it might look strange, it might even betray that he had done something bad if he turned up unannounced and then drove away without saying anything at the sight of Chris's car. He sighed and got out the Tesla, wracking his brain for a way to explain his brief, unprompted visit.

Megan heard the door close and the feint whirr of the lift taking Jay out into the freedom that he took for granted, she had missed her chance and was all alone again.

She closed her eyes, she was back in Bootle Cares and Pavel was standing in front of her in the day room, his cane folded on the back of the TV stand. A typical Wednesday morning: the residents in their enforced two-hour congregation in front of the TV whilst the staff meeting took place upstairs. As always, Pavel positioned himself to the left of the television, directly below the CCTV so that the security footage captured nothing more than a rapt TV audience. Megan smiled, the pleasure of a blind man making himself invisible to the all-seeing eyes that surveilled them never grew old.

He was wearing his favourite shirt; once the colour of irises but now faded to a dusty mauve. It was old-fashioned with a wide European fold-over collar, designed to be worn with a tie, which no-one, not even Pavel, did anymore. The only people who wore shirts like that relied on cast-offs and charity hand-outs. And even though that was most of the residents in Bootle Cares, even they still managed to assimilate something akin to contemporary Asian styling. Pavel wore that shirt deliberately. It aligned him with the liberal European culture and values England had once ascribed to; a time and place when disabled people had rights and lived in ways which were unimaginable now.

'The Right to Care Act—'

Megan heard groans behind her, Pavel had talked about this before.

He continued unperturbed. 'Is no more than imprisonment. This,' he swept his arm in a wide arc, indicating the locked door to the TV room that mirrored their wider confinement, 'Is not humane or kind, it is a travesty of our rights. Twenty forty-five was not the beginning of our right to care, it was the final and ultimate dissolution of every right that disabled people had ever known in this country. The rights to education, housing, employment. Once, we had all of these and more!'

He emanated a magnetic force that drew in even the dissenters. He had been a teacher once, and before that a researcher for what was then the British Broadcasting Corporation. That was a long time ago, before the UK had broken up and Ireland, Wales, and Scotland had formed the Celtic Union. Megan imagined him at the front of a classroom or working on an investigation, he would have been irrepressible.

'One right, a right which strips away all others, is not a right at all. We are told that The Right to Care is benevolent, we are expected to be grateful for crumbs of an existence, scraps thrown from the table of the rest of the population. Why should we be deprived of freedoms that even The New Governance permits everyone else? Our lives are no less valuable!'

Megan felt a trickle of malaise run through the room. It was one thing to say that disabled people should have some rights, but it was something else to imply a criticism of The New Governance. But Pavel didn't care, he was old enough to have lived a completely different life and had nothing left to lose.

'I'm not suggesting it was The Right to Care Act by itself that stripped us of our fundamental rights, they were being slowly eroded since two-thousand and ten. The long road to twenty forty-five began thirty-five years earlier when the government used austerity to turn the tide against disabled people, they stripped away many of our basic rights and resources, but disabled people fought back at every step.'

'Not very well, then!' someone muttered to muffled snorts of laughter.

But Pavel was not deterred. 'We fought those austerity policies that left people hungry and destitute, and we fought again against the police violence at environmental protests, we fought on as the catastrophic death toll took hold among disabled people during the coronavirus pandemic of the twenties. We battled the so-called emergency legislation that was never repealed.'

He took a deep breath and Megan sensed the pain behind his words for everything and everyone he had lost.

'Our lives were so different back then. Not perfect, by any means, but at least in principle we had the same basic freedoms as everyone else. We could work, study, have relationships and families. I am the living proof that it was possible.'

His tone shifted again. 'And not just that it was possible, but also if it can be taken away in just one lifetime, there is no reason why we can't get it back again just as quickly!'

Megan's heart accelerated, he lit a fire inside her, he made her feel strong and righteous, as if they could crash through the doors and reclaim their place in the world at that very moment. She looked around, hoping to see eyes ablaze with passion. But it was clear many of the residents thought he was making it up. They thought his speech was just the ranting of a deranged old man and there was no way that disabled people would have been able to do those things. But Megan knew Pavel was right, she could feel it inside herself just as strongly now as when he was right there in front of her. So what if she needed a wheelchair? She was sure she could manage pretty much everything she needed by herself if she was allowed to. But no-one seemed to want her to do anything, not even Jay. She was just supposed to sit in her chair and stare at the walls and feel shit about her existence. Well, that was not how her life was going to be, Pavel knew it could be different and Silvie had promised her. Silvie told her over and over again to stay strong because things would change and she wouldn't be stuck in there forever. Silvie had promised she would get her out and now all she had to do was persuade Jay to help.

Jay angled his face towards the camera and waited for the familiar click before the door swung open to admit him. He paused in the wide hallway, the house was quiet, Chris and their dad were probably in the upstairs office. The sound of his shoes clipping against the marble tiles as he moved towards the kitchen echoed around his head, why had he come here? This was a mistake.

He took a glass and filled it from the water purifier and then slid back the wide glass doors, inhaling the cool evening scent of the garden. He hovered just inside the doorway to avoid activating the lights, the darkness was comforting and he could fill the scene with whatever he chose: like the garden party the previous summer when he had finally introduced Silvie to his family. They had seen her image and heard her name for over a year by then, and it was getting too awkward to continue making excuses for keeping them apart – although he never doubted Silvie understood his reticence.

The day of the party, in the presence of his family and their opulent surroundings, was the only time he had ever seen her unsure of herself. She was uncharacteristically reserved and he repeatedly caught her eyes drinking in the architecture, the uniformed staff, the crystal glass in her hand, the lush gardens and the fleet of luxury cars lounging on the driveway. She politely shook his brothers' hands when he introduced them and made some demure comments about it being a lovely party.

She was not the firebrand he had warned them to expect and they paid her little attention. But Chris and Adam had seen him with a steady stream of different girls over the years and must have assumed she was just another temporary inhabitant on the ever-growing list, especially given her background. In their eyes she was nothing more than a rash dalliance before he settled down properly.

There were dozens of pictures on his phone from that day, but he didn't need them, his memory provided a more vivid image than any screen could produce. She was wearing an almost backless halter-neck top and trousers that fitted snugly around her hips and spread into wide swathes of fabric at her feet, all in soft grey faux Chinese silk. She had low-heeled shoes that made her almost as tall as him and her hair hung in loose waves caressing her bare shoulders. All afternoon he longed to fold his hands around her hips and pull her close to him and he let his fingers graze the naked skin of her back at every opportunity. He had considered slipping inside the house with her and taking her upstairs. But the thought of having sex with her in his childhood bedroom while the voices of his extended family drifted up from the garden below was too stifling to be a turn on. Besides, he could feel his mother watching him. She had given Silvie a friendly kiss on the cheek when they arrived, but he knew she didn't approve, especially not with Silvie in that faux silk when everyone else was in the real thing. He should have insisted on buying her something to wear regardless of her protestations about him dressing her up like an expensive ornament.

That night, he had driven back to Liverpool with a mixture of relief and disappointment. He had always known reconciling Silvie and his family was never going to be easy, but at least they had all been civilised and he was glad Silvie had seen a little more of his life for herself. An uneasy truce might not be the best starting point for the next chapter of his life, but it was not the worst either. Back then, he had thought Silvie was going to become a permanent feature of it, how could he have ever imagined this cruel twist of fate where he was landed with Megan instead?

The cool water in his throat was little solace, he couldn't face Chris or his dad now. There was no way he could tell them what he had done. He slid the door closed and placed his glass by the dishwasher and walked quietly back to the car. Clearly, he was going to have to figure out how to get rid of Megan by himself.

Chapter 6

It was still dark when stomach cramps yanked her from sleep, the sharp trills of pain accompanied by the familiar sticky feeling between her legs. She shoved the covers back and checked the sheets, thankfully it hadn't soaked through. It was hard enough getting her underwear handwashed and dried on the balcony during the day; but getting bloodstains out of white linen and then remaking the bed whilst Jay was at university would have been impossible. Still, she was going to have to say something to him, a wad of toilet paper in her knickers wasn't going to see her through her period, and it was difficult to manage with such a tiny supply of underwear and night things as it was.

She waited until his hand was on the door ready to leave for university before she spoke, to make the conversation as brief as possible.

'Jay,' she faltered. 'I need some things.'

A jolt of surprise turned him around. Whether it was surprise that she had made a direct request, or simply he wasn't expecting to see her at all at this time of the morning, she couldn't tell. Either way, she had faded into the background of his life so effectively that it never occurred to him there were all kinds of things she needed. As much as possible she fitted herself around his routine: washing and dressing whilst he was out for his run and then retreating to her room when he returned to shower and eat before university.

He looked at her blankly, he wasn't going to make this easy.

'For my period,' she mumbled.

He blanched slightly. 'Oh, of course,' he replied, swallowing hard.

He put his bag down, went into his bedroom and pulled open a drawer. 'Silvie kept everything she needed in here,' he called.

Megan followed, he looked embarrassed, as if looking in Silvie's drawer finally made him realise the whole range of things that she needed.

'Take whatever you want for now,' he told her. 'And we can go shopping later, I only have classes this morning.'

Then he turned and left.

The feint smell of Silvie's musky perfume tingled on Megan's skin as she moved towards the drawer. She picked up a bundle of folded fabric and pressed it against her face. It was almost like holding Silvie again, as if she had reached backwards in time and pulled her up from the dead. Tears damped the soft folds and she moved the fabric to her chest not wanting to dilute Silvie's precious essence. Even though everything she owned, from the clothes she wore, to the laptop full of secrets and the tiny silver pendant around her neck, were all provided by Silvie, this was different. These *were* Silvie. She piled the fabric onto her lap and reached out to take more, then hesitated. What did Jay mean by to "take anything she wanted"? Perhaps he thought she would wear some of Silvie's things – but even if they fitted her that would be impossible. But to have them close by, to be able to touch the objects that were still imbued with Silvie's essence was not something she could pass by. It would almost be as if Silvie was in her room again, like the small, childhood bedroom they shared before Megan had been confined downstairs, when Silvie would creep down in the night and slip under the covers of Megan's small cot, facing down their parents' fury when they found her there the next morning.

Silvie had fought with their parents as long as Megan could remember, refusing to accept that Megan should be treated any differently after the tumour on her spine than before. But their parents always fought back, they had wanted to put her in a home long before the Right to Care Act made it mandatory, never hiding how disappointed they were that, after the operation, their once normal child was confined to a wheelchair. They worried constantly about the consequences keeping a disabled child in a Committee house; how it would look to others and if it would affect their tenancy.

Megan squeezed Silvie's clothes tighter against her chest, trying to protect herself from the memories. But it was too late, they flooded her body as if she were back there now, reliving the crushing disappointment, the fear, rejection and then, far beyond that, the times that were so hazy it might as well have been someone else's life: another child who ran and laughed and played just like all the other kids, until she was five and the tumour changed her forever.

It had taken her parents a long time to accept that change. They stubbornly held onto the conviction that because she had some movement and sensation in her legs, she must be able to walk again, forcing her through endless hours of physiotherapy that felt more like torture than healing. She had been fitted with leg braces, an exoskeleton and electrodes, she had been forced to try endless different designs of crutches and walking frames, but whatever they did it remained impossible for her to stand for more than a few seconds or stagger a few tiny steps. Her parents compelled her onwards despite the falls and the injuries, never letting her forget that every failure to walk was her failing them. They finally gave up when she was eight, and giving up on her walking meant giving up on her. To Megan, her wheelchair was a relief, she could finally move herself around, stable and pain-free, but to everyone else her life was over.

"What do you think it's like for us having a daughter in a wheelchair?" was her mother's perpetual lament until they had finally put her in Bootle Cares.

Out of sight out of mind, like she didn't exist anymore. It was only Silvie who didn't think it made any difference to who she was or what she was worth. Silvie treated her just the same before and after the operation and regardless of her wheelchair or the physio horrors that were inflicted on her, they were sisters no matter what. Silvie alone visited her in Bootle Cares, bringing her clothes and books, sharing everything she learned at school. If it hadn't been for Silvie, Megan wouldn't have had an education at all after the age of twelve. Well, not the kind that came from the official Department of Education textbooks, anyway; there was always Pavel with the unofficial version, derived from his life experience, the things he had taught, and his irrepressible belief in justice. Silvie and Pavel were alike in so many ways, her stalwarts, and now they were both gone.

She picked up another small bundle of fabric, leaving the drawer half full, and placed it on her lap along with a box of pads she found tucked in the corner beside a menstrual cup. Closing the drawer and turning to leave, her eye caught a flash of electric pink beneath one of the pillows on Jay's neatly-made bed. She moved over and gently lifted the charcoal grey pillow to reveal a crumpled camisole with matching shorts. Her heart knotted: perhaps Jay buried his face in Silvie's things and quietly cried himself to sleep every night clutching the empty fabric. Megan touched the soft, pink cloth with her fingertips, she too would give anything for Silvie to be alive. She carefully replaced the pillow, returned to her room and lay down with her own tears.

The heat of the sun streaming onto her face woke her, it must be nearly midday if it had reached that side of the building. Grief was exhausting, it lay heavy in her body as she uncurled her limbs and pushed herself upright, the tear-induced sleep only ever a temporary respite. Silvie's crumpled pyjamas tumbled from her chest onto the sheet beside her. Smoothing them with her palms, she placed the pyjamas under her pillow and then carefully laid the rest of the fabric into her lower bedside drawer; her own meagre possessions barely filled the other two.

She wheeled across the flat and let herself out on to the balcony inhaling the warm air. It would be in direct sunlight soon, forcing her to retreat back inside to protect her fragile skin; neither she nor Silvie had the colouring to withstand even the springtime sun. Her eyes stretched across to the park; what she would give for the freedom to be able to meander along the shade-dappled paths, to make her own way in the world. She sighed, everything had changed and yet nothing was different: she was still confined indoors with access to only the tiniest outside space. She had no freedom, she was used to that, of course, but she was lonely now as well, lonelier than she had ever been. Yes, Jay's flat was a million times nicer than Bootle Cares, and she was not watched over, but at least there she had companionship, love, Jay barely even saw her.

Jay glanced at the clock on the dashboard. He had been sitting there for twenty minutes already, his mind turning over so fast he could barely keep abreast of his own thoughts. He was going to have to make a decision: either go inside and tell them that he had Megan and he was bringing her in, or drive away and think of something else. If he stayed there much longer he was going to start to look suspicious: how could he explain this to a police officer? Him sitting outside the police station in his car staring into the distance looking preoccupied, like he might really be planning an attack on them this time. He pushed the thoughts away, if he dwelt on the demo now he would completely lose his mind. All he had to do was bring Megan here and it would be over. His dad was sure to smooth over any outstanding details and it would be easy enough to get her here. She was not going to know he was driving her towards the police station rather than the shopping centre and, once they had arrived, well, she could hardly refuse to get out of the car, could she?

He could feel Silvie's outrage mounting, he pushed it down. Silvie was dead and he couldn't live in her shadow for the rest of his life. What difference could he make by himself, anyway? He was just one person, and him sacrificing everything he had for Megan was not going to change anything. It wouldn't make a real difference, it would just ruin both of their lives for nothing and, worse still, it would ruin his family's life as well. He knew things were wrong, Silvie had shown him that, but he could find other ways to help. After all, he had responsibilities, he was in a very different position to Silvie, and things weren't always as straightforward as she made out. He could do something after he had finished his MSc, when he would be able to contribute from the inside, when he would be able to take action that was considered, planned, strategic, not just him by himself pointlessly destroying his own life.

Chapter 7

Bubbles of anxiety frothed in Megan's veins as Jay wrestled her wheelchair into the back of the Tesla. She really wasn't sure how safe it was for her to go to a shopping centre. Even though she could have feasibly come from the disabled home in Netherly, she didn't have a permit and she had no idea what she would do if anyone asked to see her pass. She fastened her seatbelt and turned to Jay as he reversed out of his parking space, trying to think of a way to broach it that didn't sound ungrateful. He didn't meet her eyes, but he looked assured, like he knew what he was doing. Maybe it was best if she kept her mouth shut and trust he had it all under control, despite her heart's warning beats drumming against the inside of her ribcage.

She stared out of the window, levelling her breathing whilst she drank in the outside world. She could feel Jay occasionally glancing over at her as she committed the passing scenes to memory. What must he think of her being so captivated by the mundane cityscape that he took for granted? She must look like a child — the perpetual unwanted child she seemed destined to be.

This part of the city was new to her and it was a little shabby, downmarket from what she imagined Jay was used to. He stopped the car in an expanse of rutted grey concrete painted with faded white oblongs with a few cars dotted in between, parking across two spaces so he had room to get her wheelchair out of the boot and bring it alongside the passenger door. He gripped the chair while she transferred from the car, like he wasn't going to let it go. As soon as she had settled herself he squatted down beside her so he was just below her eye-level, resting one hand on the side of her chair. It felt both intimate and condescending, the way an adult might crouch down to talk to a very small child – so that really was how he saw her.

He tucked his hair behind his ear with his other hand.

'I know this is all really difficult,' he said imploring her with his eyes. 'And, to be honest, I'm not sure I know the best way to handle it, but I will work something out, I promise. In the meantime please just tell me if there is anything you need, for Silvie, it's what she wanted.'

His eyes moistened and he stood up quickly and looked away.

The carpark was bumpy and Jay manoeuvred Megan's chair carefully over the rough terrain as it would be impossible for her to navigate herself, it also provided respite from those eyes: Silvie's eyes that would have killed him if he had taken her to the police – although he hadn't really known where he was taking her until she was in the car beside him, all quiet and trusting, making it impossible to renege on his promise.

A flame of uncertainty flickered inside him, they were attracting a lot of attention. People stared with expressions somewhere between fascination and hostility, and he was only just now acutely aware he had driven here without thinking about how completely anomalous it was to see a disabled person in public. How had he not considered that? How had he been so complacent to assume Megan would be as unobtrusive at the retail park as she was in his flat, that she would fade into the background and pass unnoticed like she did at home? A rush of panic jarred him. Bringing Megan here was a terrible mistake and his car was so distinctive he would be easily recognised. He hesitated, perhaps he should turn back, but then he would look even more stupid. Besides, once they were in the shop it would be easier. The floor was smooth and flat and he could leave Megan to wheel herself around and keep himself at a safe distance so no-one knew he was with her. And he certainly didn't want to watch her picking underwear and whatever else she needed any more than he imagined she would want him watching her.

But, as soon as they were through the sliding doors, the atmosphere prickled like volts of electricity. He couldn't leave her, so he began pushing her towards the toiletries department the back of the shop. It looked quiet and seemed a fairly innocuous place for them to go together. A million thoughts churned through his mind, only adding to the disorientation of the danger he had put himself in.

As they moved through the aisle he thought he heard someone mutter something in their direction, but he wasn't sure and just kept moving. Then they passed two women and this time the words were unmistakable.

'Bloody scrounger, how come she's got money to spend in here when the rest of us have to work for it?!'

'Yeah, no wonder we're still in economic hardship, too much money spent on freeloaders. If it wasn't for people like her, we'd all be thriving.'

Jay stopped in his tracks. Of course he had heard people say that kind of thing about disabled people before, he might have even said something like that himself before he met Silvie and then Megan. But he would never have done so in anyone's hearing, and certainly not after the drownings in Bootle Cares. A lightening rod of fury spun him around, but Megan stopped him.

'Don't,' she said. 'Let's just go.'

She was already turning herself around and moving towards the door, he followed reluctantly, the heat of his anger making a confrontation feel enticing.

'Good riddance!' someone called as they left the shop.

Jay stopped in the open air to catch his breath, but Megan urged him on. 'Please, can we just go back to your flat?'

As he struggled to get her chair back into the boot, he felt his anger subsiding and something else taking hold. What was it? Guilt? Or perhaps even shame. Shame of association? Or shame of what he had just done? He wasn't sure. Every day that passed only confused him more and, added to that, there was now the mortification of the stupid mess he had just walked them into.

When he was finally back in the car with the doors locked he turned to her. 'I'm really sorry I—'

'I know what people think of me,' Megan interrupted.

Her eyes bored into him as if she could see right inside his mind and a heavy silence cloaked them. What could he say to that? It was true and totally ridiculous to try and pretend otherwise.

A tear escaped down her cheek and she batted it away, turning to the window.

He ought to say something, try and offer her some comfort. He lifted his hand to take hers, hovered, and then returned it to the steering wheel.

How could he console her when the honest truth was he didn't want her, either?

He swallowed and started the car.

Chapter 8

'Here, use this,' Jay angled the screen towards Megan and slid the mouse towards her fingers.

She blinked a couple of times.

It must be a long time, if ever, that she had bought something online. He glanced across at her and saw once again the strange hybrid, not-quite-person he had encountered on his first visit to Bootle Cares. The shock of that initial visit still echoed in his veins: all those strange bodies, the musty cabbage smell that penetrated his hair and clothes, and the guttural sounds ricocheting around the building that he didn't know if were cries of pain or senselessness.

'Just drag and drop whatever you want over here,' he indicated the basket icon. 'And then click twice to check out.'

He tried not to dwell on the memory.

Megan nodded, but still hesitated. Perhaps she was embarrassed to start searching with him hovering over her, after all it was personal things she needed.

'Just get whatever you need,' he offered and turned away, hoping that would ameliorate some of the awkwardness he had caused.

But maybe he was being too hard on himself? How was he supposed to have known she would have periods like other girls? It was hard to imagine her in that way, he had assumed it would be another thing about her that didn't work like everyone else. Besides, he had made a real effort since those first awful visits to Bootle Cares and she was here now, wasn't she? And he had tried hard with her and everyone else back then. And, truth be told, the more he tried the more defined everyone became, like a lens gradually coming into focus until they were no longer the indistinguishable automatons he had imagined when Silvie first told him she visited her younger sister in a disabled home. Even those with mental disabilities, like Cathy, clearly had personhood and individuality that surprised him to begin with and then slowly became more normal. One or twice, at their last few visits, he had caught himself looking at Megan and wondering if Silvie was right, perhaps Megan could survive outside if she had someone to look after her. But he never said anything, the last thing he wanted was to give Silvie ideas and, besides, he wanted to be with Silvie himself, not give her up to care for Megan, however unlikely that was. And yet, look at him now, trapped with Megan in his flat, and no idea what she needed or even really how to talk to her. And he had no clue what she did all day, she didn't even have an internet connection on her laptop. Another stab of guilt pierced his chest – yet another thing it had never occurred to him that she might need.

'Let me get your laptop online,' at least he could put

that right.

Megan handed Jay her laptop with only the smallest worm of doubt coiling inside her. She told herself it was just the strangeness of someone knowing that she had it; passing her device into another person's hands as if it was the most normal thing in the world, not a secret she had guarded for years.

When Navida first moved in to her room, Megan had resorted to typing under the bedcovers so the glow of the screen would not betray her. But she soon realised Navida would never say anything about her sitting up late into the night writing on her laptop: even if she registered what Megan was doing, it would most likely seem like just another dream in the hazy medicated half-reality she inhabited. Navida didn't really seem to care about anything, anyway, it was like she had accepted her life was over and retreated as far away from everything and everyone as possible.

It was hard not to feel angry with Navida for just giving up like that, for thinking so little of disabled people that she could not countenance her life among them. But that was probably too harsh, Megan had Pavel and Silvie who loved her, and Navida had lost everyone and everything she had built her identity around: nurse, wife, mother. But she was still a person, why could she not see that? If only she had listened to Pavel, that might have given her some hope. A bitter pain rose in the back of her throat, then again, perhaps Navida was right, what was the point of hope if they were all going to drown?

Tears threatened to overtop her eyes and she forced her attention back to the present and Jay's fingers tapping on her keypad. He looked almost guilty, or was it worry? Could it be he already knew what was on the laptop and he felt guilty he hadn't done anything about it yet? But if he knew what Silvie had given her surely he would have said something by now? Or perhaps he was worried that once she was online she would do something stupid? But he must know her better than that? Although, really, he barely knew her at all, and he spent so little time at the flat it seemed like he didn't want to either.

She forced her attention back to her search for toiletries, the kinds of things Silvie used to bring for her, but the screen kept filling with products that would probably take half a day to apply – fake tans, eyelid shaping gel, eyelashes, lip-plumping balms and all manner of brightly coloured cosmetics. It reminded her of some of the more outlandish things Pavel used to tell her: gay pride marches with outlandishly made up drag queens, glitter, rainbow flags, a mayhem of sounds and colours which, however much he described, still seemed too bizarre to be true from the confines of their drab world. And yet she believed him, even when the other residents refused.

"How would he know what was happening and what it looked like?" they would sneer.

But Pavel had been partially sighted up until his teens and would have seen enough of the world to describe it even after he lost his sight completely. Besides, only a few minutes in Pavel's company revealed his depth of perception.

"Only people with eyes can't see what is right in front of them," he used to say, and Megan believed him.

She could feel it in herself, the possibility and the potential, just as strongly now as when Pavel was right there in front of her. Perhaps Jay would see it too, eventually? Perhaps if she told him about Silvie's promise and showed him what Silvie had given her, he might think differently? After all, he was connecting her to the world of his own volition, surely that was a sign he wanted to help her?

Jay wasn't used to devices as old as this and he was struggling to work his way around it. The little orange folders on the desktop, each labelled with an incremental set of characters and numbers, were obviously not what he was looking for, but it was tempting to take a peak, nonetheless. Curiosity tugged, what might Megan deem worth saving? He could just have a quick look.

He got up to find his hard drive. It was going to be harder than he had anticipated to ger her online and there wasn't time to waste on trivialities when this thing didn't even have the most basic software installed. He reached across his desk for the drive and a chill of doubt settled inside him. Had he just made another stupid mistake in letting Megan buy feminine products with his online account? It wasn't how much money she would spend that bothered him, his parents kept all his accounts amply supplied and, given where Megan had spent most of her life, she was probably even more frugal than Silvie. But now she was filling the virtual basket with knickers and menstrual products and goodness knows what else, a new fear took hold. Was this the kind of thing the algorithms would pick up? Was this anomalous enough to expose that he was harbouring her in his flat? His chest tightened with the increasingly familiar anxiety. However anyone looked at it, there was absolutely no doubt that everything he was doing was in direct violation of the Right to Care Act and he could be punished.

Should he give up and hand Megan over after all? Realistically, he couldn't keep her in his flat forever, it was amazing he had gotten away with it for this long. So far his grief for Silvie provided the cover for his changed behaviour, but that was finite. And really, what were the options for Megan? What kind of life could she ever have?

At the same time, turning her in to spend the rest of her days in an institution that seemed only one or two degrees away from a prison was difficult to conscience. Silvie would never have done that, she never wanted Megan in there in the first place, and turning Megan in would be the ultimate betrayal. But what about him? The longer this went on the worse it would be when he finally did have to do something. Would he be arrested? Might he get sent to prison? His heart thudded at the prospect. No, his parents would never allow him to end up in prison. Not for this. And surely Adam would know the best defence lawyers even though he practiced corporate law.

Adam: that was who he needed to talk to. Why hadn't

he thought of Adam before?

He looked at the laptop, it was going to take a while for all the programmes to install. He stood up.

'I just have to go to the car,' he told Megan's back and hurried from the flat.

Inside the car Adam's phone kept ringing out.

'Come on,' Jay willed him, drumming his fingers on the dashboard. 'Pick up!'

He looked around the car park, it wasn't strange to be making a call in the car, was it? It didn't necessarily indicate there was someone in his flat who he didn't want to hear the conversation, it was just as feasible that his phone had rang as he was pulling in and he had taken the call. Thankfully there didn't seem to be anyone around to notice.

'Jay,' Adam did not conceal his surprise. 'Is everything okay?'

Jay swallowed, when was the last time he called? He couldn't remember, it wasn't going to be easy to make this seem casual.

'Yes, I'm all right.'

Silence pushed a space between them.

'How are you? How's the family?' Jay blurted, hoping it didn't sound too forced.

'Li Li has been asking when her Uncle Jay is going to come and see her again. You should, it might help to take your mind off things.'

Jay swallowed down another wave of guilt, it seemed to be all he felt these days: guilt and fear. He had always been Li Li's favourite uncle – although between himself and Chris that was hardly an achievement, but he still loved the special bond between them. He and Silvie sometimes babysat and they had taken her to the new year parade twice, now. Li Li fizzed with delight at the multicoloured dragons snaking through the streets and the brightly coloured lanterns released into the dusky sky. Jay squeezed her hand and imagined him and Silvie with their own family.

'Jay?'

'Sorry, yes, you're right, I'd love to come and see her, maybe at the weekend?'

'Yes, come on Saturday.'

Another pause thickened the air.

'Was there something else?'

Jay swallowed, it was hard to say even her name out loud, let alone admit she was in his flat. The demo filled his mind, making his head swim – that was something else altogether. It was very doubtful that even Adam would be so understanding. It wasn't something that could be explained away as easily as taking Megan to Silvie's funeral. It was pre-meditated, subversive, illegal. Now, sitting in his car with his brother on the other end of the phone, he could hardly believe that he had done it himself. The anxiety in his chest intensified, it was hard to breathe.

'Jay, is everything alright? Are you still there?'

He repeated the internal mantra that had been running though his mind since the demo: *It was days ago, nothing has happened; no-one knows I was there.* Feeling his heart slow a little, he exhaled only for another wave of guilt. He had no idea what had happened to any of the others, he had deleted everyone's contact details and the local news said no more about the demo than the EBC. Marica might know something and he could probably trust her. He would let things settle for a few more days and then get in touch.

He had to say something, 'Yes, sorry, I'm just a bit—'

Adam cut in. 'It's a difficult time for you, but you shouldn't spend all your time brooding by yourself, come and see Li Li at the weekend, that will pick you up a bit.'

'Alright I will, I'll see you then.'

Jay tottered back inside the flat, shaken by his own impetuousness, he had nearly confided in Adam, and right now he had no idea if that was a good thing or bad, he had completely lost his gage on reality. Sometimes harbouring Megan in his flat terrified him and he spent long hours in the library staring blankly at his coursework just so he could escape the reality of it. Other times, fuelled by grief and anger, he felt defiant: he had saved her life and surely no-one could object to that. But really he didn't know anything anymore.

He sat down and checked Megan's laptop, everything seemed to have installed okay and it would only take a minute or two to hook up the internet connection. As he unplugged the hard-drive, the files on the desktop caught his eye again. Curiosity tugged harder. What little secrets might Megan have concealed there? Glancing over at her, she was clearly still engrossed in scrolling though the infinite screens of whatever it was she needed to buy. His fingers hovered on the mousepad, he could just take a quick peak.

Seconds later he closed her laptop and stood up. 'All done,' he smiled.

Megan turned and met his gaze. 'Thank you.'

Her eyes were so hopeful that he could have kicked himself for even momentarily considering betraying her trust.

'Please just buy whatever you need,' he faltered, as if another flourish of generosity would compensate for almost violating her privacy.

Then, before she could kill him with more of those soulful eyes, he added, 'Do you want some coffee?' and went into the kitchen.

The beans clattered into the grinder and filled his nostrils with the bitter velvety aroma that he adored. Silvie didn't drink coffee and she never understood his devotion to it. She would often stand behind him with her arms wrapped around his waist gently teasing him as he weighed, ground, and percolated with the precision of a laboratory technician. A long sigh escaped from his lungs and his hands automatically slid to his abdomen as if there was a chance he might still find her fingers resting there, and that the last few weeks had all been a terrible dream.

Chapter 9

Megan waited until Jay had left before she opened her laptop. It was stupid really, he had installed everything she needed to get online but, even so, old habits die hard and it would be a while before she could be as casual about it as he was. Settling herself on the sofa, she rested the metal oblong on her thighs. He'd set up an automatic internet connection, but as soon as it booted up she disconnected it, she wasn't going to take any risks. She clicked through to the devices panel, her eyes skimming the screen too fast to register what was in front of her until they finally alighted on the small orange icon. She exhaled, the file was still there. Sometimes she had wondered whether it really was safest tucked away in the devices panel or if it would actually be better disguised in plain sight in one of the folders on the desktop that contained nothing more than her poems, stories, and the few photographs she owned, but she had never been brave enough to try. But what if Jay had gone into the devices folder to install the internet connection? It was unlikely, the icons seemed to be intended for setting up physical rather than virtual connections, and he would

have surely said something if he found and opened it –
unless, of course, he already knew.

After a rapid skim to make sure there was nothing
obvious wrong, she checked through everything again
more slowly. It was all just as it should be, exactly the
same as when she had transferred it from the data stick
Silvie had given her that she stowed inside her wheelchair
cushion: the copies of all her official identification
documents and screenshots from an Irish website about
the asylum process for people escaping human rights
violations in England. Silvie would never tell her how she
had got hold of it all. She would have had to request
access to the Committee databank to get Megan's
documents and only their parents would be authorised to
do that. And the other details, well, it was illegal to access
that kind of material. Sometimes she wondered if Silvie
had obtained it when she applied to the MSc in Military
Bioengineering, it was a security listed course and might
have given applicants access to different levels of
clearance, except that didn't seem to fit with the timeline.
Even in Megan's world where the weeks, months, and
years merged into a barely distinguishable sludge of time,
she was certain it was not long after Silvie had started her
undergraduate degree that she had arrived with the data
stick, and it must have been pre-Jay because she had
showed up alone.

Back then, Silvie often used to talk about taking
Megan to Ireland, but Megan had never been sure if she
meant they would go together or if Silvie would
somehow get Megan there by herself. Silvie had a lot to

give up in England, even before Jay, and Megan had often wondered if she would really sacrifice everything she had worked so hard for. And then, when she started bringing Jay to Bootle Cares, she never mentioned Ireland again. It was never clear if that was because she didn't want to talk about it in front of Jay or if she had forgotten all about it now she was in love. So, Megan had secreted the information away, along with all the stories that Pavel told her – her own hidden well of possibilities to draw on if the time ever came.

And all of it was still there, her key to freedom waiting to open the door. It didn't just prove who she was and how she was forced to reside in Bootle Cares, it also showed that their paternal grandmother was Irish and Megan was entitled to Irish citizenship and a life of freedom in the Celtic Union.

Still, on most days, the Celtic Union seemed as far away as the moon, not just the three hundred kilometres to Dublin or the Scottish border. But now here she was and the hardest part, getting out of Bootle Cares, was already done. All she needed now was get out of England and over the border. And perhaps Jay would help with that, he had a car and could go wherever he chose. It wasn't too much to ask, was it? Especially not if she showed him how much Silvie had already done.

Jay parked the Tesla in direct view of the security camera and checked the street. He and Silvie always walked from his flat to her parents' house, and it didn't feel good leaving the car in an area like this, even though it was not the worst by any means. It was a small, fairly modern estate of committee terraces where life-long leases were assigned to keyworkers. It was respectable enough, but still a far cry from what he was used to and most certainly from what his parents would expect – although everything about Silvie was a far cry from his parents' expectations.

Even when he first met her, she only eighteen and at the beginning of their degree, she was already critical and outspoken. So, despite his instant attraction to her, he gave her a wide berth and she quickly formed a circle of friends amongst the oddballs from a range of courses, a gaggle of misfits who seemed to be constantly agitated. Jay often wondered if they knew how unattractive they looked to everyone else – although Silvie always stood out amongst them, graceful in contrast to their tense bodies and she smiled a lot more than the rest.

He had slid into easy friendships with those from similar backgrounds with whom he could swap gap year stories, plan expensive adventure weekends and stock up for long boozy parties and, for the first three years of their degree, he and Silvie moved in completely different circles. It was only during their final year, when they opted for two of the same specialisms: Bio-engineering, Risks and Lessons; Bio-engineering, Military Applications, that he finally got to know her. And, the more he paid attention to her, the more he realised she was not simply loud and brash as he had assumed, but was carefully testing the boundaries, trying to find the limits to what they would be told and surreptitiously throwing the truth into doubt. He also slowly became aware that she always managed to avoid the weekly Clap For Our Heroes, even when it was directly after a lecture and the timetable ensured that all students and staff were available for the Friday demonstration of civic gratitude. But he never saw Silvie lined up with their peers, somehow she always got away.

He checked the car was locked and alarmed three times before he finally turned and opened the gate to the miniscule path that led to the front door, his heart speeding up. How were Megan and Silvie's parents going to react to what he had to tell them? Doubts swirled around inside him, after all it was three weeks since the flood they thought had taken the life of their second daughter. How would they feel about him having kept her from them for all this time? He imagined shock, possibly anger, but then perhaps tears of relief that at least one of their daughters was still alive. This could be the remaking of their family. The thought was steadying, this was the right thing to do, he was doing something good.

As soon as he reached the door, he glanced up so the camera could scan his retina before remembering where he was and pressed the doorbell instead; so many of the things he took for granted were completely alien to Silvie's family. Sometimes he thought that was why Silvie could be so outrageous, it was because she wasn't fully aware of what she was doing or the kind of the responsibilities other people had. Like the time she mentioned the 2035 pandemic in their third-year seminar on risk. And even though that was ultimately the catalyst for them getting together, the memory still sobered him: the hushed silence that descended as the lens on the camera at the front of the classroom widened to capture the image of Silvie's face and ID tag and relay it to campus security.

Up until then, they had been discussing the uncontroversial lecture material about the "Big-flu" pandemic in 2030. Even Dr Teenan was referring to it as "Big-flu", a name which Silvie always said it made it sound frivolous. She was right about that, it was an odd name for a deadly, air-born virus that obliterated millions, causing liver, kidney, and respiratory failure before finally coagulating the blood. Silvie insisted the term was a deliberate strategy to detract from what really happened, but it was just as likely that it was simply an easy moniker for "highly pathogenic avian-swine influenza: Beta 1", or HPA-SI:B1/H5N1, that combined the key elements of it: avian and swine, or bird and pig, flu. But it still seemed strange to be using that term in a university and even more so on a bio-engineering programme.

Teenan skipped over the part about how the two years of lockdown had decimated the remnants of the economic recovery promised by England's trade deal with China, and moved straight on to how Big-flu had eventually been traced to a commercial lab-meat facility that had been attempting to integrate lab-grown meat with genetically modified chickens. No-one ate anything other than plant-based proteins these days, but back then consuming animal flesh still had cultural value. "Meat" had an edgy prestige that manufacturers knew they could exploit for profit, especially if they could make virus-resistant lab-meat grow in the bodies of factory farmed birds. But they had failed spectacularly.

The horror and fear of the first few weeks that had turned into months and then years was visceral and it made it obvious why there was little resistance to the sweeping social changes that were made to stabilise the country for the emergency and beyond. Scrupulous state monitoring of all aspects of daily life was required to maintain safety and order and, in that context, the restriction of bio-engineering to state-controlled military health facilities was obvious and uncontested. Even Silvie found it hard to argue with that.

Jay heard movement in the hallway and the door opened a slither. Pale blue eyes regarded him behind frameless lenses before the door swung wide and he was pulled into a tight hug. So, he was forgiven for the funeral, that was a good start. Silvie's mum, or Ellen as she always insisted he called her, held him close and then drew him into the narrow hallway. Behind the remnants of cheap coffee and detergent that lingered in the air there was still a feint wisp of Silvie. His heart lurched in response; when would it get easier?

'It's Jay!' Ellen called up the stairs.

Silvie's father emerged tousle-headed on the landing, wrapping a robe around him, sleeping off another night shift.

Jay opened his mouth to apologise for disturbing him and to insist Liam go back to bed, but then he remembered he needed both of them present for what he had to say.

'I'll be down in a minute,' Liam mumbled and closed the bathroom door behind him.

Ellen led Jay into the cramped front room.

'I'll make some coffee,' her tone was motherly, more so than she ever used with Silvie.

Jay wanted to decline, he had almost choked the first time he took a slug of what passed for coffee in this house, but changed his mind. Rejecting her hospitality was not a good start and it would give him a little time to compose himself.

'Thanks,' he smiled, and Ellen turned towards the kitchen.

Megan closed the devices panel and reconnected to the internet, this would be the first time she had been online with her own laptop. The Badiu page opened, promising the world at her fingertips — or at least the world permitted by The New Governance. Perhaps she should start with something innocuous? But she had already seen a lifetime's worth of approved content on the computer in the dayroom at Bootle Cares and there was something much more important she needed to find out. Tremors jittered her fingers as she typed, making her almost as slow across the keys as when Silvie had first given her the laptop, the nights before she had got used to typing in the semi-darkness and when her mind had worked so much faster than she could type.

Social Eugenics, she keyed in.

It was an expression Pavel often used and she didn't know if it was a recognised term or if it was something he had invented. The search wheel turned. That is what he would call the flood, he would say The Committee wanted them to die, the useless disabled people and the migrant workers that staffed the night shift, everyone would be better off without them.

The screen stayed blank. It was still hard to believe that Bootle Cares was gone, completely destroyed, that the dirty water lapping around the roadblock had taken everyone. It felt temporary, not forever. It was impossible to imagine never seeing them again: Pavel, Cathy, Navida, the people who she shared her daily existence with. But Pavel most of all, it felt so wrong he had been swallowed by the flood and she had not.

The screen blinked, "Were you looking for *social genetics*?" It queried and then answered the question with a list of definitions: "Social science genetics is concerned with understanding whether, how and why genetic differences between human beings are linked to differences in behaviours and socioeconomic outcomes."

It wasn't an official term then, that meant it was either banned or one of Pavel's and either way she shouldn't linger on it. She closed down the search and quickly typed in "home-baking" to cover her tracks. Pavel had told her all about the days when the TV was full of cookery shows. Watching someone making food sounded boring, even from the limited opportunities of her own existence and she couldn't imagine why free people with their full capacities would want to watch that for hours on end; the past was like a different planet.

An array of recipes, websites, and videos filled the screen, she scrolled along and clicked on one that invited her to, "Home bake cinnamon rolls in less than an hour". They looked delicious and it was a long time since she had eaten a fresh, sweet pastry, her mouth watered in anticipation. Maybe she could give it a try? Maybe baking was fun, after all. Perhaps all those TV shows had been popular for a reason? And there was nothing else to do right now, she could make use of the kitchen since Jay had disappeared again. Then, when he returned, perhaps she could talk to him about what Silvie had given her.

Chapter 10

Jay shifted his body, he had taken the chair that matched the sofa, but it was difficult to sit comfortably in the sagging frame. When he visited with Silvie, her parents always deferred to the two of them taking the sofa and he would catch their eyes skimming Silvie's left hand hoping for a ring. Despite their attempts to seem casual, it was obvious they were desperate for him to commit to her. They never did manage to hide how delighted they were with him, or how far he exceeded their expectations of who Silvie might settle with even though she had managed to get into a prestigious university.

Ellen appeared with a tray of steaming mugs and a plate of biscuits, placing it on the chipped side table and offered Jay a mug in one hand and the plate in the other. He accepted politely despite the knotting in his stomach and having no desire to put anything on top of it.

Liam cleared his throat in the doorway to announce his arrival, he was dressed in a navy-blue shirt with a short upright collar and almost matching pants that might have been a work uniform. He looked around and settled himself on the sofa, Ellen passed him a mug and plonked herself down beside him.

'Tough night?' Jay asked

Liam puffed out his cheeks. 'You could say that.' He took a sip of coffee, 'I got sent up to Anfield and that's never a good thing.'

Jay didn't know a huge amount about what Liam did, he was a man of few words. Like Ellen, he worked in civic comms, hence their keyworker status, but whilst she had a low-grade admin position, Liam was some kind of engineer. He was usually based at the server banks in Speke, but occasionally he would get sent to deal with problems on the north side of the city, suggesting he had some kind of seniority.

Jay nodded with what he hoped passed for manly understanding.

'It'll be better when you're back on days again,' Ellen rubbed his thigh.

It must be hard being at the mercy of shifts that often completely separated their lives, only seeing each other in passing, one arriving home as the other prepared to leave. Perhaps that was why they had been so happy for Megan to be taken into a disabled home, at least she was never alone and there was always someone there to look after her. Another a pang of guilt prodded at him, he habitually left Megan alone for hours and days on end without a thought of what help she might need. Yet, now he thought about it, she always seemed to manage just fine by herself.

Ellen was saying something about her job, she sat at a screen all day checking communications that were flagged up for scrutiny by the algorithms, she didn't have security clearance so her role was simply to pass anything that was potentially subversive to those above her – usually Security Studies students on work placements. It was hard to imagine how she did something so mind-numbing day-in, day-out for years on end. He tried to focus on what she was saying, somehow he needed to bring the conversation round to Megan. Finally there was a pause.

'How are you feeling after, um, the funeral?' He couldn't say Silvie's name for fear his voice would crack.

A chill settled in the air and he fought the urge to fill the silence and smooth things over, the way he had wanted to in that seminar, even though he barely knew Silvie then.

Silvie had waited patiently for Dr Teenan to acknowledge her raised hand and invite her question. Then, without faltering, she spoke loud and clear.

'If the measures following the pandemic in 2030 were so effective, how does that explain the pandemic of 2035?'

She didn't flinch once, not as the camera captured her image and relayed it to security nor as it slowly rotated from her to focus on Dr Teenan. Teenan on the other hand looked petrified, her position was now as precarious as Silvie's. Students were not supposed to ask questions about things that were not on the curriculum, but staff could just as easily be dismissed for mentioning them in reply. Jay looked on in silence with his classmates as Teenan struggled to remember the protocol for situations like this.

She was young and her demeanour suggested she was one of those especially pliant members of staff who were eternally grateful for her job at The China University of Liverpool and would never do anything to put it in jeopardy. It was the only surviving university in the city and one of a few remaining institutions in the north. It survived where others had failed because of the strong links it had made with China long before any of the pandemics, The Deal, or The New Governance.

This could have been a career-ending moment for Teenan. She swallowed, her face betraying every passing thought. She would have to go straight to security after class and notify them about this breach of protocol. Even though the university recorded everything, staff were still expected to immediately report any student asking subversive questions as a demonstration of their loyalty to the institution and to avoid any suspicion of complicity. Seconds creaked by as the red light on the camera blinked expectantly at Dr Teenan.

Jay had desperately wanted to fill the silence but had no idea how he might do that without implicating himself. He imagined Teenan spending her induction at The China University anxiously learning the mandated responses, fearing a raft of radical students in every class. And then as the weeks and months went by they had slipped from her memory. This was a prestigious university and the students had as much to fear as the staff for aberrations from the approved curriculum – making Silvie either the bravest or the stupidest person he had ever met.

Finally, Teenan responded. 'University is not a place for untrue or speculative assertions. We deal with facts. The facts are,' she cleared her throat, 'The facts are that regulations were put in place so there would never be a repeat of the 2030 pandemic.'

That in itself was true, Big-flu had never resurfaced, but it still didn't explain 2035. Teenan looked at the clock, and eleven pairs of eyes followed. Ten minutes left.

'So, what does Big-flu teach us about the risks of commercial bio-engineering?'

Her voice steadied, she clearly felt back in control, she had directed the answer she wanted in her question and circumvented any further opportunities for subversion. Three hands shot up in response, one of them had been Jay's.

Thankfully Teenan hadn't called on him to speak, he didn't really want to contribute, but he was scared for Silvie and wanted to create as much distance from what had just happened as possible.

His stomach churned now with a similar feeling, except this time he had to keep pushing the conversation forwards rather than steering away from it.

Ellen sighed. 'She was everything to us, our lives will never be the same without her.'

Swallowing down the tears that were ready to ambush him at every moment, Jay nodded.

Liam took Ellen's hand but said nothing.

Jay forced himself on. 'And Megan?'

Ellen's body relaxed. 'Well, it's a blessing really, isn't

it? What life was she ever going to have?'

Jay felt the bile of cheap coffee rising in his throat, he tried to swallow but choked instead, almost slopping coffee over the rim of his mug and onto his lap.

What could he say to that? Was there even a response to a mother being relieved that her youngest daughter was dead and so soon after her eldest had been taken? And even though he could not deny the terrible thoughts he sometimes had about Megan dying instead of Silvie, it was unthinkable to hear it from their mother. It made him queasy, his own mother was incapable of being so callous, she would be devastated if anything happened to him.

Liam murmured something that sounded like assent, but Jay didn't catch his words.

Ellen looked at Jay with an expression he couldn't read, but he hoped she couldn't see how appalled he was. He forced a nod and raised his mug, letting the coffee wet his lips but not daring to attempt to swallow.

'I know you meant well,' Ellen's gaze was still fixed on him, 'But you shouldn't have brought her to the funeral, and certainly not without asking us first.'

Jay looked at his lap. 'I'm sorry,' he said and then forced his eyes back to hers so she could see he meant it – he was sorry he had come here and said anything, sorry he had misjudged things so badly.

'You don't know what it's like,' Ellen continued. 'Having to care for someone with a disability, what it does to your family, your life.'

She held up her hand to stop the interjection that

would have been inevitable if Silvie had been there.

'I know what Silvie thought about it, but she was always very idealistic. That was her one fault, and besides, it wasn't her that had to take care of Megan twenty-four-seven.'

A chill of realisation travelled up Jay's body, they probably didn't know he and Silvie had been visiting Bootle Cares. No wonder it was such a shock when he showed up with her at the funeral. They had completely closed her out of their lives, and he had just attempted to push her back in for a second time in as many weeks.

'I'm sorry,' he said, standing up. 'I should go.'

Ellen blanched slightly as if she had just realised how risky it was for her to chide him now she no longer had any claim to his time.

She stood up and moved across to him and squeezed his shoulder. 'I know you meant well, you're a good person, you've become like a son to us.'

She moved her body closer, offering a hug and he stepped into it even though it was the last thing he wanted. She smelled of old cooking, cheap shampoo, and laundry detergent.

'Come and see us again sometime,' she said pulling away. 'You're always welcome.'

Jay nodded and Liam stood up and shook his hand.

When he was finally out of the house and back in the car it took all his self-control not to collapse against the steering wheel, but their feint outlines watching at the window restrained him. He drove out of their street and turned towards the Mystery park, he needed time to gather his thoughts before he went home to face Megan and the endless unanswered question of what he should do with her.

Chapter 11

It was getting late. If he stayed there much longer he was likely to look suspicious or attract the wrong kind of attention. Even though, as far as he knew, there hadn't been squatters in the park for years, it still wasn't a good idea for someone like him to loiter there. But he wasn't ready to go back to the flat, either. Not yet, not with Ellen's words still coursing through his veins. She was glad Megan was dead, he shuddered. What would she think if she knew that not only was Megan still alive but it was him taking her to the funeral that had saved her life and, since then, he had been harbouring her in his flat?

There was no way he could make of any of it OK now, he had exhausted all his options: his family, her family, the police – well, the police were still potentially an option, but the longer it went on the worse the consequences would be for him when he finally did take her.

What would Silvie do? He pushed the thought away, it was stupid, Silvie was dead. He opened the car door, one more circuit of the park and he would make a final decision and go home. Feet crunching on the uneven path and wishing he had his running shoes with him, he let his mind pull him back to the day of the seminar, when he followed Silvie out of the building and, once he was sure they were out of view of any of the cameras, started a conversation with her.

'Your question really freaked Teenan out.'

She looked at him, not hiding her surprise he had approached her and openly scouring his face for an agenda.

'I know, I didn't want to scare her, I just wanted to see how she would react to the obvious anomaly being highlighted.'

'Well she's probably in security now sweating over the recording,' he forced a smile.

'She'll be fine, she followed the protocol.'

Her tone was flat, closing down the conversation.

'Aren't you worried?' he coaxed, surprised by how much he wanted to keep her talking.

'Not really,' she replied, a light smile finally dancing across her lips. 'It's a legitimate question. We have it drummed into us that The New Governance is to protect us from instability in the wake of the 2035 pandemic. Yet, at the same time, we are told about the success of the response to Big-flu. Anyone can see the discrepancy.'

The official history leading up to that point was uncontested: the economic depression following the first pandemic of the 2020s that had been intensified by the wars – economic and military – and the political upheaval that followed in their wake. The UK had broken up and Ireland unified, leaving England with a rapidly shrinking economy and adrift from its immediate neighbours in the Celtic and European Unions. In urgent need of trade and political partners, England had welcomed "The Deal" with China, but the country had still been on its knees when the Big-flu pandemic hit just a few years later.

'You don't believe the conspiracy theories, do you?' He couldn't conceal the incredulity in his tone.

'That depends on what you mean.'

She looked at him, piercing him with those vivid blue eyes that betrayed none of the madness he expected behind such words.

'So you think it was a hoax?' He laid it out for her to confirm or deny. 'That the 2035 virus didn't really exist, it was a *plandemic* or whatever they call it?'

'Well, it is a bit of a mixed-up narrative, isn't it? All the regulations that were put in place after Big-flu so it could never happen again, and then just three years after the end of lockdown another pandemic blows up. Did you know it's sometimes called the English pandemic – or the Chinglish pandemic depending on your perspective on The Deal? There is no report of it in Wales or Scotland. Of course, that could be because England took such decisive action to prevent the spread, but given what we know about Big-flu that seems a little bit unlikely.'

Jay was often shocked by the things Silvie seemed to know and frequently wondered where she got the information from. She certainly couldn't have found it in the University archives and she wouldn't have been stupid enough to search for it with her own devices.

A shiver ran through him, stopping him dead. Or had she? His stomach flipped and he took a long, steadying breath. Could she have made some kind of idiotic mistake that got her branded as a subversive and killed?

No, he chided himself, crunching his feet harder against the path, that's even more paranoid than the theories that the worst of her oddball mates would concoct. Her death was an accident, it was also an injustice. That was what was wrong with it, the injustice, nothing more. Just because she had been killed by someone driving a Committee car didn't mean they had deliberately murdered her. Whatever Silvie thought, things were not that bad.

Another memory surfaced before he could repress it. One of Silvie's weird angsty friends had died in strange circumstances in their second year. He disappeared after he met a guy from a dating app. His body was found a week later in a disused carpark on the outskirts of the city. The autopsy revealed a drug overdose, death by misadventure. But Silvie was adamant he never used; he didn't even drink. The profile of the guy on the app turned out to be a fake and they never did figure out who he was despite all the CCTV. Jay pushed the thoughts away, he would drive himself mad if he kept thinking like that. Even Silvie had never said outright she thought it was a state killing despite her outspoken opinions on pretty much everything else.

He turned his mind back to the day of the seminar.

'And it's a bit of a coincidence it happens at just the same time as the Arctic Melt, isn't it?' she continued, apparently warming to the topic and, he hoped, to him.

'Most of the world including the CU and the EU had been preparing for years, while England continued with rhetoric about fake news and technological solutions, reassuring the public a chemical refreeze would stop the melt. But it doesn't, sea levels surged and England goes back into a lockdown that we never come out of – except it's not called lockdown this time, it's called The New Governance.'

She was clearly on a roll, enjoying laying out the evidence before him.

'The Fixed Term Parliament Act is extended indefinitely, councils become Local Governance Committees and the National Security Bill is enacted to rid us of anyone who wants to draw attention to the unfolding climate catastrophe.'

'So you *do* believe the conspiracy theories?'

'I'm open-minded, Jay.'

She stopped walking and turned to look at him.

'Not everything is as perfect and glossy as you might believe.'

Jay opened his mouth to respond but couldn't think of anything to say. She was still watching him, her electric blue eyes sparking with something he couldn't read and, despite everything, he was hooked.

She turned and continued walking. He hesitated and then trotted after her.

Drawing alongside, he touched her arm. 'Do you fancy a beer?' he asked impetuously.

To his relief she smiled and nodded. 'Alright,' she

said. 'So long as you don't mind being seen with someone who might be peddling conspiracy theories.'

The next couple of weeks had been intoxicating, they hung around together, talking and messing about, each waiting for the other to signal it was going to turn into something more. There was a hesitancy in their budding relationship that he was not used to, he usually felt more confident around girls than he did with Silvie. There was something about her which made him question himself in ways he had never done before. He always felt an easy assuredness with his previous girlfriends: assured of their interest in him and assured of himself. But Silvie pierced though all of his layers and it felt scary and exciting. She challenged him and made him think about himself and the world differently, as if she was taking him on an adventure, a bit like the seven labours of Hercules, except that she was testing his mind not his body.

The memory of her was so vivid he could almost inhale her scent and trace her the curve of skin beneath his fingers. Yet, she was also so far away from him now that it felt like a different lifetime, a different person. These days it felt like he was watching his former self on a movie screen; the only person who couldn't foresee the inevitable tragedy as the plot sped towards Silvie's death.

He turned back towards the car, if only he was more like her: braver, more certain.

Chapter 12

The EBC news was coming to an end and their empty plates rested on the low table in front of them. Jay took a sip of his beer, ready to spring up and stack the dishwasher the minute the evening bulletin finished. The news provided an easy rationale for their silence and he was more and more afraid of the conversation that must be inevitable as time went on. He took another slug from his bottle and glanced at the glass of water he had placed on the table in front of Megan. Never in all these weeks had he thought to offer her a beer, assuming alcohol, like so many things, was not for her. She had never said anything about it but, in fairness, anytime it seemed like she was about to start a conversation he made his excuses and left as quickly as he could. He could manage her being here when it was like this, when they sat in silence like an old married couple who lived at arms-length, accepting the other's presence but avoiding intimacy as much as possible in the tiny space of his flat. It was like they had reached an unspoken understanding that on the nights when he came home directly after Uni, they would eat together quietly in front of the news and then retreat to their separate rooms. Mostly he picked up something on the way home, but occasionally he would cook. Other nights he left her to her own devices, to reheat left-overs or whatever she could find in the fridge. It was far from ideal but it was the best he could manage right now.

The news trundled towards its conclusion and the night sky closed in around them. He looked across at Megan and then, for some reason, he could not take his eyes away. She was sitting at the other end of the sofa with her legs tucked underneath her and her wheelchair obscured by the dusk. Luscious red hair tumbled around her body and her eyes danced with promise. In the half-light she could almost be Silvie, especially when she pushed her hair back from her face exactly the same way that Silvie used to do. Something stirred deep inside his body and propelled him towards her.

'You're so like her,' he whispered, tilting her chin upwards and leaning forwards to bring his mouth to hers.

Surprise, and then something else, registered in her eyes, something that made her look even more like Silvie.

Megan could feel Jay's breath against her skin and the intoxicating mixture of his scent and cologne wrapping around her. A fireball sped downwards from the pit of her stomach. They hovered, their lips about to touch. Then, with all the strength in her body, she shoved him away.

'No! Don't try and kiss me because you want Silvie. I'm not Silvie! She's dead!'

It took all her power to push him away, she wanted

him to kiss her so much, but not this much, not so much that she would let him pretend she was Silvie. She flung herself into her chair and sped to her room, slamming the door behind her. A scream curdled in her throat, she wanted to scream so loud that the walls would crumble. But all she could do was throw herself face down onto her narrow bed and sob into her pillow. It was so unfair, so cruel, he could be touching her now, it could be just the way she had always dreamed it would be. Except that it wouldn't be her he was touching, it would be Silvie. And however much she wanted him, she could not sink to that. She could not have sex with her dead sister's boyfriend whilst he imagined she was Silvie and she longed for him to want her for herself, she would not let that be her first real experience. It had to be with someone who cared about her, otherwise it would be just the same as before, like she didn't matter, like she wasn't a person at all.

She was fourteen the first time it happened. She heard the lock on her door turning and scrambled to hide her laptop. A heavy outline filled the doorway and then moved into her room, locking the door behind him. Ben, he said his name was, but she knew that wasn't true. He sat on the side of her bed, bowing the mattress towards him and she pushed herself as far away from him as possible, pressing her body against the wall. In the gloom of the night light she could see a strange smile on his face as he leaned towards her and the air soured with the smell of his armpits. He took her by the shoulders and dragged her back across the bed towards him. She struggled to pull herself free, but he punched her in the face, knocking her flat and springing tears of shock from her eyes. Then he clamped a hot, meaty hand around her throat so she could hardly breathe. She scrabbled at his fingers, but he only strengthened his grip.

'Stop it,' he had whispered in a tone she instinctively obeyed.

He loosened his grip just enough that she could still breathe whilst his other hand worked its way underneath the bedcovers. She struggled at first but his fingers tightened again.

'Stop!' he hissed and she feared for her life.

His rough fingers scrabbled at the waist of her pyjamas and then forced themself between her legs.

'You're going to learn to behave like a normal girl,' he rasped.

Pain tore through her as he rammed his big, dirty fingers inside her.

His eyes sparkled with hateful joy, 'That's better,' he said leaning so close to her that the oniony heat of his breath was damp on her face. 'You'd better be a good girl otherwise you don't know what else might happen to you.'

She closed her eyes. It felt like he was tearing her apart, destroying her so that she could never be whole again, trapping her in a prison of pain and hate and shame. She hated him, but she hated herself more, for lying still and doing nothing but weeping pathetic, silent tears and wishing herself a million miles away. Her pillow was soaked with tears when he left, locking the door behind him.

The next day she pretended that the blood in her pyjamas was her period. But she couldn't keep the secret forever, not from Pavel. As the nights of Ben took their toll, Pavel gently coaxed the truth out of her. He trembled with rage when she finally told him. She had never seen him so angry, it was not the same as when he was all fired up to lecture the residents about the rights of disabled people. This was a primal rage, like he could kill someone with the power of it, it almost scared her. But the complaint was a disaster. The manager twisted it all around and started accusing Pavel of doing things to her until she cried hysterically and begged him not to say anything else. She couldn't lose him, she would tolerate Ben every single night of the week so they wouldn't take Pavel away. But in the end she didn't have to, Ben, or whatever his name really was, got transferred to another home and she never dared to think of what he might be doing there with his big dirty fingers and his hateful ugly lies.

In the months that followed, Pavel told her over and over again that whatever twisted lies Ben had told her, what he did was not normal, it was not the same as when someone cared about you. When someone touched you with love it felt like they had turned every millimetre of your body into diamonds that were sparkling in the sun. He told her about the boyfriends he had had when he was young, and that sex was beautiful when you were with someone that cared about you. As he spoke she could almost see his young self behind the creases in his skin and his thinning grey hair, he must have been very good-looking back then, she could see why he'd had lots of boyfriends. Pavel told her she would find someone who would make her feel that way too, but she had no idea how that would ever happen.

Later on, she wondered if it would feel the same way as it did when she touched herself. Some nights when Navida had fallen into her drugged sleep she would think of Jay and let her fantasies unfold beneath her fingers. Then she would feel awkward the next time he showed up with Silvie as if it was visible on her face. Could he see that she liked him or, worse still, could he see all those fantasies playing out behind her eyes? Was that why he had tried it on with her just now? Had he assumed she would be that easy?

She thought about what they could have been doing together and felt a rush of desire. And then she thought about him imagining she was Silvie and she felt sick. She could not do that to herself, she had to value herself more than that. Anyway, she could never compete with her sister, Silvie could probably do all kinds of wild things in bed she had no idea about and no possibility of matching, how would she even know what to do at all?

There was a gentle knock on her door. Half lifting her face from her pillow, she waited to see if it repeated, hoping he would go away. She didn't want him to see her all red and tear stained, and she definitely didn't want him in the tiny sanctuary of her room. He tapped on the door again and then opened it a crack. Pushing herself into a sitting position and smoothing her dress over her thighs, she braced herself for whatever was coming next. A slither of his face appeared through the gap in the door, but at least he didn't open it any wider.

'I just wanted to say I'm sorry,' he said quietly.

She nodded, she couldn't think of anything to say. But she didn't have to, he closed the door and padded into his bedroom and shut the door. She thought she heard a sob but she couldn't be certain.

Megan opened the oven door and hot, sweet air buffeted her skin. Eight perfect, golden-brown almond croissants smiled at her as she lifted the tray onto the wooden chopping board and picked up the next in line. It was laid out with six symmetrical sweet potato pies, raw and naked-looking beside their gently crisped neighbours. She knew it was a little wasteful to cook them in separate batches, but she wanted each to have perfect positioning in the centre of the oven. Besides, Jay was barely here anymore and he hadn't cooked in weeks, he was hardly likely to be worrying about his energy bills. She batted the thought away, there was no point in feeling resentful towards him, he was, after all, her last hope of escape.

The glance of her fingertip against the hot crisp surface of the pastry confirmed it was cooked to perfection, she seemed to have a knack for baking and she was becoming more experimental with whatever ingredients and equipment were within her reach. Up until now she had only ever created with words on a screen and it was surprisingly satisfying to turn disparate ingredients into an array of sweet treats and savouries.

She had started out with the simple recipes she found online but quickly grew tired of following instructions and instead trusted her instincts as to what would work, and most of the time she was right. She always left her creations on the kitchen worktop for Jay to sample whatever time of day or night he came home and there were only ever crumbs left in his wake.

They hadn't spoken since that awful night, but he had been making a noticeable effort with the shopping, keeping the fridge and the cupboards stocked and always placing them within her reach. At the same time, she lived in complete solitude, and no amount of baking could overcome the trapped isolation that threaded through her veins and grew a little deeper every day.

Sometimes, after she had gone to bed, she heard him watching the late-night news and willed herself to get up and talk to him, but so far she had just lain there, unable to summon the courage. Hiding in stasis was so much easier. At the same time, it was obvious they couldn't go on like this, she had to talk to him. If only he would help her to leave, get to Ireland, she would be free and all of this would all be over. Could he simply drive her to Scotland and over the bridge from Portpatrick to Larne? It couldn't be too difficult, all the trade and energy treaties meant it was a soft border between England and Scotland and people crossed from country to country every day, openly, legally – albeit for very different reasons than the English authorities would admit. Pavel had laughed out loud when he read Silvie's school text books describing how England continued to invest in CU solar and wind power to help support the economic development of its former regions, who would inevitably move on to sheal gas production when their economies were advanced enough to do so. In truth, long before the melt, and as soon as the Celtic Union had formed they began preparing for a future based on renewable energy and sea freight. They built sea defences and refigured their ports to withstand the rising sea-levels and they generated more power than they could use through tidal, wind, and solar energy. England had chosen a different path, reopening coal mines and fracking for gas, leaving them dependent now on the Celtic Union that they sought to separate themselves from in every other way.

Megan swallowed down a shard of pain, reconciling what she knew with being here was getting harder and harder, if she didn't get out soon she would go mad or die. There was no option but to talk to Jay. But how much he would be prepared to help and what was okay to ask of him was another matter altogether. On the other hand, what choice did she have? And although there were no doubt limits to what he was willing to risk, he must be just as eager to get her out of his flat as she was to be gone. Even if he was only prepared to take her as far as Scotland, she would be safer there and she could probably figure out a way to get to Ireland by herself. It would be hard, but she could do it.

At the same time, she could not deny that he had risked a lot for her already. He had let her stay in his flat when he could have turned her in; he went on the demo of his own volition; and, of course, he had taken her to

Silvie's funeral in the first place. Perhaps he would feel better about helping her to escape when he knew Silvie had already done most of the work and he saw the documents she had?

She slid the warm croissants onto the cooling rack and arranged them into a circle, decision made. It was up to her now, she would wait for Jay to come home and then she would tell him everything and they could make a plan.

Chapter 13

It had been dark for a couple of hours already and Megan could feel the last of her resolve ebbing away. Jay still wasn't back, and her plan that they would talk after the early evening news was completely redundant. It was now looking like she would have to face him after he had been out with his friends and her confidence was waning – a night out would only exacerbate the chasm between their lives and make her proposal seem even more unthinkable.

At eleven PM she gave up, closed down her laptop, switched off the lights and went into her room. As she climbed into bed she heard the front door opening. She sat still, summoning the courage to go face him, but there was another voice, he had someone with him. It was a woman, jealousy spiked her. Then she tensed, had she left anything in the sitting room that would betray her presence?

Clattering sounds and spurts of laughter ricocheted out from the kitchen – they must have found the pastries she had made earlier. There was a loud blast of music.

'Shssh, Marcia!' Jay slurred. 'The neighbours!'

He laughed and drunken footsteps tumbled towards the sitting room. Silence followed and then the sound of a bottle being kicked over. Jay's voice filled the air but not loud enough to make out what he said, then there were more erratic footsteps and the soft clunk of his bedroom door closing.

Only a thin wall separated her room from his and she could hear more stumbling around and then silence. Then she could hear them again, except now it was just noises, grunting and gasping. She knotted herself under the duvet, pulling a pillow tight around her ears, but it made no difference, she could hear them as clearly as if she was in the room with them. They were getting louder and louder. It was worse than torture. How could Jay have sex with someone knowing she was in the next room and it was only weeks since Silvie had died? The grunting, gasping, and moaning was relentless, she clutched the pillow tighter around her ears, longing to be anywhere but here.

Eventually silence descended, but Megan lay awake, her mind racing. Who was that woman? Had he just picked her up or had he been seeing her for a while – maybe even while Silvie was alive? Fury curdled inside her, he was a prick, an arrogant, selfish prick. What had Silvie ever seen in him? The sooner she got herself out of here and away from him the better. She would find a way with or without his help and she would be glad to get away from him forever.

Sleep must have eventually overtaken her because she woke the next day with her bedside lamp still alight. She was about to get out of bed and use the bathroom when she remembered the night before. The hot torch of anger reignited inside her, she was trapped inside her room until that woman left, trapped by Jay's selfishness and stupidity.

Minutes dragged like hours, the weight of her bladder grew more and more urgent, how long was she going to have to endure this? She tried to comfort herself that at least she wasn't having to listen to them having sex again, but it did nothing to dilute her fury. After an eternity, muted voices seeped into the silence, quickly followed by footsteps and, at last, the sound of the front door closing. Ears straining, Megan waited another moment, was she alone again at last? A kitchen tap turned and a solitary pair of footsteps, Jays, receded behind his bedroom door which closed with a soft click. Finally she could move.

With her bladder mercifully empty, she ran herself a bath, undressed and carefully lifted herself from her chair to the side of the bath and then lowered herself into the water, glad of her strong arms. She had been doing exercises from a website that detailed how to use items from the kitchen as weights and resistance. It was designed to be a home workout for times when lockdown restrictions were in place, to ensure everyone was taking responsibility for their health. To begin with, she thought it was silly, but she tried it a few times and quickly realised she enjoyed the feeling of working her muscles and, as the days went on, she liked the impact it was having on her body.

She sank into the hot water, if only it would dissipate

the venom that was boiling inside her. Her anger was raw; how could she ever look him in the face after this? Humiliation, jealousy, and hatred swirled inside her. She hated being dependent on him, she hated the disparity between them, she hated him. Just because he was rich and gorgeous and going to university he thought he could do whatever he liked regardless of anyone else. He was a spoilt, selfish prick and she was stupid for liking him. He must think she was a useless, ugly blob. He must hate her being alive when Silvie was dead, although, what could he have really felt for Silvie if he could do that so soon afterwards? Silvie would be so hurt if she knew. The rage curdled tighter in her stomach, he had betrayed Silvie and that was the most unforgivable of all.

After she was bathed and dressed she went out onto the balcony with her laptop to make the most of the fresh air before the sun made its way round to that side of the building. But it was impossible to focus on the page in front of her, her mind was spinning threads of fury faster than she could think, and that only added more fuel to her rage. He had even stolen her ability to write, one of the few things that was hers and she loved. She closed the story and clicked onto a recipes page, still not focused but her drifting attention mattered less. If there was any way she could leave the flat she would throw her belongings in a bag and be gone in an instant, but she was stuck. And now, to make it worse, she could hear Jay moving around in the background and it was impossible to get to her room from the balcony without crossing his path. She kept her back to the living room, her eyes on the screen, ignoring him as best she could. Then he was leaning in the doorway of the balcony beside her and she had no choice but to look up. He was wearing baggy pyjama bottoms and a dark blue t-shirt that clung to the gentle undulations of his muscles. His hair was tousled and there was a dark shadow of stubble across his face. He was paler than normal, but a glow of appreciation stirred in her stomach, she still responded to him, regardless of how humiliated she felt by her stupid, pointless feelings. He passed her a mug of coffee.

'I hope I didn't wake you last night?'

It was more like a plea than a question.

She took the mug and looked away, unable to control the flush creeping over her face.

He exhaled. 'I'm sorry.'

He let his back slide down the doorjamb so he was squatting in the doorway. He was blocking her path and she couldn't get away from him.

'I'm sorry, Megan,' he said again.

He sounded like he actually meant it.

He put his face in his hands. 'I'm normally better than this. I just,' he paused and swallowed, 'I just don't know what I'm doing anymore. It feels like my whole life is turned upside down and I just don't know what to do.'

Megan looked at him, part of her felt sorry for him, but another part of her was furious. She closed the lid of the laptop and turned to face him.

'Your fucking life?'

It came out louder and harder than she expected and she hadn't meant to swear.

He looked up at her in surprise.

'Your fucking *life*!?'

She said it again, now that her anger was uncorked she couldn't hold it back.

She waved her arm in the direction of his flat. 'You look pretty fucking comfortable to me! You go to Uni, you come and go as you want, you do what you want with whoever you want almost like Silvie never existed.'

She knew that would hurt but she didn't care, she wanted to wound him.

'She might not have meant much to you, but she was my sister and a better person that you could ever be. And I've not only lost her, but I've also lost all the people I loved. We might all look like useless lumps to you but they were my family. And I've got nowhere to go and no life ahead of me apart from hiding in your spare room while you get on with your life and go around fucking whoever you want. You're a spoilt, selfish bastard, Jay, so don't ever try and tell me how hard your fucking life is!'

The words suddenly ran out, she hadn't meant to say any of that, it had poured out in a froth of anger and now she needed to get away from him, only she was stuck on the balcony with him blocking the doorway. He saw her hands on her wheel rims, stood up and silently moved out of her path. She pushed herself past him and into her room and slammed the door behind her, shaking with anger. She felt like throwing her laptop at the wall, but she didn't have the luxury of being that impulsive so she picked up a pillow and flung that instead.

There was no choice but to apologise. She had prepared what she would say while he was out for his run and waited until he had washed, dressed, and eaten before she forced herself into the living room to face him. He was slouched on the sofa, thumbing his phone but as soon as she came in he put it down and sat upright.

'I'm sorry,' she said. 'I shouldn't have said any of that. I know you don't have to do this, and that you are risking a lot by having me here and I do really appreciate it. It's none of my business what you do with your life.'

Tears welled in her eyes, she felt stupid already, crying was the last thing she needed. There was more she had planned to say, but if she spoke again her voice would crack and betray her. Jay looked at her for a moment. Then, to her surprise, he got up and moved over to her and, a little awkwardly, leant down and hugged her. Fighting her tears for all she was worth she kept her arms pressed to her sides.

He pulled back from her and perched on the edge of the sofa.

'No, you're right, I am the one who should be sorry. I brought you here without telling you what I was doing and then I just sort of left you. And I know it looks like I am carrying on with my life as normal, but I don't really know what I am doing most of the time. Silvie dying, Bootle Cares flooding, the demo, it all feels overwhelming and I suppose Uni is my last bit of normality to hang on to.'

He swallowed and looked at the floor. 'And I know how it looks me sleeping with Marcia, but it wasn't like that.'

He stopped, embarrassed, obviously he wasn't going to talk to Megan about sex. He looked towards the balcony and changed the subject.

'I can see it seems like I am acting like you are not here, and I don't mean to, I just don't know what else to do. I have been trying to figure it all out and I'm just getting more and more confused.'

'But you don't need to work it out on your own,' the tears were subsiding and her resolve was returning. 'I can figure things out as well.'

She held his eyes and took a deep breath, now was the time to tell him.

'I have other information, too, a plan Silvie started. It could be a way out of this for both of us. Please don't assume I am completely helpless.'

He looked away for a second and then returned to her eyes. 'I don't think you are helpless, Megan.'

He said it with conviction, like he meant it.

He sighed. 'I guess I just feel like all of this is my responsibility and I should fix it. I don't want you to suffer because of what I did.'

'Well, I would be dead if you hadn't kept me out.'

'I know.'

He moved over to her and rested a hand on her shoulder. 'I'm glad you are still here.'

Megan couldn't fight back her tears anymore. Jay wrapped his arms around her and she sobbed into him finally returning his hug. He held her tight, their bodies pressed together so that she could feel light convulsions in his chest as if he was crying too.

Eventually, when she had no more tears, they parted and Jay quickly wiped his eyes on his sleeve.

He gently squeezed her shoulder again. 'I'll make some coffee and let's talk.'

Megan nodded, went into her room and picked up her laptop, at last they were going to make a plan.

Chapter 14

Megan stared at her reflection in the mirror. With her hair tucked up under the big, floppy cap and the tinted lenses dulling her eyes to pale grey, two of her most distinctive features were erased. The glasses also partially covered the dusting of freckles over the bridge of her nose – there was still plenty of time to buy concealer, but it didn't look like she would need to.

June seemed a lifetime away, but in her heart of hearts she knew it was the best Jay could manage. He had to be extra careful not to do anything that might provoke questions or arouse suspicion, and asking for time off from his course before teaching had finished would do both. There was also a bio-engineering conference in Dublin that provided a handy rationale for him taking leave and requesting his passport before he had submitted his dissertation. And at least they weren't going to have to wait until after the August deadline before they could travel, she would definitely go mad if she had to stay shut in his flat until then. But, to be fair, he had become noticeably more considerate these days and he was trying to make things easier for her. He had put money into a debit account so she could buy whatever she needed online, and he encouraged her to make lists of ingredients for her baking experiments that he went out of his way to fulfil. He regularly brought her books from the library and often spent evenings at the flat with her. She liked the change, it was like he was finally starting to see her as a person and, now they were actually relating to one another properly, it helped to put her silly fantasies to bed, there was no way there could ever be anything between them, they were a million miles apart.

Shifting her weight from one side of her body and then the other, she pulled on Silvie's black pyjama bottoms, cut off at one knee to accommodate the chunky medical boot she bought online along with the cream-coloured sling that rested around her neck. It was a little awkward to get her foot inside the boot and she couldn't wheel herself when she had her arm in the sling, but the transformation was remarkable. She looked like someone who was temporarily injured rather than permanently disabled and, if she held her nerve, this would enable her to travel alongside Jay for most of the journey. She had created a story to accompany them: she and Jay were cousins, she had been visiting from Scotland and she had fallen down stairs at a party and now Jay was taking her home. It shrank her visibility to that of a normal person, someone who could move around freely wherever she chose.

A scorch of anger burned inside her. Why did her wheelchair matter so much? Why did it negate everything else about her? She was a person just the same as everyone else, she had the same needs and feelings and desires, yet no-one seemed to believe that, it was like she was nothing and could do nothing. It wasn't just Bootle Cares that confined her, they had made her own body into a prison.

'Ireland will be different,' she consoled herself, trying to imagine what her life there might be like and whether it would be anything like the story she had created: a life that involved traveling and going to parties; a family of people who wanted her. It seemed impossible, too much to hope for, just to be able to live with a bit of autonomy and dignity would be enough. Shaking the anger from her mind, she wheeled into the living room, slipping her arm into the sling as she entered. Jay laughed.

'God, Megan, that's very good, you don't look like you at all!'

He looked her up and down, shaking his head and smiling.

'It makes a difference, does it?' she blurted before she could think better of it, 'To what you think of me?'

And then quickly correcting herself to make it less of an accusation, 'To what *people* think of me? I even seem different even to myself,' she confessed.

Jay clearly understood exactly what she meant and was trying to work out a reply that didn't sound awful.

'Yes,' he said eventually. 'It shouldn't make a difference, but it does.'

Megan inhaled, she wasn't sure whether that was what she wanted to hear or not, she was glad of his honesty, but didn't like the answer. She definitely didn't want him to lie to her, but she wished he didn't see her the same way that everyone else did. It made her long for Silvie and Pavel all the more, the people who saw her and loved her for who she was. Then she smiled to herself, Pavel was blind and yet he could see her better than anyone else.

Jay noticed her smile and his face formed a question.

'I was just thinking about Pavel.'

He studied her, probably trying to work out what Pavel had to do with the disguise and bracing himself for the tears that usually accompanied her memories of him.

He sighed. 'I'm sorry, Megan, I can't imagine what any of this has been like for you, but it will get better, it will be different in Ireland.'

He looked at her, his eyes deep pools of concern that softened the room.

'Thank you.'

She said that a lot these days.

'It will get better, I promise,' he said again, as if that made it true.

Then, to her surprise, he got up and folded his arms around her in a gentle hug, his hair tumbling against her skin, his body resting against hers and his cologne seeping into her pores. As soon as she could, without it seeming like a rebuff, she released the hug and returned the bathroom, but it was too late to avoid the surge of longing that pushed tears towards her eyes. She took off the glasses and unwound her hair from the cap, damp blue eyes stared forlornly back at her from the mirror.

She was small and stupid again, ridiculous for loving someone who would never love her back. If only there was a way to get rid of these feelings once and for all, to be done with them forever. Ireland, Ireland was the answer. In just a few weeks he would be back in this flat all alone and she would be in a different country and they would never see each other again. A whole new life far away from this torture was just around the corner.

Jay glanced across at Megan, she looked completely normal sitting beside him in the passenger seat of the Tesla. Why hadn't he thought of this sooner? It was easy enough and it gave her a change of scenery. All he had to do was check that none of the neighbours were around, wheel her down to the carpark and, once she was safely in the passenger seat, stow her wheelchair behind the bin unit, and then he could take her for a drive just like anyone else. It was nice doing these little things for her and she was a constant surprise, smart and resourceful, good company in many ways. It felt good to show her Liverpool, too, taking her to some of the places he and Silvie used to go and discovering more of the city for himself. So long as they stayed in the car it was fine, no-one could see she was disabled and there was nothing notable about it – well, aside from the car, but that attracted attention to him rather than her.

Park Road was quiet, probably because they were heading towards the old city centre that had once skirted the waters' edge but was now submerged by it: the Albert Dock with its heritage apartments, the conference centre, hotels, and museums were all lost to the risen tide. He stopped the car and stared out trying to imagine the waterfront as it had been in the early part of the twenty-first century, before he was born, full of people and thriving businesses, a tourist hotspot with the Mersey an attraction rather than a source of devastation and fear. It was hard to picture Liverpool as anything other than it was now, a crumbling city with the anomaly of a well-resourced university. The past was never something he had dwelt much upon before, well not until Silvie, and now Megan.

He pointed to the lichen-green Liver Birds perched on the roof of the partially submerged Royal Liver building.

'They were built with one facing out to sea to watch over the sailors and the other facing inland to watch over city.' Repeating something he had only recently learned himself – it was almost ironic, the devastation they must have witnessed.

'Yes,' Megan half-smiled. 'I remember my parents brought Silvie and I to see them when we were very small. Before—'

For a moment he thought she was going to say *before the melt*, but that couldn't be right, she would have barely been two years old then and surely she wouldn't be able to remember that far back? A thud of realisation landed in his body, she meant before the tumour, before she was disabled, when her parents were happy to be seen in public with both of their daughters. A lance of pain cut into his chest for everything that had been taken away from her – if it wasn't for that she could have had a normal life, she might have even gone to university like Silvie. It was unfair, cruel almost, the way her life had been stolen from her. What would she have been like if she wasn't disabled?

Silence stretched between them, he needed to change the subject, quickly. 'Apparently The Committee wanted to try and save the Liver building in the early days.'

Megan nodded. 'Yes, Pavel told me about that. They were going to try and reconstruct the whole city centre further inland, but there wasn't the money. I think they even tried to auction some of the most iconic buildings, hoping that a big corporation like Rind Holdings might fund the dismantling and relocation if they got them cheap.'

'Really?'

That was very surprising, most of Liverpool had such an intense feeling of abandonment it was hard to imagine anyone had ever wanted to rebuild it. She could be wrong, of course, but she seemed pretty certain.

'Yes, but there was only one bid, from a Saudi prince who wanted it for his private compound. The Committee decided the buildings might just as well stay waterlogged in Liverpool than disappear to the other side of the world.'

She smiled, broadly this time. 'And they were probably still hoping that the tide would go out again.'

A bubble of laughter rose up from his gut and spilled over, it had been a long time since he laughed like that and it felt good. Megan had clearly inherited her satirical sense of humour from Silvie, although she was softer, easier to keep up with – and of course, his time with Silvie had sharpened his wit.

Chapter 15

A burst of rain pummelled the car roof and hit the rutted tarmac around them with a hiss. Even though it was only the very beginning of May, the sun-baked road absorbed the globes of rain the instant they landed. He was already having to take it slowly, winding through rucked up streets of Toxteth towards Grafton Street and the sky-burst wasn't helping. At least he knew the way, they had been here before and landed upon the perfect spot to gaze down at the creaking flood barriers that bordered Sefton Drive. There was something compelling about the flimsy barriers that protected the orange-brick Ellerman estate whilst the slate-grey Armstrong Quay apartments, once in the enviable location on the waterfront, had been surrendered to the tide. It was rumoured to be the same all along the waterfront, but there was no vantage point he could find from which to verify it. A thrill of morbid fascination warmed his veins every time he thought about it: the exclusive quays developments and yacht club all reduced to waterlogged squats, the docklands middle class wiped out in a single tidal surge.

The rain stopped as suddenly as it began, bright

sunshine splitting the grey clouds and momentarily blinding him. He reached for the sun visor and slipped on his shades. One more turn and they were out of the direct sunlight and peering down at the scene below through the windscreen. The sludge-brown water was close to topping the flood barriers but the ground on the estate side was still dry. Clearly someone had wanted the Ellerman development protected and they had got their way for the time being, even though it looked unlikely to stay dry for much longer.

Why someone would want to save such a mundane estate was a complete mystery to him. It could hardly be an investment that retained any value with a flood barrier so close and barely restraining the water. Or maybe it was about something else altogether? Silvie used to feed him stories about the city's reputation for murky power structures long before The New Governance. Many of the formerly-elected councillors had been directly co-opted into the local Committee, their interest in power subsuming any democratic principles they might have once espoused. But Silvie had a knack for over-hyping everything into a dark conspiracy and why would Liverpool be different to anywhere else? Although it was probably true that any formerly elected representatives who challenged The New Governance quickly fell foul of The National Security Act and ended up in prison. He could remember his parents talking in hushed tones about a number of cases that had been appealed to the International Court of Human Rights by a foreign organisation. He was only a child, but the fear behind their words caught his attention, he had never heard such uncertainty in their voices before, or since. But now he could see how catastrophic the consequences could have been if there had been some kind of UN intervention. In the end, they needn't have worried, international condemnation counted for little and there was never mention of those people again. He had never thought of them either until just now. What had happened after the furore of foreign interest died down? Perhaps they had revoked their stance or plea-bargained their way out. Or maybe they were still in jail somewhere, their lives ebbing away whilst they stubbornly held onto a long-dead point of principle? That's the sort of thing Silvie would have done, sacrificed herself in a battle of principle that she was certain to lose. It was insane and yet weirdly attractive at the same time, to act according to your beliefs regardless of the personal consequences; simultaneously heroic and stupid. He had never doubted what he would do in their position, it was an obvious choice: look after yourself and your loved ones regardless of what you compromise; or act in accordance with your beliefs and suffer the consequences. It was obvious, and yet, all of a sudden, it didn't quite feel right.

A blast of police siren ricocheted through the air, jarring him into the present, his heart accelerating as it did so often these days. He looked around, but the road remained deserted, perhaps they were heading towards the squatters below who leaked out an existence in the upper floors of the waterlogged Armstrong Flats. From this vantage point on Grafton Street they were in clear view as paddled battered inflatable dinghies across the floodwater, making their way inside through holed-out windows and doors. There was no running water or electricity, but at least they had somewhere to shelter where the police and army rarely followed. The siren retreated into the distance, he and the squatters were safe for another day.

Megan gasped, accelerating his heart again.

He turned to face her, 'What is it?'

She was swallowing hard like she was trying not cry.

'Are you o—' he stopped and followed her gaze.

There was a young woman with a small baby swaddled against her chest rowing across the filthy water towards the Armstrong flats. Tears glistened on Megan's cheeks, did she know that woman? It seemed implausible, but why else would she be so upset?

'Who is it?'

Megan shook her head. She was crying full force now and had to take a few breaths before she could speak.

'I don't know,' she gulped. 'I don't know her. It's just—' her voice cracked. 'It's just that I thought Bootle Cares was the worst thing possible, but this…' she tilted her head towards the woman who was now using her hands to squeeze her dinghy through an old French door, her baby pressed tightly against her. 'It's just so cruel.'

Jay inhaled slowly, that was not what he had expected and discomfort riddled his bones, propelling him back into the unease he felt the first few times he met her. It wasn't normal to react like that, was it? Especially when she didn't even know her. Maybe there was more wrong with Megan than her legs after all? Maybe he was making a terrible mistake? He had grown used to Silvie's challenges to injustice, but Silvie put forward rational arguments, and often he agreed with her, but Megan's response was pure emotion – childlike.

Sleep eluded him, it was past two AM and the day's events were replaying through his mind like an old movie-reel on loop. He couldn't shake free Megan's reaction, only now threads of self-doubt intertwined the memory. How come he was never affected by other people's plight? He could see it was wrong, but he didn't *feel* anything. It wasn't that he was hard-hearted, he cared deeply about a lot of people and he had loved Silvie more than he thought possible. Yet he could look on others suffering from a cool distance. Why was that?

It was hard to form a coherent answer, but it was almost as if their circumstances made them *other*, not quite culpable for their fate, but certainly not deserving of the same empathy as his own loved ones. Did he really believe that? That people who were suffering somehow deserved their fate because of what they had done or who they were? In the dark hours of night and, with Megan in the next room, it seemed a terrible way to think, but it was the only way he could make sense of his feelings. Megan, on the other hand, responded to everyone the same, regardless of who or what they were, and despite her own life being so limited. The fact she knew nothing about that woman no difference to how deeply she felt or how much she cared about what was happening to her. His own pool of concern seemed small and mean compared to hers.

Chapter 16

Megan could feel the tension in Jay's thighs as he squeezed the pedals to navigate the potholed road, gently cursing every bump he failed to avoid. His hair was tucked behind his ear giving her a full profile view and his long, manicured fingers were folded around the steering wheel. His watch and signet ring glinted in the sun and his sleeves had slipped back to reveal the fine dark hair on his arms. She imagined his touch on her skin and turned away, she didn't want him to see her staring at him or to notice the flush rising in her cheeks. But in reality, there may as well have been a brick wall between them for the likelihood of him ever noticing her.

He pulled over to the side of the road. 'I don't think I can go much further,' he smiled. 'Not if we want to be able to turn around and leave anyway.'

'Okay,' she smiled in reply, surveying their surroundings.

The overtopped river stretched out in front of them. Riverside Drive was permanently under water, not helped by the trees having been felled for a dual carriageway in the late twenty-twenties. It seemed such an odd decision to make in the face of impending climate breakdown, but Megan found much of the past incomprehensible: the choices people made; they had known so much and yet carried on as if none of it was true. Everywhere she turned she was confronted with yet more waterlogged monuments to the inaction of the past – here the Riverside Gardens housing development that hadn't even lasted a decade before it was permanently submerged.

Megan was slowly mapping the city together from Pavel's stories and her journeys with Jay. She was writing it all down, if she really was going to leave, she needed something concrete, a memorial to the past and all the people she had loved, a reminder of what she had left behind. This definitely looked like one of places Pavel had told her about, close enough to the image in her mind's eye to create a wave of satisfaction in her chest as she stared at the small cul-de-sacs of detached houses nestled on the brink of the encroaching river. Rough access roads had been built after the flood and people still lived there, even though they were no longer the desirable residences they had once been. According to Pavel, these were some of the first to be hit by the scavengers and squatters when disaster struck. Many of the residents had fled to their second homes far inland when the river began to surge and the newly homeless quickly made their way to the vacant properties.

'Have you been here before?' she asked Jay

He shook his head. 'No, never,' his tone suggesting that was obvious.

It was strange how little Jay knew about any of it. Of

course, he would only have been six or seven when it happened and living a long way from the disaster zones. But he was well-educated and surely his parents or his brothers would have talked to him about it? Or perhaps they never dwelt on the suffering of ordinary people, their lives as remote to them as a foreign land.

Megan tried to imagine the shock and the chaos as the displaced set up camp in parks or empty buildings that quickly degenerated into lawless shantytowns. It had taken the army to restore order and clear the squatters and scavengers from the parks across the city. Thousands had died. Although, in the end, no-one knew exactly how many died because of the water and how many were killed in the military interventions that followed.

'Where would you like to go next?' Jay asked, clearly bored and already inching the car between the potholes to face the direction they had come.

She kept her voice cheerful. 'Let's see if we can find the place where Pavel used to work, it's somewhere in Wavertree, by the park.'

It was probably not that far from where her parents lived, although she had no recollection of it as a child and her place-memory was hazy now.

Pavel had rented a ground-floor flat with his boyfriend, Carl, just a short distance from The School for the Blind. His work options had diminished soon after the break-up of the UK. It wasn't just that his previous employer, the BBC, no longer existed, it was also that the equalities legislation which gave disabled people some nominal protection was rapidly being repealed and the only remaining places that employed disabled people were disability charities. So Pavel had ended up teaching at the blind school. He told Megan how he hoped he would be able to teach subjects similar to those he had encountered as an undergraduate: the critical approaches to power, history, and politics that had inspired and energised him, but he had been sorely disappointed. Resources were being stripped away from special schools and they were struggling against an increasingly hostile current; the curriculum was limited and expectations of disabled children were low.

Megan glanced over at Jay trying to read his expression. Did he believe the things she told him? Or did he, like the residents in Bootle Cares, think she was repeating the ramblings of a mad old man? Could Jay ever understand what it had been like for Pavel as his life deteriorated from the freedoms that Jay took for granted to abject confinement? Could Jay imagine what it had been like for her to be shut away in Bootle Cares for all those years? She let out a sigh, perhaps no-one except Silvie would ever really understand.

Jay looked across at her. 'Go on,' he encouraged. 'It's interesting.' Then he added, '*And* my favourite coffee stop is very close to where you are describing.'

Megan glanced back at him, was he listening to her or thinking about himself? Her heart willed the former, but it was more likely the latter. A few minutes later he pulled over at a street vendor on Smithdown Road and returned to the car with two thick paper cups and a bag of pastries.

'Best coffee in Liverpool,' he smiled passing her a

cup. 'Not that you'd know from the surroundings!'

He looked genuinely pleased to be sharing something with her.

Megan sniffed the dark liquid, sipped and smiled, 'Mmm,' she agreed, sinking back into her seat.

Jay bit into a pastry. 'These are definitely not as good as yours, but maybe a decent second.'

Her eyes ran involuntarily across his stomach. He told her he had been adding an extra half mile to his runs every day to try and counterbalance the impact of all her baking. If he was, it was working, he still looked taught and lean. She turned and looked out of the window towards the park and nibbled the corner of her pastry, ignoring the swell of desire in her belly.

Her parents lived in the maze of streets somewhere off the western side of the park, so she guessed Pavel's flat and the blind school must be to the north east. In any case, it was far enough away from the river and the city centre to be safe from the immediate danger when the melt occurred. But everyone had been scared, makeshift shelters had sprung up on the park and violence broke out as people fought over the last scraps of their existence. Pavel told Megan how he and Carl had stayed up all night armed with household implements, fearing the violence would spill over into their block. Luckily, it had never spread that far, but some of the houses on Grant Avenue had their windows smashed and the shops on Smithdown Road had been shuttered up, most never to reopen.

The fear and the chaos in Bootle Cares the night of

the flood filled her mind, the night when she had been safely snuggled up in Jay's bed. It was the second time round for Pavel. What had he done in those last minutes of his life? What had he thought and felt? He would have gone to Cathy, she was sure of that, he would have been able to navigate his way through the darkness better than anyone and he was a surrogate brother to Cathy in the same way he had been a surrogate father to herself, a force of love and strength in the face of crushing bleakness. He would have tried to comfort Cathy, to make her last moments less terrifying. At least neither of them died alone, but that was little solace. What a waste. Such a generous, wise, and loving person condemned to a vile death simply because he could not see. Was this really what humanity had become? It seemed so cruel and pointless. Did human beings deserve to exist at all if this was the best they could manage?

She looked across at Jay and remembered the demo, she could not let herself think like that for long. There were all those people, including him, who had risked their own lives to demand that the lives of disabled people counted for something, and what about everything Jay was risking now so she had the chance of a better life? She would not give up hope, she had to believe she had survived for a reason, that there was some purpose to her being alive when everyone she loved was dead. She would do something, she would find a way to honour all those people and to make things different.

Chapter 17

Jay opened his laptop and angled it towards Megan as she nestled into the corner of the sofa. As well as taking her out in the car, he had started sharing his photos and memories of Silvie. It hurt, but it was also soothing to talk to someone who knew her and loved her as much as he did. Sometimes they imagined what Silvie would have said if she had been there with them, laughing out loud when they echoed her words in chorus.

An image stopped him in his tracks, it was from the early days, one of his very first visits to Bootle Cares. His hands had trembled as he captured the image, belying the façade of casual composure he had worked so hard to create as he resisted every urge to stare in fascinated horror at the strange bodies which populated the freakish otherworld and, all the while, reassuring himself that Silvie didn't know him well enough to sense his thinly veiled repugnance. He had been incredulous at them wanting a picture at all, why would people like that want to look at themselves, especially the blind one?

A flush of shame spread through his body and he glanced across at Megan, could she tell what he had thought of them? But she was staring at the screen and Silvie, Pavel, and herself smiling into the camera with interlinked arms. Her brow was knotted and her chest rising and falling as if she was in physical pain. At least she had not been looking at him.

'Are you okay?'

She nodded, cleared her throat, and then exhaled into a crescendo of sobs.

He stretched out his hand and hesitated, his instinct was to touch her, but he wasn't really sure if that was okay. He hugged her occasionally, but she often felt tense, as if she didn't like physical contact with him. But now she was sobbing on the sofa beside him and he couldn't just sit there and do nothing. He brought his hand to her back and gently circled between her shoulder blades, she curled forwards in response, weeping into her palms.

Her grief was like an assault, cracking open the pain in his chest and wetting his eyes before he knew it was happening. This was the worst, when it caught him off guard and the only hope of keeping it under control was by taking long, deliberate, slow breaths. He needed to be stronger than this, no matter how often he told himself he was grieving and it was normal to cry, he couldn't just break down in front of Megan, he had to keep it together. Reaching for his handkerchief he glanced the back of his wrist against his cheeks to make sure they were dry before he pushed the folded oblong of fabric into her hands.

It was an eternity before she had finally cried herself

out and he could seek respite in the kitchen. Standing in the cool, bright air of the fridge he felt solid again, the chill of the glass bottles against his fingers offering a reassuring physical sensation, sometimes it felt like Megan was crying his tears as well.

In the semi-gloom he turned onto his side and pulled his knees to his chest. Another sleepless night, his mind painting frantic scenes across the blank white ceiling. How often did this happen? It felt more and more frequent, but then again anything could be possible in the sleep-deprived delirium of the early hours.

Was it really true that all those people had been taken by the surge and nothing had been said or done about it? Even the demo seemed to have been wiped from public discourse, and if Marica knew anything more about it she certainly wasn't letting on. He sat up and picked up his phone. It was pointless trying to sleep with his mind on overdrive. He clicked onto the *Liverpool Voice* site and started skimming though key dates, even at this hour he wasn't deranged enough to type Bootle Cares directly into the tab. Nothing about the flood appeared, but there were almost weekly headlines about escape attempts – people with makeshift boats trying to reach Ireland, setting sail from the old port channel even though it was so badly damaged there was no real advantage in trying to leave from there as anywhere else along the devastated estuary. But the constant lurid reporting of the drownings and detentions only heightened how scant coverage of the flood and the deaths in Bootle Cares had been. He clicked onto 13th March to re-read what little of it there was, but it came up blank. Frowning, he tried again and then picked a couple of days either side, but still nothing. Finally, fingers trembling, he clicked onto the date of the demo.

Nothing.

A chill of realisation crawled up his body, it had all been erased. Silvie was right, the incessant reports about the failed escape attempts were a warning – a constant reminder about the futility of trying to leave. Nothing more had been said about Bootle Cares because no-one was going to be upset by a bunch of dead cripples and there was nothing to warn people against. And the demo, well, perhaps it was easier to erase it altogether than to risk anyone investigating the names and the faces on the banners or those who had been detained.

Staring at the screen, it felt like the world was tipping on its axis. If only he had given Silvie's words more credence everything might be different now. A surge of memories deepened the chill in his veins: all those times she had taken him walking towards the port after they had visited Megan, she had been silently telling him something, showing him, and he had done nothing. He had seen the water lapping around the oil salvage plant that buffered Arctic Road that was so close to Bootle Cares it seemed criminal now, but he hadn't thought like that at the time. It had no more impact on him than the squatters he was vaguely aware of or the precarity of the rudimentary flood defences that had been built along the waterfront to try and protect what remained of the Baltic

Triangle and the south east of the city. He never questioned that the barrier stopped when it reached the boundary of the north tunnel, since it was flooded and the port and water treatment plant were already lost, it seemed obvious that there was nothing else to protect.

But what about all those people in the path of the surge? The water was already only metres away from the back wall of the compound that contained Bootle Cares. Once, Silvie had shown him where the original entrance was, on Summer Road, facing the port, rather than Derby Road where he had always known it. The street entrance had been moved and the back wall sealed up. That was the most that the residents had been offered as a flood defence: a blocked up back wall that also conveniently hid how close the water crept.

The ice in his body knotted into a sickness in his stomach. Back then, he had been more unnerved by the people who lived there rather than the sea water rising only metres away. And he had only ever wanted to leave it all behind, he didn't even like going to North Liverpool. It was bleak and barren compared to the southern half of the city which, despite everything, still retained some of its former beauty: tree-lined streets, large redbrick houses, parks and gardens, even though much of it was now succumbing to the same fate as the rest of the city.

But the truth was, each time Silvie had led him towards the oil salvage plant to witness the sea water creeping ever closer to where Megan lived, he knew there was something she wanted from him. She had never said anything directly but he could feel her watching, waiting for him to say or do the right thing, but he had never been bothered enough to figure out what it was, dismissing it as just another of her quirks. Now he understood that she was waiting for him to voice something about getting Megan away from there. She had been waiting for him to offer some indication she could trust him with the half-made plan she and Megan had devised. The wound in his heart cracked open. If only she had been more explicit, why hadn't she just asked him?

But then, before she had been killed by a Committee car, before he had seen the flood and the demo would he really have been open to something like that? He doubted it. It was true he could be a spoilt, selfish, bastard just like Megan had said, but it cut deep inside that Silvie had thought it too and however much she said she loved him she didn't fully trust him, either.

He inhaled, the rise in his chest tearing his heart.

At least he had done the right thing by Megan, he had got her out for Silvie's funeral and, in doing so, he had saved her life. And he would help her get away for good, surely that was some consolation? He could prove himself in that way, even if it was too late for Silvie, even if it had taken losing Silvie to finally make him open his mind.

Chapter 18

Megan stared uncomprehending. It was dark and Jay had led her down to the carpark at Merebank and was now standing in front of a battered old black car looking pleased with himself.

'It's for Ireland,' he said, and then, noticing her incomprehension, added, 'We can hardly go in the Tesla.'

The last of her romantic dreams crumbled away: Jay, gorgeous as always, driving her to freedom in his expensive red car.

She opened her mouth, but he rushed on.

'I can barely get your chair in the Tesla as it is, let alone hide it and you as well.'

His smile was fading, but she couldn't think of anything reassuring to say.

'And the Tesla is too distinctive, there's only a handful of them in the country,' he coaxed.

He was right about the Tesla, there was no denying that the size of it, its rarity, and the personalised number plates all made it impossible, but the decrepit metal lump in front of her was still a jolt. She looked from Jay to the car and back again. It was hard not to be disappointed by the battered oblong that looked like it had spent at least a decade in barn.

Before she could ask where he got it from he said, 'It's so old it's not even an electric hybrid. It's a Skoda diesel, one of the last that was made. But I've checked and there are a couple of service stations on route that still have diesel pumps where we can fill up.'

Appreciation stirred in her chest: he had recently started going out more often and she had assumed he was just socialising, getting on with his life, but clearly he had been making plans as well. Smiling, she moved around the car, trying to find something to admire.

'It's got archaic hand-shift gears so it's a bit weird to drive, but I'll get used to it with some practice.'

He was enjoying explaining it to her and now she had got over the initial shock his energy was infectious.

'The most important thing is that it has loads of room. We should be able to hide you and your chair easily. But we need to try it first.'

Megan nodded, a renewed fizz of excitement overriding the blow of what her journey to Ireland was actually going to look like. She wheeled to the passenger side and swept the seat with her hand before she manoeuvred herself into the car, it wasn't much cleaner on the inside than out. Jay went round to the back and lifted her chair in the boot as easily as a paper bag – he was right about the extra space, at least.

The car bounced and lurched as Jay steered out of the carpark, his face a mixture of concentration and embarrassment as he drove unsteadily along Penny Lane and onto Church Road. Then he turned abruptly and brought the car to a jerky halt behind high, overgrown walls. It was pitch black, there were no lights and seemingly no security cameras winking at them through the darkness. Megan's eyes followed the beams of the car headlamps, it was just possible to make out the partial blackened silhouette of what could have been a large Victorian building. Whatever it was in its heyday it was now completely derelict, apparently ravaged by fire – perhaps squatters had moved in and accidently set it ablaze. Now, it was completely ruined, desirable to no one, neither the squatters desperate for shelter, nor a corporation like Rind Holdings who were usually quick to claim any abandoned space and turn it to profit. The walls around the perimeter were in barely any better condition than the building, only remaining upright because of the sprawling trees and shrubbery weaving through the cracks and holding them in place.

Scanning her surroundings a thought fluttered in her chest. Might this be the blind school where Pavel had worked? She didn't have a clear sense of precisely where they were, but it was possible, they were in the right vicinity. A warmth spread through her body, as if she had summoned Pavel's essence from the embers of the long dead fire. For a moment, she could feel him pulling her into a deep, warm hug, filling her with love and cheering on her escape.

She turned to Jay to ask if he knew what it used to be, but he seemed preoccupied, the earlier buzz of energy replaced by something more sombre.

A quiver of doubt ran through Jay's spine and there was no way he was going to tell Megan how he knew about this place. It felt very different now he was there with her in the Skoda compared to the times when he had been with Marcia in the Tesla.

Marcia had directed him there the first time she told him to pick her up. They couldn't go to Marcia's place because of her husband, and Jay wasn't going to bring her back to his flat again. Even without taking Megan into account, it felt weird to have an almost-stranger in the bed he had shared with Silvie for so long. He wasn't ready for that yet, so he told Marcia his brother and sister-in-law were staying while they looked for a place in Liverpool and he had given up his room to them. It wasn't a very convincing lie and he didn't think Marcia believed him. She had probably seen some of Silvie's things in his room and assumed he had a girlfriend, but it didn't matter, they both knew it was just a physical relationship. After the first time they didn't even kiss, he had reached up to pull her mouth to his as she straddled him in the car but she reared away. So he folded his hands around her hips, sliding them upwards and around her waist whilst she moved on top of him; perhaps kissing was an intimacy too far for an illicit liaison. Either way, she knew what she was doing, and he got a kick out of it too, he couldn't deny that.

But other times, like now, he felt seedy about it. Being pursued by an older, married woman seemed cheap and sad rather than exciting, and he couldn't look at

Megan without hearing her words in the flat. Was she right? Was he that bad? Was it better or worse that this was so completely different? Did it make it more or less of a betrayal? At least doing it in the car meant he could drop her home afterwards and there wasn't the awkwardness of the next morning to deal with and then he could quickly put it out of his mind. Still, if he really thought about it, and the circumstances that had given rise to Marcia's interest in him, the deaths in Bootle Cares, the demo and its catastrophic consequences for nearly everyone except him, then he probably wouldn't like her much at all – and he certainly wouldn't like himself, either. So he didn't dwell on it, and each time it happened he told himself that was the last and pushed it to the back of his mind. Then, she would message him and he would go and pick her up in the Tesla, reassuring himself it didn't mean anything, it was just a distraction and a bit of fun and surely he was allowed that much?

He double checked the lights were off, killed the engine and got out of the car and shut the door without looking at Megan. The last thing he needed were those eyes boring into him. In the dark outside the car, the cool evening air steadied him, he was alright, he knew what he was doing.

The thud of the car door closing reverberated through Megan's body and Jay was quickly swallowed by the gloom as he moved to the back of the car despite his light-coloured clothing. The sprawling greenery completely obscured the last of the remaining streetlights.

A dim glow lit the car as Jay opened the boot and she watched as he effortlessly removed her chair. He unfolded it, flattened down the cushion and wheeled it round to her side of the car. She stared at him through the darkness, trying to read his expression, why had he brought her here and what did he want her to do?

'We have to try it out,' he said, reading her hesitation. 'We have to make sure you and your chair can be hidden from view. You don't have any of the documents that you need to get through any of the borders.'

'Of course,' she faltered.

She had always known that, but in reality she hadn't thought much beyond her dream of driving away with him in the Tesla. It was only now as he wheeled her to the back of the car with the boot lid raised that she realised what that meant – she was going to have to hide in the boot of the car. She looked inside and then back at Jay, even in the darkness she could tell that it was filthy inside. The car must be at least twenty-five years old and it looked like it hadn't been cleaned for more than half of that. Jay followed her gaze, he paused for a moment and then took off his jacket and spread it over as much of the boot as it would cover. It was light grey, new and expensive and now it would be ruined.

'Sorry Megan,' he seemed unconcerned about his jacket. 'I'll get the car cleaned properly before we go. And we can put a duvet and some pillows in to make it more comfortable for the journey. For now I just need to be sure that we can get you and your chair hidden in the back.'

It was still not clear what he planned to do with her chair, but she could at least get herself into the car, it was flat right to the edge and looked easy enough. She shifted herself forwards, but there was nothing, she was slipping into the gap between her chair and the car. In a second Jay's arms were around her, halting her fall and gently easing her towards the edge of the boot. He held her for a moment so she could steady herself and then carefully released her. His touch was surprisingly gentle and, despite how much she hated being physically handled, the way he helped her felt kind. Usually when people touched her it was demeaning, as if she was an unpleasantness that had to be dealt with. The touch of her parents, the physiotherapists and the staff in Bootle Cares all told her she was nothing more than an object. But from Jay she felt something completely different, he held her with tenderness and restraint, a touch that acknowledged and respected her femininity. It reminded her of a truth she had always known about him: it wasn't just his good looks that drew her to him, there was something else very special deep inside. Most of the time it was buried under the layers of entitlement that sprawled around him like dense undergrowth, choking out the light. But every now and then she caught a glimpse of it, like a jewel on the forest floor that only needed to be polished a few more times before it shone more brightly than anything else.

'Are you okay?' he asked, concern shading his face.

'Yes, I think so,' she pushed the thoughts aside and forced a smile. 'I'm just not used to getting in and out of the boot of a car!'

'I should hope not,' he smiled in response. 'Don't get any ideas about making a career out of being a fugitive!'

Megan laughed and curled up onto his jacket. The fabric was imbued with a mixture of his scent and the cologne he wore. If only he would hold her again, reach out and take her in his arms because he wanted her, she inhaled, losing herself and then stopped, embarrassed. He was right there in front of her and she was sniffing at his clothes like a dodgy aftershave advert. She cringed. What would he think of her if he saw her acting like that? It was all too easy to imagine how mortified he would be at her longing for him, his recoiling at the possibility that he could ever reciprocate feelings for his dead girlfriend's disabled little sister. After all, regardless of those hidden gems of tenderness, he was still rich and gorgeous and could have anyone one he wanted and she, well, she was practically from another planet.

She forced a glance in his direction to see if he had noticed. Thankfully, he had turned away and was occupied with folding up her chair. He picked it up and turned around to face her. For a moment she thought he was going to lay it down on top of her. But he held it just above her, bringing one foot to the edge of the boot and bending his leg so he could balance the chair on his knee whilst he scraped some marks into the dirt on the inside of the car with his free hand. For a few precious seconds their bodies were almost touching.

'I think it will work,' he affirmed, absorbed by his balancing act. 'Will you be alright like that, maybe for more than an hour at a time?'

'Yes,' she said before she could think better of it.

It was uncomfortable to lie there and it was hard to imagine what it would feel like when the car was in motion, but it didn't matter. She would put up with almost anything for the promise of a different future in Ireland even though it meant she would never see him again – and precisely because she would never see him again. Surely distance and time would eventually cure her of this hopeless longing.

'Okay, good.' He put her chair down and offered her his hand to help her out of the car.

She didn't take it, as much as she loved the way he held her, she didn't want him to think she needed his help, and didn't want that to be the reason he touched her.

Chapter 19

Jay decided to take a detour on the way back to the flat. He needed more practice driving the Skoda, he still crunched the stick-shift gears incessantly and it felt like he stalled at nearly every traffic light. He looked apologetically across at Megan to check if she was bothered by all the grinding and jerking, but she laughed.

'It's going to look like I am driving at this rate!'

He smiled tentatively, was it okay for him to laugh as well?

Megan was hard to read and sometimes it seemed like there was more going on behind those neon blue eyes than he really understood. Still, he appreciated the way she made light of it. Aside from that one time in the flat when she shouted at him, she had never been angry with him and, after everything she had been through, it would be easy for her to be bitter and resentful, but she never was. He was glad he was helping her; she deserved a better life and he was going to do the best he could to make it happen.

Every day he made himself practice driving the Skoda, he

could hardly smuggle Megan to Ireland grinding and lurching the car all the way. It also occupied the times when he might otherwise be tempted to see Marcia. It was better all round to end it now, it would save things from getting messy later and awkward questions about his trip to Dublin in a strange car, especially since he had been refused permission to attend the conference. Besides, there was something he wanted to do for Megan before they left.

Finally, two days before they were due to leave, he found the right moment. 'Is there anywhere you would like to go for a last drive?'

Megan looked at him for a moment, as if weighing up the wisdom of her own suggestion before she committed herself.

'Can we go Bootle, to the roadblock by the flood?'

'Are you sure?'

That was not what he expected, he assumed she would want to stay as far away from Bootle Cares as possible. She still had nightmares about it. He sometimes heard her in the kitchen in the early hours of the morning and went to check she was okay. The first time, she was ashen and shivering, whether it was from cold or fear he couldn't tell. So he fetched Silvie's robe from the back of his bedroom door and wrapped it around her like a hug from her big sister. She had kept the robe and it was probably going to end up in Ireland now.

Megan nodded. 'Yes, I'm sure. Is that all right?'

'Of course, whatever you want,' he smiled.

'I have to see it one last time, to say goodbye before

we leave.'

Her words felt strange. Despite the weeks of meticulous planning it was still hard to believe they were actually on the verge of leaving. It was surreal, his life seemed to have split into completely different planes of reality. There was the top layer where he carried on much as before, going to university, living in his flat, visiting his family and seeing his mates now and again – albeit less often since Silvie had died. Below that was the plane which was blackened and broken from losing Silvie: the wound and the absence that he might never recover from. And finally, beneath it all, was this secret churning space where he was a subversive, committing illegal acts and hatching plans that could send him to prison for a very long time. It was strange how easily he could slip undetected between these different worlds. Perhaps that would also make it easier to return to the top layer once all of this was over?

He looked at Megan, his last piece of Silvie and soon she would be gone forever too.

The Tesla purred along Stanley Road, the overtopped Mersey snaking beneath them. The sky was clear and sunlight sparkled on the water making it almost pretty and inviting rather than poisoned and deadly. He turned down Marsh Lane towards the river, passing the half derelict shopping centre and the old station that had been taken over by squatters – one more surge and they would be in need of new shelter.

They were drawing close to the flood site when he realised Megan would have no idea how close they were to Bootle Cares and this would be her last chance to change her mind.

'Are you sure about this?'

She looked at him and nodded, anxious but determined.

He wasn't going to question her again, even though he still wasn't convinced about the wisdom of it. What might she be expecting? The site was going to look a lot different from the initial wreckage the day after Silvie's funeral. It would probably have also changed since the last time he was there, just before the demo. By then, the water had already receded a little and the police and the floating debris were gone – that wasn't even three months ago, but it felt like a different lifetime.

At the junction with Baltic Road, the remnants of the road block lay abandoned on the wet ground but Derby Road, everything below remained completely submerged. Jay pulled over and turned to face Megan. She was staring out the window as if she was seeing it for the first time, a series of pained expressions crossing her face. Turning back to face the water he waited, wishing there was more he could offer than companiable silence. After a few moments she dipped her head forwards and unfasted the thin silver chain with the tiny heart-shaped pendant that she wore around her neck: a gift from Silvie.

She turned to face him. 'Will you put it in the water? It's for Pavel.'

Jay held his hand out and she let the chain coil into his palm. She didn't need to say anything else. This was the nearest to a memorial that Pavel or any of the others would get. There hadn't even been an attempt to recover the bodies as far as he knew, and after the demo there was no-one left to fight for the rights of their loved ones. This was the only way Megan could honour them and it seemed right that it was with a gift from Silvie – the sister whose death had given her life.

He climbed out of the car and gently shut the door. Checking there was no-one around and no security cameras trained in his direction, he began to walk towards the water. He got as close to the water's edge as he could without soaking his feet and turned round and looked at Megan. Her eyes were fixed on him and he held her gaze and inhaled, wishing he could breathe in what she needed from him. Then he turned back towards the flooded road and squatted down. Extending his arm as far as possible over the water he gently released the chain and watched it disappear below the sludgy brown surface. He waited a moment and then stood up and walked slowly back to the car. Megan was weeping softly as he climbed in beside her and he gently rubbed her back until her tears subsided. Then he drove them back to his flat for the very last time.

Chapter 20

Jay steered the Skoda northwards along the back streets out of the city. The tightness in his chest only slightly mollified by the jarring ride resulting from the rutted roads and not his driving. It was just after 4PM, they had planned their departure to ensure it would be nightfall when they reached the first of the border crossing points. He picked up an old A-road as it skirted the eastern flank of Bootle, avoiding the motorway out of the city and the security checks that might spring up without warning on the outbound lanes. Even though it felt like they were a safe distance from Derby Road and Bootle Cares, the flood was still visible, stretching outwards from the old estuary below.

Remnants of the docks and the industries they once served protruded above the water in a macabre dance. In the corner of his eye he glimpsed the old redbrick warehouse that had been converted into the Titanic Hotel back in the twenties, but which was now sinking into the sea just like its namesake nearly a hundred and fifty years before. Flaking white lettering declared its presence, except now as a memorial to the same conceit that had condemned its predecessor, rather than the bold redevelopment of the docklands it had once proclaimed.

Eventually the road veered away from the estuary and faded signposts directed him onwards as the Lancashire countryside unfolded around the car. The road was quiet and Megan was staring transfixed at the passing world. Most of the landscape looked like it had barely changed in decades and, compared to the chaos of the cityscape, the parched brown hills and remote villages could almost pass for a rural idyll. They might be driving back in time: the quaint, idealised English past in living colour, like a government produced picture post-card.

Inside the car tension thickened the air, growing stouter the further away from the city they drew. He needed a distraction, light chatter was hardly appropriate now and if they talked about what really lay ahead he might turn the car around and drive straight back to Merebank. Relaxing his grip on the steering wheel, he fiddled with the audio controls in the car. He hadn't managed to connect his phone to the ancient sound system, and he had no idea if the in-car device would work, but the speakers crackled into life with surprisingly alacrity and unfamiliar music filled the car. A man and a woman singing to each other.

"*Are you living for love?*" their voices harmonised.

A love song, a bit old fashioned, but it was better than silence.

Then, without warning, the tone changed and the male voice took over, chanting rapid rhythmic vocals.

"*Where the street folds round and the motors start, and the idiot wields the power."*

Did he hear that correctly? *The idiot wields the power.*

He glanced at Megan, her expression a mix of surprise and concern. It must be a CU channel, the car was awash with lyrics that would never be permitted on an English station.

"Where the chosen hold the highest card, on the field of honour where the ground is hard, so the highest hand is joking wild."

He switched it off. 'Best to be on the safe side,' he said, trying to sound casual.

Megan nodded, even though she would have no more idea than him whether or not they could be picked up listening to a banned station in an old car.

The tightness in his chest was spreading behind his eyes, as if his whole body was wired up to some kind of electrical current that was slowly burning through him. In the silent ache of his anxiety it felt like an eternity before he saw signs to the A6 where he joined the teatime traffic heading into Preston. From there he would join the last section of the M55 and merge into the M6 northwards, avoiding any of the possible security checks just outside town – although here the security would probably still be mostly focused on the western rather than the northern exit.

Megan's gaze followed the westerly route out of Preston, was that it? Did that lead to the place she knew so vividly in her mind's eye from Pavel's stories? It seemed more incredible than anything else he had told her: that public protest had briefly closed down the whole fracking enterprise in the days before the UK had broken up and the CU was formed. It was hard to believe people had so much power they could change things, even though they had paid a heavy price for it. She had felt Pavel's terror as he described being thrown face-down to the ground and his hands roughly cuffed behind him – police violence had been shocking back then.

Would it be the same if they were caught now? Would they hurt her even though there was no possibility of her escaping? And what would they do to Jay? Had he even considered that? He always seemed so sure of everything, she glanced across at him, albeit less so now.

But there was hope, after all the protesters had won and, for a brief period, Pavel said it felt like the whole tide of history was turning in a different direction – until the pandemics, the wars, and the collapsing climate put paid to all of that. Nonetheless, maybe this was her moment, the brief interlude when change was possible?

Fracking had been reinstated under the emergency energy security measures as soon as the UK broke up. There were no protests then, mass gatherings were already illegal and even had the permitted ten gathered at the Preston New Road fracking site – or any of the other sites that sprang up across the north – they would have quickly been detained under the National Security Act.

Without thinking, Megan let out a long sigh and regretted it as Jay's eyes flicked anxiously in her direction. She didn't want to see how on edge he was, for once she longed for his slick self-assuredness.

It couldn't be much further until they reached the first border. It felt like they had been driving for an ice-age, as if they were locked in time and would never actually arrive at the short stretch of tarmac and concrete that was the passage to her new life — the kind of life Pavel had once lived and wanted Megan to believe was possible again. What was it that enabled him to maintain his hope in spite of having witnessed all of his worst fears come true? What gave him the energy to continually fight back in any way he could: his organising in Bootle Cares, his unwavering commitment to those who were even more powerless than him? How come he had not given up like Navida and so many of the others? Maybe it was because he had lived a completely different life and knew other things were possible? Or maybe it was something special about him? Tears welled in her eyes and she turned to the motorway speeding alongside them so Jay would not see her blinking them away, she had to be strong.

Pavel would have relished a conversation like that, teasing out the social origins of resilience and resistance and challenging her when she strayed towards simplistic predetermination. His perspective sometimes made the world feel harder to bear because it seemed that people were so complicit in the very worst injustices. But, at the same time, it always left room for change and hope, however terrible things might be at the time.

She turned to Jay, it also explained him. Even though he was rich and gorgeous with a perfect life laid out for him, he could act in ways that went against it all. When he had begun to see what other people experienced he had started to change, and he was still changing, that was clear. And he was trying to make change happen for others as well – for her. A warmth ignited in her stomach and spread up to her chest. She let her gaze rest on him, his eyes pinned to the road, absorbed in his own thoughts.

I'll never forget this, she promised silently. *I'll remember you and what you have done for the rest of my life.*

Chapter 21

Megan watched from the passenger seat as Jay fumbled with the fuel cap and lifted the nozzle from the diesel pump. He jumped as a squirt of liquid splashed onto the concrete floor, spinning around to make sure no one had noticed. It was unnerving to see him so unsure of himself, vulnerable. He steadied himself and his confident demeaner slowly returned as he refuelled the car. He tucked his hair behind his ear and turned towards her as if he could feel her watching him. She held his gaze and smiled hoping he could feel her reassurance, he needed to be confident now, they were going to have to stay here until dusk and the Southwaite services were a lot busier than either of them had imagined.

With the car slotted neatly in a parking bay in a sparsely occupied zone at the back of the services, Jay lifted her chair out of the boot. Checking that no-one was watching, she transferred into it before slipping her arm in the sling and then let Jay push her towards the main entrance. They were barely though the doors when they were assaulted with questions.

'Gosh, you've been in the wars!'

'Aye, silly girl, what have you done to yourself?'

The Scottish lilts did not soften the impact of their words and Megan wasn't going to be able to use her prepared story now, her voice would instantly betray that she did not share their native land. She had never considered that Scottish people might be travelling south of the border, in her mind it was only ever a northwards exodus. He heart thudded, there was so much they had not considered. Mumbling something about a party, she twisted round to Jay, willing him to jump in and corroborate her account but he looked ashen. Then, as if reading her mind, he forced a chuckle.

'Yes, I told her to keep off the Tsingtao but she wouldn't listen!'

The old couple chortled, throwing knowing glances at them as if she and Jay might be a younger version of themselves. Then, thankfully, they moved on. Jay wheeled her towards a quiet corner of a large canteen, both of them keeping their eyes downcast to avoid the stares as they passed – eye contact would only invite more questions.

'I think you should just wait here.'

He looked shaken.

Megan nodded, there was no need to explain, neither of them wanted any more encounters like that. It was all so much harder than they had imagined.

Jay remained standing. 'Is there anything particular you would like to eat?'

He tilted his head in the direction of a wall-mounted menu that was too far away for her to read.

'Not really.'

She had no idea what kind of food would be available in a service station but it smelled like everything was fried.

'I'll have the same as you,' she forced a smile. 'Just less of it.'

Jay strode across the canteen, his confidence increasing with every step further away from her. It was like a metaphor for their lives: everything would be so much easier for him without her, how could she ever have been stupid enough to think anything else?

Pressure was growing in her bladder and she had no idea what to do. She had nothing more than a few sips of water all afternoon, but it made no difference, she was still going to have to go to the bathroom. And worse still, she was going to have to tell Jay. She waited. But as soon as they finished eating, he got up and went off again only returning what felt like an age later with Celtic Union phones for them both, complete with Wi-Fi, call, and bank credit.

'Look at this,' he leaned across showing her an Irish news site: '*England facing new economic sanctions after further human rights violations.*'

Megan thumbed down the article on her new phone, skimming rather than reading, unable to focus on anything other than the need to empty her bladder – she wouldn't be able to hold off much longer. Jay glanced at his watch, the sun was beginning to set.

'We should get going again in the next twenty

minutes, is there anything else you need whilst we're here?'

Megan looked at him, willing him to understand without her having to say the words. But he simply smiled encouragement at her as if he was coaxing a greeting out of a shy child.

She took a deep breath. 'I need the toilet.'

She could feel heat rising in her cheeks, it was excruciating.

He stood up. 'Okay, I'll go and have a look,' he said and walked off.

Her head snapped upwards. What was he doing? Surely he wasn't going to go and look in the women's toilets? And what for? She wouldn't be able to get her chair in there. But he was gone before she could ask.

He returned a few minutes later. 'There's a baby change with a toilet, which looks like it has enough room for your chair.'

He moved around behind her. 'I'll take you,' he added, as if it was a choice.

This felt worse than anything, why was everything such a humiliation? And the constant staring made it unbearable, she may as well be naked. He stopped in front of a wide door that was painted with a cartoon image of a baby on a changing mat. Holding it open with his foot he steered her through and then finally let go of her chair. Megan removed the sling from her arm and turned herself around.

'Is this okay?' he asked. 'Can you manage?'

She looked at the space in front of her, there was a

large changing table, nappy and soap dispensers, a sink and a bin. In the corner there was also a toilet with space to one side of it that she could manoeuvre her chair into.

'Yes,' she replied, confused. 'How did you know there would be something like this?'

Jay's face softened. 'I went on holiday with Adam and Shuang a couple of times just after Li Li, my niece, was born and I changed her a few times. I guess I was the free help.'

He smiled at the memory.

'I'll wait outside.'

Megan watched as he closed the door. A teenage Jay babysitting and changing nappies was like another blow to her already battered heart, she couldn't bear much more of being around him. The more she knew him, the bigger the gulf became between her feelings for him and the barren ground where they smashed to pieces. And now, on top of that, she had to endure him waiting outside while she urinated. Loving him felt like a long cruel joke at her expense.

Staring at her reflection in the mirror as she washed her hands, she noticed a couple of strands of hair had escaped from her hat. She tucked them back inside and pushed her glasses up her nose. Not much longer and it would all be over for good.

Chapter 22

Jay left the motorway near Kingston and turned back in a southerly direction towards Brunstock Park. They had agreed that somewhere rural and unpopulated would be the safest place for Megan go into hiding. He drove steadily down the road on the eastern side of the park and pulled into a farm track behind a copse of trees. Leaving the door open, he climbed out of the car and started walking, straining his eyes over the fields and the surrounding landscape. Even though it was well into the evening there was a chance a farmer could still be at work, making the most of the last moments of the summer light. A burst of noise ripped through the quiet and an old-style motorbike sped past on the road below. Body rigid, he waited to see if any more vehicles followed, allowing his heart to decelerate. One last look around was all there was time for now, he just had to trust that the trees by the road shielded them from view. He walked back up the slope and opened the boot, this was it, they had to do it as quickly as possible.

Half an hour later he slowed the car at the approach to

the border checkpoint. A car was stopped at the booth in front with its boot lid raised and the driver standing aside whilst two customs officials rummaged through the contents. Panic surged through his body, was it a random search? Did they search everyone? Or were they already looking for him and Megan?

He looked over at the other booths, mostly it seemed to be a few quick questions and a wave through, it must be random. He could switch lanes, but that might look suspicious. Anyway, if it was random, and they had already stopped the car in front, that made it almost one hundred per cent certain they would not search his car as well. Watching the scene in front and trying to calm his breathing, he fought back the horror that if he had driven even slightly faster it could have been him standing there as his car disgorged its secrets. Taking a deep breath he checked his documents, ID card and passport with conference flyer enclosed. Everything was there as planned, but he was uncertain now, unnerved by what was happening right in front of him.

Finally, the officers finished with the driver in front and signalled Jay forwards to the booth. The officer eyed him and he tried to arrange his face into a causal expression.

'Passport or ID card, please.'

He hesitated, he wanted to use his ID card even though that was not what they had agreed. But it was obvious now there were so many possibilities they had never considered, that threw all of their plans into doubt. He tried to focus, the ID card felt less risky, but there were only seconds to make a decision and hesitation would look suspicious. Holding onto the passport, he handed over the card. The officer studied it.

'Destination?'

A surge of adrenaline rocked his body, he couldn't mention the conference in Dublin now, he had to commit to a new, spontaneous, lie. He remembered the story Megan had invented.

'Glasgow,' he said, as confidently as he could.

If he was only going to Scotland there would be no need for him to show his passport as well. The officer looked at him for a moment and then the picture on his ID and then scanned it against his monitor.

'Very good, have a pleasant journey.'

Jay's smile was heartfelt. 'Thank you.'

Forcing himself not to snatch the card out of the officers hand in his hurry to get away, he slid it back into his wallet, put the car in gear and drove through the check point. Megan was curled up in the boot, what could she hear? Probably nothing, but she must be able to feel the car moving again and know that they had just illegally entered Scotland.

Chapter 23

After the border, the motorway regulations switched to kilometres per hour and the signs were in Gaelic as well as English. Jay exited after the Gretna Green services and continued northwards on a minor road until he reached a crossroads and turned left towards Kirkpatrick. It was dark now and the thickening cloud made the night feel heavy. He followed the signs to the parish church and turned the car into the adjacent plot where the old graveyard had been extended, following the tarmacked surface until it came to an abrupt halt. He stopped the car and switched off the lights and engine. A graveyard seemed foolish now, and it felt a lot more exposed than he had imagined, but there wasn't time to search for an alternative. He got out of the car and surveyed the surroundings. The feint hum of the motorway whirred in the distance, and he could see the lights at the crossroads where he had turned towards the village, but other than that it was dead still. He went to the back of the car and opened the boot.

A moment later and Megan was looking up at him wide-eyed from her nest of bedding. He nodded, there were no words. She pushed herself into a sitting position and unfolded her legs, wincing slightly as she rubbed them. She must be in pain, but at least she could travel in comfort for a while now. Her plait had loosened and long amber threads slipped free, glowing in the night. She reached down and opened the small bag that was tucked in beside her.

'I need to change,' she said. 'There's no point in putting the disguise back on again now.'

His eyes rested on her, transfixed, it felt like he was only just waking up to the reality of who she was and what he was doing. She looked at him with a strange expression and then hooked her fingers to the waistband of Silvie's one-and-a-half-legged pyjama-bottoms and began to shuffle backwards. A burst of realisation propelled him to the front of the car horrified it looked like he was deliberately watching her undress.

Staring out across the gravestones whilst his mortification subsided, his mind wandered over the lives of the occupants beneath the stones, had any of them had done anything as strange and risky as this? It was weirdly comforting to imagine all the wild and wonderful things that other people had done in their lifetimes: the risks they had taken and the mistakes they had made. It made him feel a little less insane and a bit more like he was just part of the wider confusion of humanity, making their way through life the best they knew how.

The sound of Megan's tyres crackling softly against the debris blown to the ground from the nearby trees made him turn around. She had changed into black leggings and thick woolly socks, and wrapped a long, faded cardigan around her, she must be cold despite the mild evening. Wordlessly, she transferred herself into the passenger seat and Jay returned her chair to the boot of the car. With Megan out of her disguise and back in the car, the reassurance evaporated as quickly as it had arrived. There was only the stark truth: he had committed a number of major felonies and he was about commit even more, and all for a promise that might not even be true. What if Ireland turned out to be no different from England, after all? Would they have to do this whole journey again in reverse? That would double their chances of being caught and, at best, only return them to the same impossible situation they had left. Panic rose through his body, and yet there was no other way out for either of them, this was the only thing he could do. He rested his head and forearms against the back window of the car, willing the reassurance to return. It didn't. Taking a deep breath he climbed back into the driver's seat. Megan looked at him, her face betraying that she was feeling it too. He swallowed and switched on the engine, turning the car carefully out of the graveyard and following the road through the village towards Anan where he could pick up the main westerly route.

Despite being a primary route, the road was an unlit single carriageway that twisted and turned through what seemed to be mostly unpopulated countryside – although it was hard to be sure in the dark. Navigating the road was tricky and this section of the journey was going to take longer than the couple of hours he had imagined.

About an hour and a half after they left Kirkpatrick, the road looped down towards the coast, offering the first glimpse of the inky sea that promised Megan's freedom. He glanced over at her, she was so quiet she might have been sleeping, but her eyes were wide, pinned to every detail the night revealed as the road led them towards the bridge. After Barlae the road widened and illuminated signs for the bridge dotted the highway. In a few more kilometres there would be security cameras so he turned off the main road and headed south towards Milton and Auchenmaig.

It was just before midnight, a short slip road led to an abandoned car wash and he pulled in and switched off the lights and the engine. Megan looked at him, he could sense her fear taking over. Reaching over, he gave her shoulder a quick squeeze, it was the most he could offer.

'Okay,' he said, forcing himself to make eye contact with her and not be subsumed by their fear. 'This is it.'

His jaw was tight.

'You have to hide from here on.'

They had planned this part of the journey relentlessly, but had never expected it to feel like this. It had seemed logical and straightforward then, but now, despite how easily they had got through the first border, the whole plan seemed fragile and fallible. They had to pass through customs and immigration checkpoints at each end of the bridge. Had they really believed they, two young people, could outwit the security of three states with such a simple plan?

Megan inhaled. 'Okay,' her voice was shaky.

A twinge of hope ignited in his solar plexus, perhaps she was about to change her mind and decide not to go through with it? He could just turn around and drive back to Liverpool and think of something else that was less risky; less absurd. After all, he had a lot more to lose than her, her life in England was pretty much a prison anyway – although no doubt actual prison was multiple times worse than Bootle Cares. But for him? It was unthinkable. Yet that was the trade-off he was gambling: free her from a life of confinement at the risk of both of them being imprisoned for years.

He forced himself out of the car and brought Megan's chair round to the passenger door. She lifted herself across, checking carefully she had not left anything inside that would betray her and then he wheeled her over the rutted ground to the back of the car. They looked at each other, this could be the last time they ever saw each other. Megan lifted herself onto the edge of the boot and curled herself into a tight knot and pulling the duvet around her. Jay covered her with the decoy shelf and checked the supports were in place for the last time and then folded her chair and placed that on top and then put the original boot shelf over it.

He had tried to invent an elaborate lie to tell the joiner who had fitted the extra shelf into the car but he wasn't very good at lying – he could avoid the truth reasonably adeptly if he had to, but actually constructing and maintaining an outright lie was too difficult. If he knew something was untrue himself, it was almost impossible for him to convince anyone otherwise. In the end, he had simply paid so much money in cash that the guy didn't feel the need to ask any questions and he simply worked to the specifications Jay had given him. But money wasn't going to help now, he was going to have to lie his way through two sets of customs and immigration checks and both of their lives depended on him getting it right. And no matter how much he had rehearsed it with Megan or in his own head as he lay awake at night, he was still terrified. It suddenly seemed obvious he would not be able to pull it off, he would falter and expose himself.

Why did he not say anything to Megan? That could have been their last chance before it was all over. Wracked with fear, he shut the lid of the boot, gulped in the night air and checked his pockets one last time: passport, ID, conference flyer; the three small documents that told the lies both of their futures hinged on. He forced himself back into the car and started to drive, his hands trembling on the wheel. *I'm just driving to Ireland*, he repeated over and over again, *hundreds of people do this every day*.

Chapter 24

'Passport, please.'

This was it, the first of the immigration barriers on the bridge, no more option of passport or ID. It was a soft border here for CU citizens only, and the English plates on the car had already proclaimed he was not in that lucky category. Taking a discreet, steadying breath and trying to appear nonchalant, Jay handed over his passport with the conference flyer folded in the back page as if he had forgotten it was there. The customs officer glanced at the paper flyer and Jay suddenly realised it was a terrible mistake. What if he checked the conference registration list? He hadn't told Megan he had been refused permission to go. It had felt insignificant then, an unimportant detail in the wider scheme of things – he was still going to take her to Ireland and the conference was irrelevant to that. Only now it was obvious that it could blow everything apart. He fought to maintain a blasé countenance while his heart hammered in his throat. The officer handed back the flyer and studied the passport, looking at it and then at Jay. The picture was not a good likeness.

'How long will you be in Ireland for?'

'Two weeks – a conference and a bit of a holiday.'

Could the officer hear the strain in his voice? Was leaving the conference flyer in his passport so crass that it was an instant give-away? And what about the picture? The passport was a few years old, was that enough to excuse the poor likeness?

The officer thumbed through the pages, it was taking forever and blood pounded in his ears.

'Right-oh,' the officer bent the spine of the passport so that two pages were spread open.

'This stamp is your fourteen-day visa,' he clunked a small metal object against the pages. 'You will be stamped with an exit visa when you leave.'

Jay winced, he hadn't expected a physical mark on the passport, he had assumed it would be digital, not hard evidence of the illicit journey marked forever on the paper.

'Fourteen days is the maximum you can stay on this type of visa,' the officer continued. 'And you cannot apply for an extension during your visit.'

He scanned the back pages of the passport against his monitor and then finally returned it to Jay.

'Thank you,' Jay forced his voice as level as he could.

It felt like his lungs didn't start working properly again until he was half way across the bridge. One more checkpoint and they had made it. Tremors of pent-up adrenalin took hold of his limbs, shaking him so hard it would be impossible to change gear if he needed to. He wanted to pull over and collect himself, but stopping on the bridge would arouse concern or suspicion, or both. So he carefully monitored his foot on the accelerator, keeping a strict sixty miles an hour, just under the one hundred kilometre an hour limit.

A car sped towards him in the outside lane. Police? Immigration officers? Had his deception been discovered? The car hovered alongside him and he stole himself for the inevitable, then its tail-lights disappeared into the distance. He exhaled, alone again on the bridge.

The lights from the bridge glinted on the dark, churning water below. It was like being suspended between worlds in an eternal limbo. But eventually, the speed limit began dropping by ten kilometres an hour every few hundred meters in preparation for the border controls at the Larne exit. He slowed to a crawl as the booths appeared, spanning the lanes of the bridge in both directions like piano keys. There was a car ahead of him, perhaps the one that had overtaken him earlier? Either way, he didn't bother to switch lanes, he simply took long deep breaths and waited to be waved forward to the cubicle.

He forced a smile. 'Evening.'

'Good evening, sir, can I see your passport, please?' Jay handed over the document. 'Thank you. Purpose of visit?'

'Conference and a short holiday.'

'Where will you be staying?'

'Dublin, The Distillery Hotel in Smithfield.'

'In Dublin for the whole of your visit?'

'Yes, maybe a day trip here and there: Kilkenny,

Wicklow, but I will be staying in Dublin the whole time.'

'This visa is for fourteen days only and you cannot apply for an extension while you are in Ireland.'

'Yes, I still have my dissertation to finish in England so I can't afford to be away for any longer than that!'

Why did he say that? He was babbling, his nerves were getting the better of him precisely when he needed to be the most in control. Everything hinged on this moment: Megan curled up in the boot; all the lies to get this far; he couldn't mess it up with stupid unplanned chatter. The customs officer looked at the passport and then at Jay. *Please don't question the picture*, he wished into the distant heave of the waves.

'Very good, sir, enjoy your visit.'

He handed back the passport.

That was it, it was done. Jay hoped the officer didn't see his hands shaking as he put the car into gear and drove away. Tears sprang up without warning and tried to force their way out of his eyes. But he had to keep going, even as he lost his battle with his tears and his cheeks were wet.

Fáilte go hÉirinn, Welcome to Ireland, emblazoned in large green letters on a sparkling white sign: the land border. The road was brightly lit, he hoped his reaction was not visible on the cameras. Imagine if the whole plan was ruined because he had been seen crying on security footage, destroyed at the very end by his own weakness? He kept driving. Thankfully there didn't seem to be many cameras after the exit from the bridge. It was nearly over, there was only one more stop planned now and that was to release Megan before they reached the motorway towards Belfast and then on to Dublin. Even though she didn't have any documents other than the copies on her laptop they were safe now, in Ireland disabled people were free to move around without question.

At Millbrook, he exited from the roundabout following the sign that pointed towards a garden centre. He drove steadily into the carpark, heading towards the back corner where there was a tall hedge and it was dark. He switched off the lights and the engine and got out of the car, checking for security cameras. There were none in sight, there hardly seemed to be any at all on the Irish side of the bridge, there seemed to be much less interest in monitoring the population here – and there were certainly far less restrictions to be complied with. Even so, he had a story in case he was asked why he had stopped: he had been overcome with tiredness and needed to stretch his legs and get some fresh air. He scoured the carpark again. It seemed safe, it was dark and there was no-one about. He opened the boot and removed the first shelf and lifted Megan's wheelchair out and unfolded it, laying the cushion flat against the seat and then checked around him one more time. A shadow moved further along the hedge. He froze, holding his breath. A fox stepped out and trotted across the carpark. Jay exhaled and waited to see if any lights were activated, but everything remained dark and still. Reassured, he lifted the second shelf of the boot and Megan looked up at him.

'We're in Ireland,' he whispered.

Megan gasped and began to unfurl her body. She was stiff, wincing with pain, sitting on the edge of the boot while her body eased.

'Thank you,' she said, staring into his eyes with an intensity that made him feel like she could see right inside him.

He sat down beside her and she twisted around to face him.

'You've saved my life for the second time,' she said. 'Thank you.'

He turned and wrapped his arms around her and they held each other tight, not quite believing what they had just done.

Chapter 25

Jay could feel Megan's body softening against him as if the confines of her old life were melting away in his arms. He released the hug. 'You're a free woman,' he smiled.

'I know,' she whispered. A tear slipped from her eye.

'I can't quite believe this is real.'

She inhaled deeply as if she could breathe in her freedom from the Irish air.

'It's real,' he assured her and reached forward and wiped the tear from her cheek with his thumb. 'We did it.'

His touch hung in the air between them.

He stood up and stretched, pulling the tightness out of his limbs. Hunger churned his stomach and he rummaged on the back seat of the car for something to eat. He took a gulp from a bottle of water and then passed it to Megan. She looked almost ethereal perched on the back of the boot in the darkness, her hair tangled around her and her bright blue eyes damp with tears sparkling against her pale skin. His heart knotted for Silvie and everything that was gone.

The rustle of paper wrapping of a service-station pie rewarded his searching fingertips and he stretched forwards and pulled it from its hiding place. Dutifully, he offered it to Megan, disproportionately relieved when she shook her head. He took a large bite and chewed, watching as she lifted herself into her chair and wheeled herself around the carpark. She looked like she was testing the limits of her freedom, trying to see if there really were no boundaries to where she could go and what she could do. How long was it, if ever, that she had been able to do something as simple as that?

It was strange seeing her like this, on the verge of independence. Doubt snagged in his throat – would she really be okay? What if her parents were right? What if she needed help every day and he had taken her away from the only support she had? He put the last crust of pie in his mouth, each bite a minor disappointment compared to Megan's creations. The inevitability of nothing ever matching her baking made him smile, of course she would be alright.

He glanced at his watch. 'It's nearly three AM,' he called, enjoying the audacity of speaking to her aloud and unconcerned in a public space.

She turned and smiled and began moving back towards him.

'It will be light in a couple of hours,' he added, even though it didn't matter anymore if it was light or dark, there were no more checkpoints to pass through, and nothing more to hide – well, not in Ireland, anyway.

Megan settled herself back into the passenger seat

and he turned the car back onto the main road and headed south. It was unlit and deserted. As he stared into the night, shapes began to form in the darkness beyond the silver pools of the headlights, and a leaden weight of tiredness bore down on his eyes. He blinked a few times but it only made his eyelids heavier, if he closed them again he probably wouldn't be able to reopen them. Squinting into the distance, he could just make out a road sign ahead, Carrickfergus. He turned the car in that direction, glancing at Megan.

'I need to close my eyes for a bit before we hit the motorway.'

Megan nodded, peering into the night as they drove along the coast road. The cliffs had been reinforced and there were viewing points along the way. He pulled into one of the small parking bays, it didn't feel quite right that people went to look at the sea for pleasure rather than avoiding it in fear, but it must be okay with all that infrastructure around it. He killed the lights and the engine and there was nothing but the sea and the night sky. The sound of the waves beneath the car felt a little ominous, but eventually the slow, rhythmic drag and splash of the water on the rocks became soothing; a lullaby pulling him closer and closer to sleep. Megan looked amazingly alert considering what she had endured over the last twelve hours and not at all like she needed to sleep.

'Do you need anything? Your chair?'

'No, thanks,' she reached around behind her seat. 'I'll just do some writing,' She unfolded her laptop.

'What are you writing?' He angled his seat into a horizontal position and closed his eyes.

'Just bits and pieces,' she said vaguely.

'Read me something,' he smiled, eyes still closed.

Megan faltered.

'I'm waiting,' he encouraged.

'Okay,' she replied, uncertainly. 'I'll read you something I wrote a while ago.'

There was a long pause and then her voice again returned. She was reading in verse, weaving a gentle rhythm into the car and painting images inside his head that he could not quite understand. She seemed to have brought him under the ocean, telling the story of a group of creatures, whales perhaps, in their final struggle for survival as the waters around them were desecrated. But it was not desperate and violent, it did not seem like the like the last battle for existence he would have imagined, it was full of love and wisdom, a group of beings holding together as their world caved in around them. It was not what he had expected at all. Her voice faded. He forced his eyes open and looked at her.

'Don't stop,' he said. 'It's beautiful. I've never heard anything like it in my life.'

They looked at each other for a moment and then she returned her eyes to the screen and continued reading.

Megan swallowed hard and took a deep breath to steady her voice, she did not want to betray how much his words meant to her. Giving all of her attention to each word on the screen, she continued reading, not thinking and feeling anything beyond the flow of the story. Thankfully, he was asleep by the time she reached the last verse. She sighed and closed the laptop and looked out across the waves to the dark horizon. To the east lay her old life, a life of confinement, pain, and death. North, south, and west of her lay a whole new world. She turned to Jay, the midwife to her new life. His chest was rising and falling with the slowness of his breath and she could see his eyes flickering behind the lids. What dreams might be filling his mind? He looked so innocent whilst he slept, she could almost lean over and plant a kiss on his forehead. Instead, she turned towards the horizon and watched the sky as it gradually turned from dark-slate to grey-blue and then as the first light from the sun began to appear. Rays of white light peaked over the water, followed by the first slither of the orange sun.

Jay woke in the rising light and they watched in silence as the sun ascended.

'It's a beautiful day,' he murmured, his voice still thick with sleep.

Megan reached over and squeezed his hand. 'Thank you,' she said. 'This is the best day of my life.'

To her surprise, his eyes moistened.

'It's nothing more than you deserve,' he replied and quickly looked away.

A moment later he climbed out of the car and stretched his arms above his head, circling them in wide arcs before reaching down to his toes. He peeled himself back to standing position and twisted side-to-side from the waist, letting his arms flay out from his sides. He must have felt her eyes on him because he stopped suddenly, looking awkward, probably self-conscious about moving around like that in front of her, no doubt comparing her to Silvie and pitying her for all the things she would never be able to do regardless of what country she was in – after all, whatever hopes and dreams might be coming true right now, there was one thing that would never change.

Chapter 26

Jay climbed back inside the car, sensing a shift in the atmosphere between them.

'Come on,' he said keeping his tone light. 'Let's find some services and get some coffee and a wash. I feel like I have slept in an old sock!'

Megan smiled with warmth and the equilibrium between them returned as quickly as it had disappeared. His body relaxed, he hadn't noticed until now how much her happiness meant to him.

Despite longing for coffee, he waited until they had passed Belfast and were safely on route to Dublin before taking a slip road to a service station, certain that nothing could go wrong now. As he turned the car towards the back of the carpark, he noticed a sign with a crude approximation of a wheelchair pointing in the other direction. He glanced at Megan, but she would have no more idea what it meant than him, so he said nothing and followed the signs. They arrived at the front of the services where extra-large parking bays had been painted with similar symbols.

'Look at this,' he could hear the incredulity in his own

voice. 'Car parks that are especially designed for disabled people.'

Megan was smiling with delighted surprise, clearly Ireland was a lot different to what she had imagined, too. He opened the boot and brought her chair around to the side of the car and she transferred into it keeping her laptop pressed against her thighs. He moved to take the handles of her chair and then stopped himself, she was free to move around without him now, no-one here even gave her a second glance.

A car drew into the bay beside them with a single male occupant. In just a few seconds the man opened the door, lifted a wheelchair frame from the passenger seat onto the tarmac beside him and added wheels and a cushion and transferred into it. The man must have felt Jay staring because he looked him square in the face. Jay forced a smile and turned away only to see Megan had been watching too – and she had never looked so happy.

The building was cool and there were only a handful of people inside. Megan went to the bathroom – something else that was also especially provided for disabled people – while he bought breakfast of coffee and freshly baked berry muffins. As they ate, he checked both of their new phones again and a flicker of doubt crossed his mind, would Megan know how to use it? Had she had ever had a phone like this before? It would be a complete waste to give her something she had no idea how to use, at the same time he didn't want to patronise her, she was capable of so much more than he had once imagined. And she had seemed quite adept with it at

Southwaite, but they were both nervous then and she might not have wanted to say or do anything that would draw even more attention to them.

He slid her phone back across the table towards her. 'Does it all look okay to you?' he asked, pleased with the subtlety of his question.

She picked it up and thumbed through a few screens. 'I think so, but I don't know much about phones, although it's fairly similar to one that Silvie had a few years back.'

Silvie's name cut into the space between them like a shard of guilt. This had been the longest time he hadn't thought of her. Was he forgetting her? It was a terrifying idea, he would rather have the pain of losing her raw and weeping every day than allow her to fade into the distance.

Megan placed her hand on his, her touch was comforting, as if she was absolving him. She didn't take it away until he began to gather up their cups and plates and return them to the counter. They were both quiet for the rest of the journey, Megan with her laptop clutched against her thighs staring out of the window, not risking a second of her new life slipping by without her full attention.

Most of the drive was easy, but as they drew closer to Dublin the motorway ended and the signs to the city centre sent him into a maze of suburbs, where gnarled old trees shaded large redbrick houses. Once, there had been a tunnel into the city, but the rising sea-level and the refigured port had put paid to that. The traffic was slow as they neared the centre of Dublin, most of the lanes were taken by cyclists, hydro-buses, and electric trams that criss-crossed the city. The car crawled around the outskirts of Smithfield and then the road doubled back on itself, bringing them to the one of the three remaining river crossings in the city centre. The first glimpse of the river almost stopped him in his tracks. Enormous, rusting tidal defences towered over the water and the streets below, stretching in either direction as far as he could see. These were nothing like the shoddy defences in Liverpool, they rose up like giants, brutal and crude yes, but strong and defiant, protecting the city and those who lived there.

Almost instinctively now, he changed down a gear as the road inclined steeply onto the bridge that traversed the flood defences and the original, ruined crossing at Christchurch Cathedral.

Megan pressed her face to the window, scouring the water below for the signs of the original stone bridge but it was completely obscured beneath the sludge-coloured water. She looked up again as they passed the stone archway that connected the Cathedral to the Synod building across the road. The formality of the architecture added to the tightening in her chest, the map on her phone showed it was not far, they were very close to the asylum centre where she would turn herself in. She twisted around and looked back, there was something poignant about the old archway, the new bridge and the rusting flood defences, it seemed to capture the gap between the potential of human achievement and the reality they created. She tightened her grip on the laptop, hoping that was the story of her life in reverse.

After Christchurch, she matched the street signs to her screen as Jay turned right on to Thomas and then James' Street. The traffic had thinned to occasional cyclists and intermittent buses and trams heading west out of the city. Large signs to the hospital loomed in front of them and her heart thudded. The Citizen's Asylum Centre had been co-located with the hospital because so many people arrived from England suffering years of medical neglect. Even though Jay was driving slowly into the hospital campus, following signs in Gaelic and English, it felt like everything was speeding up, their surroundings blurring in front of her eyes. It was a moment before she realised that had Jay brought the car to a gentle stop in front of a squat yellow brick building with large dark-tinted glass doors and solar panels on the roof. They had arrived.

Bile rose in her stomach. This was it, everything she had ever dreamed of was right in front of her. This could just as easily be the end as the beginning – if they had got any of it wrong her life was over. She inhaled slowly, swallowing down the bitterness in her throat and willing herself back to calmness while her fingertips formed damp pools on the metal surface of the laptop.

Jay turned to her. 'Are you okay? Do you want me to come in with you?'

Megan nodded and then shook her head in answer to

each question. This was something she needed to do alone. It was the end of one life and the beginning of another, if it were to be everything she dreamed of, then she had to do it by herself. Her new life had to start without Jay in it. She took a deep breath and turned to meet his gaze.

'I'm just a bit nervous, that's all.'

'That's only to be expected,' he smiled gently. 'This is a big deal. This is enormous.'

He squeezed her hand, his fingers warm and dry against her clammy skin.

'But you're strong, Megan. You can do this, and I'm here for you,' his tone was full of gentle reassurance.

She squeezed his hand in return, not trusting her voice to respond.

'If you need anything or if you change your mind and want some company, just message me.'

His attentiveness was almost too much to bear, thankfully, he kept talking and got out of the car.

'Either way, let me know how you get on as soon as you can.'

He brought her wheelchair round to her side of the car and lifted her bags from the back seat while she transferred into it. He attached the larger bag to the handles at the back and passed her the lighter one to put on her lap, she slipped her phone into the front pocket and tucked her laptop behind it. That was all she owned in the world, two bags and an old laptop – Jay had brought more than that for two weeks.

They hugged briefly and then she pulled away from

him, she could feel him watching her as she wheeled herself towards the wide glass doors. She paused for one last look at him before she entered, the man who had risked so much to get her here, leaning causally against a battered old estate car with crumpled clothes and tangled hair. He looked different now he was stripped of all the markers of good fortune that usually surrounded him, like he was just a regular guy with a decrepit car yet, in that moment, he was more special than he had ever been.

'Thank you,' she said, locking eyes with him for just a second, and then forcing herself through the doors.

He would be gone soon and that would be the end of it.

Jay watched Megan disappear behind the shiny, opaque doors and inwardly wished her luck, she was on her own now and there was nothing more he could do. He turned to open the driver's door and the horizon seemed to tip on its axis, his knees buckled and he pressed his body against the car to stay upright. Pain knitted inside his chest, compressing his lungs, if anyone ever found out about this his life was over. He breathed slowly and deliberately, steadying himself against the car as the wave of anxiety crested, *you're just tired*, he told himself over and over again, *no-one even knows she is alive*. Even so it took all his resolve to force his body back into the car and start the engine. His hands were unsteady on the controls as he began to drive back across the river towards his hotel.

Chapter 27

The doors slid closed and Megan found herself in a multi-sided, asymmetrical room with a light wooden floor and brightly painted doors set into a number of walls. Two corridors laid with the same light wood flooring stretched away from her in opposite directions. The rich bitter scent of freshly brewed coffee battled with a sweet detergent to dominate the air. A few chairs were scattered in the centre of the room but Megan was alone. To her right was a reception counter sealed with a Perspex screen, behind which a small number of people sat at desks with computer terminals. There was a woman in a wheelchair beside one of them, she must have arrived even earlier and have started her application already. A phone on the adjacent desk trilled and she picked it up and, turning her chair to face the terminal, she began tapping information into the computer. A somersault of delight turned in her stomach: she worked there! Ireland got better and better by the minute. Buoyed, Megan wheeled closer to the screen and a middle-aged woman with greying hair and an emerald green salwar kameez approached from the other side – her name badge read

Udaya McCarthy.

'Hello, can I help you?' she smiled.

'I have just escaped from England.'

Hearing herself say the words, Megan felt her strength disintegrating, every hurt and humiliation, every grief and loss, was suddenly alive in her body, battering her from the inside out.

She forced herself on. 'My grandmother was Irish and I would like to claim asylum and apply for citizenship.'

A wave of desperation pushed deep, guttural sobs through her chest that swallowed up all the air in her lungs. She gasped for breath, she had to speak, she had to explain the documents she had, this was her once chance. She tried to lift her laptop as evidence, but she couldn't do anything other than cry. She put her face in her hands and tears streamed between her fingers, splashing on the smooth grey surface of her laptop.

'It's okay,' Udaya reassured her, disappearing from behind the screen and reappearing at her side. 'We can talk in another room.'

Megan nodded, fighting to regain control of herself, she could not ruin it now and make it all for nothing.

'This way,' Udaya smiled. 'Do you want me to carry that?' she nodded towards the bag on Megan's lap.

'I can manage, thank you.'

Udaya led her across the lobby and opened the orange door. Inside two low, wide chairs faced each other across a table with a box of tissues. This time Megan let Udaya help unload her bags from her chair.

'Make yourself comfortable and I'll go and get some

water,' she said and left the room.

Megan transferred herself into one of the chairs and curled into a tight knot as if she could squeeze out the last of her tears, breathing into her knees to summon her self-control. Udaya returned with a jug of water and some paper cups.

'I'm sorry,' Megan began, unfurling herself. 'It's been an enormous journey and I'm a bit overwhelmed by it all.'

'I'm sure you are. No-one gets here easily,' Udaya replied sitting down and pouring each of them a cup of water.

'Thanks,' Megan gulped. 'I'll be alright in a minute. I have to start getting things sorted out today.'

'Don't worry, you will, there's plenty of time. Just take a few minutes to see how you feel first.'

Udaya sipped her water and smiled softly, her presence was comforting.

'I had to get in the boot of a car to get here,' Megan blurted, it barely felt real already, even though it was only minutes since she got out of the car and her body still hurt from the journey.

'A friend helped me.'

'It sounds like you have a very good friend to help you get here.'

'Yes, he is my sister's boyfriend. Was.'

'Was?'

'Yes. She's dead.'

More sobs forced their way through her body. How could she even begin to tell everything that had got her to this point when she couldn't even stop herself from crying?

But somehow she did. It took most of the day, Udaya carefully tapping everything that Megan recounted into a terminal, occasionally checking and reconfirming details. After many hours, when the initial application was complete and copies of the documents on Megan's laptop were verified and transferred into the system, Udaya finally issued her an interim right to reside ID card.

'There's a lot more we have to do,' Udaya warned her. 'But we should be able to get most of your essentials sorted out this week,' she smiled reassuringly.

Megan nodded, delirious with exhaustion.

Udaya led her to a minibus that would take her to her temporary accommodation. She stared blankly out of the window letting the world slip by in a haze, too tired to care of which part of the city she was in or to try and track the journey on her phone. After a short time, the minibus came to a halt outside a modern, low-rise building with a sloping roof covered in solar panels and greenery planted in every available patch of surrounding earth. The upper windows boasted miniature gardens of trailing plants. A tall man with sandy coloured hair appeared at the front door as soon as they arrived. He climbed on board and introduced himself to Megan, shaking her hand and welcoming her with an accent and a name she struggled to understand.

'Everyone calls me Paddy,' he added, taking her bags whilst the driver lowered the ramp for her to disembark.

Paddy led her inside and gave her a short tour of the ground floor of the building and briefly talked through the regulations. To her relief, he also handed her a printed sheet of paper containing the information she had barely understood, before finally showing her to the room which she would occupy. It had a smooth wooden floor, a wide bed, a desk and chair, a rail and drawers for her clothes and an adjoining bathroom. It was clean, fresh, and easy to move around, much nicer than anything she had had before.

'You should get something to eat,' Paddy coaxed her. 'The main kitchen shuts at eight, but you can help yourself in the kitchenette at any time.'

Megan agreed just to be rid of him, he was very kind, but all she wanted to do was lie down and sleep. When he finally left her, she locked the door, stripped down to her underwear, climbed under the bed covers and closed her eyes.

Clattering cutlery, the low hum of voices and the smell of coffee drew her from sleep, she looked at her phone, it was just after seven and she was ravenous. She showered quickly and pulled on the first set of clothes she could find from the top of her bag, not caring how crumpled they were, and headed out to the kitchen.

Chapter 28

The next few days were a marathon of bureaucracy at the asylum centre, completing applications for all the essentials of life as an Irish citizen that would spring into being once her status was confirmed. There was universal basic income, social housing, bank account, registering with the different services. She messaged Jay and they agreed they would meet up when she had got through the bulk of the applications – there was so much to do that she barely had time to miss him. Life at Bootle Cares and then waiting in Jay's flat had been slow and un-taxing, now everything sped along at such a pace it felt like her whole future was passing through someone else's hands before she had even seen what they were holding.

By the fourth day it was impossible to avoid the compulsory medical examination. She had resisted as much as she dared, making every excuse she could contrive to escape it, but ultimately she had no choice. Her body was rigid as she wheeled herself down one of the long corridors to the medical wing, she hated this more than anything. Reluctantly, she knocked on the door and was welcomed into a consulting room by a woman with died blue hair and multi-coloured clothes who didn't look much older than herself. The room was clean and bright, with comfy chairs, an examination table and a desk with a terminal where the doctor indicated her to sit.

'I'm Doctor Rielly,' the woman said, reaching forward to shake Megan's hand like this was a normal interaction. 'But please, call me Jo.'

Megan forced a smile and offered her hand. 'I'm Megan,' she said pointlessly given the information the doctor already had about her.

Megan braced herself, waiting to be told to undress so her back could be prodded and her legs pulled around. But the doctor just chatted away in the same friendly tone, taking her pulse and blood samples and typing notes into the terminal. And then, just as she was just starting to relax, the doctor said she was making an appointment for a mobility assessment with a physiotherapist. Megan froze, of course, that was when it would happen. Her head pounded, was there a way to avoid the physiotherapy appointment? But it was too late to say anything, the doctor had already typed the details into her terminal and was now talking about a carer.

'Your caseworker at the asylum centre can help you apply for some support with your mobility or day-to-day living needs.'

Her tone implied that this was good news, but Megan knew otherwise.

'No,' she managed to get the words out, this was one thing she was not going to back down on. 'I don't need a carer.'

'It's not just for care, they are a kind of personal assistant, we call them PCA's, personal and care assistants.'

'No,' Megan said again, she didn't want anyone near her, making excuses to touch her and push her around.

'All PCAs are fully trained and professionally accredited,' the doctor continued, her eyes were earnest. 'It's a respected profession over here – not like the stories I hear from England. You interview and select the PCA yourself, it's all in your control,' she coaxed.

'No,' Megan repeated. 'I don't need a PCA, I can manage everything I need myself.'

The doctor looked at her for a moment and then nodded and made some more notes.

'Well, if you change your mind, or if your situation changes, you can apply at a future date.'

'Thank you,' Megan said with feeling, getting back to Udaya and the endless train of applications would be sweet relief compared to talk of physiotherapists and carers. And there was the access to education course at Trinity College she was excited about, that really did counteract the dread of what the physiotherapist would do. It was an opportunity that had been especially introduced to help returning citizens integrate and, if Megan did well, she could go on to a degree programme. Udaya told Megan she had also studied at Trinity College, arriving as a young woman from the Punjab to complete a Master's degree and she fallen in love and then married straight after her graduation.

'I went to Trinity for an MSc and I got a husband as well!' Udaya's eyes twinkled. 'You never know, you might too!'

'I don't think that's very likely,' Megan faltered.

Until then, Pavel was the only person who had ever suggested that someone would want her in that way. Yet Udaya said it so naturally, as if it was just the same for Megan as anyone else; as if her wheelchair made no difference at all.

'You're a beautiful girl and very clever,' Udaya coaxed in a motherly tone. 'You will make someone very happy.'

Megan swallowed back tears for what must be the millionth time since she had arrived. Because, despite everything, she couldn't help wishing it was Jay who thought she was beautiful and who she could make very happy. But as she thought it, she knew it was a pathetic, ridiculous fantasy, he would be gone in less than two weeks and that would be the end of it.

Chapter 29

Every morning, Jay got up early and ran for at least an hour, there was a gym at the hotel but he preferred to be outside. He liked the morning light and it gave him a chance to get to know the city before it was crowded with people going about their daily business. His feet pounded the pavements and the city began to map itself out in his mind's eye. There was something comforting about Dublin, a warmth and an ease that seeped into his pores and made him feel like he really was on holiday.

After his run, he showered and ate and spent some time catching up on his dissertation or messaging friends on his English phone. They all thought he was staying at his parent's holiday home in the Peak District. His previous summers there made it easy to fabricate stories about the routes he ran and places he visited, but as much as possible he kept the chat to coursework or friends in common, that way he didn't have to risk concocting lies that would eventually trip him up.

His CU phone beeped and a glow spread through him before he even read the message. Megan was being taken to see a flat today, he loved hearing all her news and how fast things were happening for her – how could he have ever doubted this was the right thing to do?

'*Be sure to take some pictures,*' he tapped in reply. '*I want to see it!*'

It was a shame he wouldn't view it with her, or even share the pictures in person – it felt like a such long time since he had left her at the asylum centre. Initially, he had been relishing the prospect of having his own space for a while, the relief of solitude and not having to think about anyone else after months of forced closeness. And the hotel was nice, he had access to all the exclusive facilities and he was well attended to, but it was still strange not to have Megan around, it felt like there was something missing, something he had grown accustomed to.

'*I will,*' she replied. '*I might even be able to move in next week if all the admin gets sorted!*'

Megan in her own flat, what would that be like? An old doubt echoed in his mind, but he pushed it away.

'*Amazing!*' he replied. '*If it's early next week I can help move your things in for you before I leave.*'

He pressed send and winced, she hardly had enough stuff to need any help moving, and no doubt the people at the asylum centre had that organised already.

'*Only if you want me to,*' he added quickly.

'*That would be lovely, thank you.*'

More and more he felt like he was playing catch-up with her, and not just in the way she thought about things, her moral compass that made him seem lazy and shallow in comparison, but in her adaptability to life. For someone who had spent most of her life confined to a wheelchair and then trapped in Bootle Cares she was remarkably capable.

He looked at his watch for what felt like the millionth time. The minutes crawled by and he wasn't getting anywhere with the papers that he needed to analyse for his dissertation. It was hard, he grasped the edges of what the data was telling him, but so much of the content was a haze. It had been so much easier when Silvie had been there to talk it through, everything was clearer then. A pang of grief squeezed his heart, it still felt too hard to be forever. It seemed more like she had been taken away from him for a while as a test, and if he did the right thing he would get her back – her return was his reward. He would save Megan and then he would be transported back to Merebank and find Silvie sprawled on the sofa engrossed in some research paper or other, peppering the air with excerpts interlaced with her own relentless critique.

He put his screen on the table and stood up. It was no good, he couldn't concentrate, maybe a walk around Smithfield or along the quays towards the park would help. He picked up his bag and slid his devices into it heading towards the exit, he was in soft shoes and no jacket, but he needed to get out.

The doors slid open and he automatically turned towards the car rather than the direction of the quays. It stopped him in his tracks, the old Skoda had never seemed more out of place, utterly alien to his life. Anxiety twisted in his chest, what would he do with it when he got back to Liverpool? Selling it might be an option, but who would want to buy it? He had paid practically nothing for it and it would probably be a very long time before he found anyone else who had either the desire or need for it. Perhaps he could leave it at one of the tent villages on the outskirts of the city? Except that might make things worse – the car would still be registered in his name and it would seem very odd for him to buy a car and then leave it at the wastelands.

What about selling it in Ireland? Of course! He could do that and then get the boat or the bus and train back to England. That way he would return with absolutely no evidence of what he had done. Megan might even be able to find out how to go about it. He reached into his bag for his CU phone and then stopped. He couldn't expect Megan to help, she was hardly going to be able to ask anyone with everything that was going on for her. Another thought knotted in his stomach. It wasn't just the car, there was the passport with the visa stamp in it: permanent, damning evidence of what he had done. It was his responsibility to sort it out, not Megans.

His CU phone beeped, jolting him back into the present, and then tightening the thread of anxiety, he hadn't messaged Megan about the car before he thought better of it had he? He thumbed the screen.

'*Photos*!' she had typed and then, '*I love it!*'

He scrolled to the images, the first showed a large hallway with stark white walls and pale flooring that reflected the glare of the camera. Next was a bathroom which looked similar to those he had seen in Bootle

Cares, albeit in much better condition. There was a lot of space, but instead of it being taken up with a bath there was a shower with a seat fixed to the wall. The shower, toilet, and sink had rails beside them, all pure white on slate grey tiles. He registered a hint of surprise as he flicked to the image of the bedroom and the large double bed. It had been made up with pale blue linen which offered the only relief from all the white. But a double bed, for Megan? The bedroom easily accommodated it with enough room to manoeuvre her wheelchair all the way round, but still it seemed a bit unnecessary. The floor looked like it was the same material as the hallway, and there were low level storage units built into the walls. The final pictures showed a combined living room and kitchen which included a grey sofa, a coffee table, and a small wooden table with two chairs as well as the kitchen units. The last photograph showed a door leading onto a wide balcony which must have been designed especially accommodate a wheelchair, perhaps even two given the double bed? That was a strange thought, he pushed it away.

His phone beeped again. *Isn't it amazing? I love it already! I'm so happy!'*

He skimmed back through the pictures, even though the flat was much smaller than his place at Merebank Towers, she was right, it was still pretty amazing that someone in a wheelchair could live in a place like that. He chose his words carefully.

'You seem to have everything you need! I'm really pleased for you.'

'Thank you! You'll get to see it for yourself very soon too! I'm signing the tenancy tomorrow morning!'

Sometimes the contrast between Ireland and England was almost too incredible to be true, if he hadn't seen it for himself he would never have believed it was possible.

'That's fantastic! I can't wait to be your first guest.'

He slipped his phone back into his bag. He was still standing beside the Skoda, the bridge between these two worlds. It would be okay, he would work out what to do about the car, and then no-one would ever believe this could have really happened.

He turned and walked across the plaza towards one of the narrow streets that sloped gently upwards away from the river, he would have a wander to clear his head and then head back for lunch. It was strange to think that in a week or so all of this would live only in his memory, a fantastical secret he could never share. Perhaps long into the future, he and Megan would be able to get in touch, maybe when they were old it would be safe for them to do so, or perhaps one day he would tell his kids the story and they would make him find out what had happened to her. It felt good to see it through the eyes of his future children, he had been brave, he had done the right thing at huge risk to himself and he had transformed someone else's life forever.

Chapter 30

A trace of uncertainty feathered his arms as Jay steered the Skoda out of the parking bay and turned towards the river. Megan had asked him to meet her at the Dublin Physiotherapy Centre, which was somewhere called Tallaght, where she had an appointment that would take up most of the morning – her life was so busy already and he barely grasped a lot of what was going on for her. At least they had the afternoon, their first chance to spend some time together and he had planned a drive, like they used to do in Liverpool, but up into the Wicklow mountains. It would be good for him to get out of the city and see something else of Ireland before he left, and he had told the border guard he might spend a day in Wicklow, so it seemed a wasted opportunity not to go. But he still felt faintly uneasy, perhaps because it was only days now until his return to England and the nagging problem of what to do with the car.

Glancing at his phone, he followed the directions through the south of the city and onto the N81 towards Blessington. Megan had refused his offer to take her to her appointment, presumably because the asylum centre had organised the transport – anyway, he had to get used to the idea that she didn't need him anymore, however unreal it sometimes felt. Tallaght sprawled out on either side of the N81, an ugly, late twentieth century development, that seemed to have been designed to replicate inner-city deprivation, despite having been constructed on a completely empty, greenfield site. His phone indicated the physio centre was immediately to his right in a large, square building that, at first glance, appeared to be a repurposed mall. Faded letters confirmed its former life as the unimaginatively named "Square Shopping Centre".

He steered towards the complex, the last trace of uncertainty dissipating from his limbs. It was easy to find a parking space, hardly anyone seemed to drive a car here. Was it because they couldn't afford it, or because car-use was tainted by the rising sea levels? Either way, it made it easy for him. It probably wasn't even necessary to lock the Skoda, no-one here would want the ancient diesel with English plates – it would be easier if they did, stealing it would be a massive favour, as long as it was never recovered and traced back to him. He clicked the button as he walked away, not checking it was secure, everything would be so much better when he was rid of it.

Automatic doors slid open and a bright space opened up before him. This was not what he had imagined at all, it was not the rundown remnants of the heyday of cheap chain stores and fast fashion that the outside of the building suggested, it was more like a craft market or an arts installation with a warming smell of freshly baked bread and ground coffee. A jumble of second-hand shops, local produce, and workshop spaces for learning about everything from growing vegetables, to installing solar panels and mending cookers and clothes spread around him and people stopped and chatted and laughed with one another – no one seemed worried about surveillance and there were no cameras as far as he could see.

'Are you alright there, son?' a voice appeared beside him.

A man, probably at least a decade older than his father, leaning on a brightly coloured walking stick, regarded him curiously.

'You're looking a little lost.'

'Oh, am I? I'm fine, thank you.'

'Are you looking for something in particular?' the man persisted.

Jay looked around and saw huge letters above a corridor to his right that declared The Dublin Physiotherapy Centre.

He pointed and smiled. 'That's where I'm going!'

The man nodded. 'Well if you need any help, you only have to ask.'

'Thank you,' Jay faltered.

'You have a lovely day, son.'

The man smiled and shuffled off in the direction of a seed-share workshop and Jay stared around him one more time. Was this what a circular economy really looked like? It was so different from the school text books that had made it seem bleak and frugal, with people squeezing out a pitiable existence from the waste left by previous generations, barely better off than if they had been living on a rubbish dump. He had expected it to be cold and grey, damp with desolation and despair. Yet, compared to what he could see in front of him now, that bleakness was a much more apt description of the English economy. Was nearly everything he had learned a lie?

Mustering his confidence he strode towards the Physiotherapy Centre and another set of automatic doors slid open to admit him. For the second time he was stopped in his tracks. Windows, which must have once belonged to individual retail outlets, displayed a vast array of completely incomprehensible equipment, like the set of a science fiction film. He stared, and slowly some of the items began to take shape as recognisable objects. There were prosthetic limbs, strange-shaped crutches and wheelchairs, but still a vast array of objects that slightly sacred him – it was almost as disorienting as the first time he had visited Bootle Cares. How would he even begin to know where to find Megan in a place like this? He reached for his phone, but before his fingers touched the screen he heard her voice.

'Jay!' She was speeding towards him. 'Look at this!'

She was using a completely different chair. It had cambered wheels and sleek black lines and fitted compactly around her body. She turned and whizzed away from him again, moving back up the polished corridor almost as fast as he could run. The back of the wheelchair was low and there didn't appear to be any handles. She stopped abruptly and pirouetted on the spot with her hair flying out around her and one hand in the air like a flamenco dancer. She came to a stop facing him, her eyes dancing.

'Now this is what I call a set of wheels!'

She laughed, and then pelted back towards him, swerving around him at the last minute and completing another pirouette at his side.

Her laughter was infectious, he couldn't help sharing her delight. It was so good to see her this happy, fused with energy she was radiating out all around her. But there was something else, too, she looked different. He was suddenly acutely aware of the curve of her waist into her hips and her compact round breasts. Her face seemed to have taken on new detail, there was something seductive about the scatter of freckles over her nose and the curve of her lips. He caught himself imagining those softly toned arms wrapped around his body and desire opened out inside him. He squashed it down, appalled at himself, it was Megan, Silvie's little sister. Silvie's disabled little sister. Except she didn't seem that way now, she seemed…

'What?' Megan demanded.

He had been staring at her, he felt himself flush as if she could read his thoughts.

'Do you get to keep it?' he blurted the first thing he thought of.

'Yes, it's amazing, isn't it? This is the standard for people over here, not like the shit you get in England.

The physio said it would feel like I'd had square wheels once I got a decent chair and she's right, this is amazing! And even better, the physio is also a wheelchair-user herself!'

'What?!' it was Jays turn to ask.

He had noticed quite a lot of disabled people around since they had arrived but he didn't think they had jobs, or not like that anyway.

Megan skimmed through her phone and held it up to his face. The screen showed a dark-haired woman sitting in a bright orange wheelchair with highlights of her professional biography overlaying the image which included teaching wheelchair sports as well as physiotherapy – he had no idea there even was such a thing. That must have been why Megan had been keen to come here, and on her own, this was all part of her new life.

'Yeah,' she was saying. 'Disabled people can do everything here, go to uni, work, travel, whatever they want. It's like a different universe. And apparently all of Europe is the same, it's *normal*. England is the anomaly. Come on, let's go for a spin!'

She tugged at his wrist and then spun around and headed down the corridor in the direction he had come. He trotted after her, breaking into a stride to catch up.

'Come on, keep up!' She laughed and sped off ahead of him, through the automatic doors and then waited at the main entrance so they could leave together.

'This is going to take some getting used to!'

Walking along beside her, he risked another glance at

her and then immediately dragged his eyes away, he could not believe where his thoughts were going.

Chapter 31

Megan watched from the passenger seat as Jay lifted her new chair into the boot of the Skoda, she had shown him how to remove the wheels and fold down the back to make it more compact, but he didn't need to. It was so small and light compared to her other chair he could lift it with one hand. He closed the lid of the boot and climbed in the driver's seat.

'What time are you getting collected?' he asked.

He was looking at her normally again now, earlier he had stared at her with an expression she didn't recognise, but he must have just been surprised by the chair.

'What do you mean?'

'To go back to the hostel?'

'They're not collecting me.'

He looked confused. 'How did you get here, then?'

Megan pointed to a tram just pulling to a halt in front of them, he was definitely acting a little strangely today, perhaps he was preoccupied with the journey home, even though there was nothing at stake for him now.

'Oh,' he responded, still not sounding quite right. 'Do you need to be back at a particular time?'

'Doors close at ten PM, but I'm sure we'll be back well before then.'

'To the mountains, then,' he smiled.

She smiled back holding his eyes, whatever strangeness there had been was gone, they were back to normal again.

The main road through Tallaght was quiet, it was six lanes wide in places and even with one lane on each side repurposed for cycling and the central reservation taken up by the tram line, the other four lanes were still mostly empty. In some stretches, the outer lane was being dug up and planted with nut trees. The buildings on either side of the thoroughfare were mostly ugly late twentieth century blocks that were being retrofitted with solar panels, wind turbines, and green walls and, as they drew out of Tallaght towards Blessington, new estates sprang up all around them as if Dublin was scurrying westwards away from the rising sea. There was a marked contrast between the new estates and the pre-existing ones. Old Tallaght had been constructed with the feel of urban desolation, clusters of identical redbrick houses squatted along mazes of roads that led to more of the same. But at least the old houses had gardens that could be turned over to growing food, and pitched roofs that could be layered with solar panels. The new estates were designed for solar and wind generation and small spherical white turbines with bite-shaped cutouts to catch the wind dotted the roofs and balconies. Plants grew from every wall of the new builds and interspersed the solar panels. It was so unlike what was happening in Liverpool – and presumably the rest of England – it was like a totally different world here not just a neighbouring island separated by a few miles of sea.

Blessington main street was yet another contrast, it was quaint old Ireland, with low, grey stone buildings and an austere church at the top of a long street of brightly painted shop fronts. Each sign declared the name of the owner: O'Malley's, Kennedy, O'Toole, Jay started as they passed Connolly's.

'There's thousands of them,' Megan smiled. 'It's a very common name here, I don't think I'm going to find any long-lost relatives.'

'It would be good to get some coffee, though,' she added, pointing to a small pavement café beside Connolly's. 'And maybe we should pick up something for lunch?'

Jay drew the car to a gentle stop outside a small delicatessen and brought Megan's new chair around to the passenger door. They crossed the road headed back towards the café, peering into shop windows stuffed with second hand books and toys, or offering repairs of everything from clothes to refrigerators and solar panels. The ease which Megan could now move was a transformation, he kept expecting to have to help her, but with her new chair she could traverse the environment almost as easily as him. How had she lived like that? So restricted, unable to do anything. A surge of admiration filled his chest, she had a quiet, stoic resolve in spite of everything that life had inflicted on her, holding out for the time when things would get better. She didn't compromise her values yet, at the same time, she did not expect others to reciprocate, she simply stayed true to what she believed no matter the obstacles she faced. He had always assumed Megan had learnt her resolve from Silvie, but now he began to wonder if it was the other way round.

'Take a seat,' she pointed a to a small table. 'I'll get these.'

She seemed so confident now, too, smiling and talking to the barista, not the timid little mouse she had always seemed. She opened a wallet and paid in cash – Megan with money, that would also take some getting used to.

'Thank you,' she smiled again as the barista deposited two steaming, bowl-shaped cups of coffee on the table as if it was the most natural thing in the world.

'Thank you,' he added, just to hear his own voice saying something normal.

Megan glanced up at the sky, this side of the road must be south facing, but a breeze sent clouds skimming across the sun with such alacrity that even her skin was not at risk. He pulled his eyes away from her and inhaled the bitter, rich aroma of the coffee and thumbed his phone for the best route over the mountains, this was their last drive together, it had to be special.

Megan insisted on going into the deli by herself while he started the car, and she exited a few moments later with a paper bag leaking the scent of freshly baked bread. It was strange how everything here seemed so simple yet so lush at the same time, fresh, clean, and authentic in a way he hadn't experienced despite all the luxury that surrounded him on a daily basis.

Back in the car, he turned left off the main street, crossing the bridge at the tip of the lake and then turning right towards Ballysmuttan and the Sally Gap. The road pulled steeply upwards, dotted with the occasional old stone cottage or gratuitous late twentieth century bungalow, but soon it was completely empty. The car was straining, he changed down a gear, had he been stupid to assume it would cope with the inclines of the Wicklow Mountains?

The road twisted higher, the landscape becoming sparser with every turn. The mountains that were once famed for their purple heather and thick yellow gorse were now a bleak moonscape baked dry under the perpetual sun. What a place this would be to be stranded. But there was a sinister beauty to this scorched earth, too, the solitude of the mountains, high up, away from the city where the air felt light. Turning right at a crossroads, he followed the road snaking towards Laragh and Glendalough. It was a good job there was no other traffic, there was little room to pass and it was taking all his concentration to navigate the winding road without the additional worry of other vehicles. Eventually, the road drew alongside a marked parking area and he turned gratefully into it. He switched off the engine and lifted Megan's chair from the boot and brought it alongside the car.

The silence was intoxicating. Across the valley rose

the peak of Tóin le Gaoith and at its base a lake that had formed in the shape of heart.

Megan watched as Jay walked to the edge of the tarmacked area, gazing out across the landscape as if he was standing on the prow of a ship and it was the ocean spread out before him. He would be gone in two days and she would never see him again. Even though she knew it was for the best, her heart still hurt.

She committed the image of him staring out into the mountains to memory, a private photograph in her mind's eye, a keepsake and a lament, infused with all the conflicting feelings she harboured for him. Almost as if he could read her thoughts he turned around to face her, the breeze tugging his hair across his face. He brushed it away with his hand, tucking it behind his ear as he walked towards her.

'Are you okay?' he asked, his face etched with concern.

Before she thought better of it she said, 'I was just thinking that I'll never see you again in another couple of days.'

'I know, it feels strange after all of this,' he sighed. 'It will take some getting used to.'

'I'll miss you,' she said. 'And you know I will be eternally grateful for what you have done for me.'

He leant forward and hovered in front of her before wrapping her in a tight hug, resting his face against the back of her neck. A tingle of warmth spread through her, the energy between them felt so intimate, so special, if it was anyone else but Jay she might have believed this could be something, but it was Jay, and he was just being brotherly. As if in confirmation he pulled away from her and went to get the bag of food from the car.

Lying across his bed at the hotel Jay reflected on the day, he had two more nights left in Ireland and then all of this would be over. He was glad he was going to help move Megan into her new flat before he went home, even though she had little to take with her and did not really need his help. But seeing her to her new home made it feel like he had completely fulfilled his promise in a way that even Silvie could not dispute. Megan was safe and had a whole new life stretching out in front of her – and what a life it was going to be, far beyond anything either of them had imagined.

Those odd feelings from earlier in the day resurfaced in his body; he had almost kissed her on the mountains. As he had drawn close to hug her, he had felt an overwhelming urge to bring his mouth to hers as if it was the most natural thing in the world. He shuddered, it was definitely the right time to be leaving, there was no way he should be having those kinds of thoughts about Megan. He had pushed the impulse away and wrapped his arms around her and she had held him tightly in return. Did she know? And what would she have done if he had kissed her? Would she have shouted at him the way she did in his flat? She was right to be pissed off with him then, it was so soon after Silvie had died and it was only because he had been thinking of her. Was that what it was now? Was he missing Silvie and seeing what he had lost in Megan for the very last time? It didn't really feel like that, but what else could it be? Either way it certainly wasn't right. He had released the hug and made an effort to seem relaxed and causal, hoping she hadn't noticed his near indiscretion.

His English phone beeped and he picked it up. It was a message from his dad.

'Where are you and what is going on? The police have been here asking questions about a demo and a missing passport. Your mum is distraught. I want an explanation now.'

He just made it into the bathroom in time to vomit into the toilet bowl, his stomach emptying with such force it felt like his insides were stripped bare. He groped for the handle and flushed the mess away, disgusted and retching even though there was nothing more to bring up. He knelt, shaking, his forehead burning against the cool porcelain outer bowl feeling the world crashing down around him.

Chapter 32

Jay was sitting on the sofa staring at her laptop with an expression she couldn't read – although, he was clearly unhappy. Earlier that day, she had sent him a link to her article in the *Irish Times* and for the first time in ages he had replied instantly, arriving at her door shortly afterwards.

He looked up at her. 'How did you get to write for the *Irish Times*?' he asked, and then, with an almost accusing tone, 'I didn't know you were going to do that.'

She thought he would be happy for her, although it seemed like he was angry, but why? Was it because she had written about her life in England before he was safely back in Liverpool? But he was not supposed to be in Ireland anymore and she had no idea why he was still there. Every time she saw him or he messaged her, he assured her that he was on the verge of leaving and he would be back home in a couple of days. Except he never was, he was always still in Dublin long after.

'I did tell you!' she retorted, her tone as sharp as his.

It had an impact, he looked away from her, returning his eyes to the screen and then the floor before he met her gaze again. His expression had softened and for an instant he looked vulnerable, almost scared, but then the shutters came down again.

'I'm sorry,' he said. 'My head's been a bit all over the place with trying to get the car fixed and everything.'

He averted his eyes again, looking guilty. She didn't believe the story about the car, it had been fine when they went up the mountains and again two days later when he helped her move into the flat and nothing could have happened in the short space of time between then and his scheduled departure that would take this long to sort out.

Perhaps he had met someone and started a new relationship? After all, he had slept with that woman in Liverpool not long after Silvie's funeral and he was never short of attention from women. It was something she couldn't help noticing whenever they were out together, all the admiring glances he attracted and the efforts to make eye contact while she remained invisible at his side. Jay neither ignored nor overtly responded to the attention, well, not whilst she was there anyway, but he must have countless opportunities when he was on his own. He seemed to take all the admiration for granted – yet another aspect of his good fortune he was utterly oblivious to. Either way, he was definitely lying about something.

A surge of anger burned in her chest, he was just as selfish and entitled as he had always been. He was messing up their plans so he could get laid, and then he had the nerve to be unhappy when her dreams finally came true after all those hellish years. Her first piece of writing had been published and all he could do was sit there and frown! She wanted to wheel over and slap him, hard, right across that gorgeous face. It was shocking how much she wanted to hurt him, to jolt him out of his selfish reverie. She pushed the urge away, it shouldn't matter to her that he was sleeping with someone, Silvie was dead and he obviously couldn't resist fucking around whenever the opportunity arose. If only he would just go back to England and stop tormenting her with his presence. She had prepared herself for him leaving, the acidic mixture of pain and relief that she would never see him again, but at least secure in the knowledge he would recede into the past and she would eventually be free of these feelings. But now he wouldn't even give her the double-edged peace of his absence.

He was watching her, how much of what she was feeling could he ever imagine?

'Tell me about it again,' he invited.

Megan sighed and prepared to recount her story, but it was joyless now, he had poured cold water all over her success.

It was her application for the access course at Trinity College that had set the chain in motion. There were entrance assessments for her to complete before she could enrol, most of them were straightforward numeracy and literacy tests, but she also had to write an essay on a contemporary political issue. Initially, it had felt like hopeless task, what did she know about politics in Ireland? But as she re-read the instructions she realised it didn't have to be about national politics, in the list of suggested topics was human rights. In an instant, she went from having nothing to say, to more than she could possibly condense within the word limit. Her mind fizzed with ideas, and she felt Pavel hovering close by. Yet, despite having so much she wanted to say, she could not get it right. The first draft read like a shopping list of rights that disabled people were denied in England and a criticism of The Right to Care Act. It felt dead, if only she could be as powerful and persuasive as Pavel. She closed her eyes and he was in front of her, drawing her in to a narrative that was simultaneously personal and political, integrating his personal experiences with the wider evidence. She tingled with excitement as she wrote, she was finally using her voice and the thrill of a platform to speak from was intoxicating. The result was a first-person account of a typical day in Bootle Cares interspersed with critical reflections on state power and public complicity in human rights violations. But she was also nervous, this was not the dry academic essay she imagined they must want from her. This was part memoir, part critical analysis, part political treatise. At the same time, from the moment she started, she knew this was the way she wanted to write. But was she risking her opportunity of a university place writing like this? Should she be cautious and try and mould herself into what she imagined they expected of her? Pavel re-appeared in her minds eye, the latter part of his life, and pretty much all of her own, had been shaped by other people's expectations. The whole point of her escape was to free herself from confinement, not to re-impose it on herself. So, she trusted her instincts and the advice she knew Pavel would have given her and submitted the essay as it was.

It was only a few days before she opened the email with her assessment grades, heart-pounding. She had passed everything easily and would be admitted to the course, but that wasn't the best bit of news. Tears blurred her vision when she saw what she had been given for the essay: ninety-five percent.

She looked over at Jay again. She had got the results the day she moved into the flat and she had told him all about it while he was helping.

He was looking at her now with an impenetrable expression, like part of him was somewhere else.

'I remember that,' he reassured her. 'But I don't understand how that has anything to do with you publishing an article in the *Irish Times*.'

'That's it,' she replied, jabbing her finger in the direction of the laptop. 'That's my essay!'

She pulled the laptop from his hands and clicked into her emails.

'I told you already,' she said thrusting the screen back in front of him so he could read for himself.

Dear Megan,

My name is Ciara Finlay and I am the head of the Access Programme. Part of my role is to moderate the entrance assessments and your essay was brought to my attention. I wanted to email you to let you know that I was truly astonished by your work. It is some of the most powerful writing I have ever encountered and I think it deserves a wider audience. With your permission, I would like to pass your essay to a friend of mine who is one of the editors at the Irish Times. *They have recently started running special features on the situation in England, but of course it is very difficult for anyone to be able to provide a first-hand account. I think they might be interested in publishing your essay and I certainly think it would make a wonderful contribution.*

Please let me know if you are happy for me to forward it and your contact details to him.

Best wishes,

Ciara.

Megan had replied instantly, her fingers shaking on the keyboard, not quite believing what was happening. Someone might publish a piece of her writing! She had been in Ireland just two short weeks and already it felt like every dream she had ever dared to imagine was coming true.

She regarded Jay for a moment, well, not every dream, but most of them. The ones that really mattered.

'It's going to be a regular thing,' she told him for the second time.

She felt like adding that he had better get used to it if he was going to stick around but she stopped herself. She didn't want to be mean to him however much he irked her at the moment. After all, it was him who had saved her life and shepherded her to this a new one. Yes, he was acting strangely now, but that didn't take away from everything he had done for her — or how much she really liked him underneath.

'They have asked me to write a regular column called *Life Over the Water*,' she continued.

'That's amazing, I'm really happy for you, you always wanted to be a writer!'

How did he know that? Maybe Silvie had told him, but it was odd he would remember when he had not bothered to pay attention to something so important that had happened so recently.

'They are paying me as well, so I actually have a paid job!'

A warm glow spread through her and she couldn't help beaming in delight. Jay smiled back at her, but it wasn't heartfelt, it was a cool and damp blanket over her fire of excitement.

'How often will you write for them?'

There was an edge to his voice that made it seem like a loaded question, but she had no idea what he was angling for.

'Once a week,' she replied, smile fading. 'For the mid-week feature.'

He nodded. 'Well I'll probably be back in Liverpool by the time the next one is out.'

He looked relieved.

He really didn't make any sense at all, if he wanted to go back so much why didn't he just leave? She opened her mouth to ask him about his travel plans, but as if sensing the turn of conversation he folded up her laptop and got up.

'I'd better get going.'

He moved over and hugged her briefly. Even with his arms around her he felt a long, long way away.

Lying awake in bed that night, she knew she had to do something, they couldn't go on like this with him lying and her pretending she believed him. There had to be a way to have a proper conversation, although every time she had tried he managed to shut her out so effectively she never knew how to begin. She also had to be careful not to challenge him too much about why he was there in case she seemed ungrateful, as if she had quickly forgotten everything he had done for her, or implied she didn't welcome his presence – even though he didn't seem very happy about being in Ireland, either. None of it made sense, would he really be there just for the sake of a new relationship? But there wasn't any other reason why he hadn't gone home she could see, and it certainly wasn't because he wanted to spend his time with her.

Chapter 33

Finally the buzzer sounded, it had to be him. The viewing panel confirmed the grainy image of Jay's face and Meagan buzzed him into the block. She turned back into the kitchen and switched on the kettle, she had already boiled it three times, certain he was just about to arrive. He was late, which was not like him, or not how he used to be, anyway. His behaviour was increasingly erratic these days, but tonight she was going to find out what was going on once and for all – no more messing around or evasiveness. He never used to be like this and, despite all his faults, he always used to be honest with her.

She wheeled back to the door, waiting for the feint ping of the lift in the hallway and his steps on the tiled floor.

When exactly had he started to change? He had been fine for the first week or so after they arrived, happy, relaxed, confident and seemingly pleased with how well things were going. The first time she remembered something odd about him was the day he picked her up from the physio centre and they went up the mountains, but he wasn't sombre and cagey then like he was now, but there *was* definitely something different, a weird energy she couldn't put her finger on. Whatever it was, that seemed to be the start of it. Yet he had still insisted on moving her into her flat, repeatedly telling her how much he wanted to, only to turn up on the day distant and distracted.

Footsteps echoed in the hallway followed by a light tap on the door. She turned the handle and Jay stepped inside and hugged her. She studied him while he removed his jacket and hung it on the peg. There was definitely something different about him, his face looked drawn and guarded and even though he was well dressed in his usual chic, expensive clothes he somehow looked dishevelled. Perhaps he was ill? One thing was certain, he didn't look like someone who was in the flush of a new relationship.

'Tea?' she smiled.

He nodded and followed her into the kitchen. Her stomach churned in anxious anticipation, a bit like the day he was supposed to leave for England and hours had creaked by with no word from him. She had been dreading the goodbye, knowing it would shatter her heart, but the possibility of him leaving without her seeing him one last time was more than she could bear. Late that night, when she was distraught with rage and anguish, he had messaged to say he hadn't gone home because of a problem with the car and he was going to be in Dublin for a few more days. Then, a few days later he told her he had given up on the car and bought a ferry ticket, but the only available place from Dublin to

Holyhead was in two weeks' time.

But that didn't make any sense, even if it was true the ferry was fully booked he could have got a train to Larne and taken the shuttlebus over the bridge and been back in Liverpool in hours. And then those two weeks came and went and still he stayed on without explanation.

He leaned on the counter beside her whilst she poured boiling water into the teapot.

'You can sit down,' she said inclining her head towards the sofa.

He moved over and took off his shoes and crossed his legs under him, apparently oblivious to how late he was. On the other hand, it was a bit of surprise she had managed to get him to the flat at all with just a few hours' notice. He was slow to answer her messages, it often took two or three days before she got a reply, and he seemed to avoid anything more than a fleeting meet-up or conversation.

He caught her watching him.

'Have you eaten?' she asked.

To her surprise he shook his head.

She went to the fridge and cut a large slice of pie and put it in the microwave. Watching the pie turning slowly in the orange light, she gathered the courage to confront him, the same courage that had propelled her to his hotel that morning to finally have it out with him, only to discover he wasn't there and no-one knew who he was.

She put the plate, teapot, mugs and a bottle of oat milk on a tray and carried it over on her lap. She lifted the tray on the table and passed him the plate of pie.

Then, taking a deep breath and steadying her gaze she asked, 'What's going on?'

His eyes widened and he looked away taking a large bite of pie.

'Jay?' she prompted, he had to tell her the full truth this time.

He swallowed. 'What do you mean?'

He still didn't meet her eyes and his tone was wary, but he wasn't going get away with treating her like she was stupid.

'I'm not an idiot.'

He took on a pained expression to indicate he knew that but kept on eating.

'Jay, I know something is going on,' she persisted. 'I went to your hotel and you weren't there. They didn't even know your name, they only knew you by the room number, and they said you checked out weeks ago.'

Jay choked, his hand flying to his mouth so he didn't spray pie across the room.

'How did you do that?'

'What?'

'Get to the hotel?'

'I took the tram, what does that matter anyway? That's not the point.'

Even in the midst of the dire mess Jay was in, this new reality where Megan could do whatever she wanted and move around with the same freedom as everyone else was still a shock. No disabled person in England would have been able to do that: to leave their home on a whim and go wherever they chose, and especially not on public transport. Even if they had a pass to go out it was physically impossible to get a wheelchair onboard. It was so different here, even seeing Megan in her own flat took some getting used to: here she was making him tea and feeding him just like anyone else. Sure, the flat looked a bit different, with the sit-under kitchen units and revolving storage system instead of cupboards – but lots of flats had them. The bathroom was different, too, but mostly it was just a normal flat. It was weird, as if putting her in a different environment made her a completely different person, almost like she didn't have a disability at all, of course he could still see her wheelchair, but somehow it didn't really mean anything anymore, it was irrelevant.

Megan was watching him intently, those pale blue eyes fixed on him, expectant, and there it was again, that feeling when he looked at her which made his insides somersault. *It's Silvie I can see in her,* he reminded himself. Except she didn't look anything like Silvie anymore, she looked like no-one else he had ever seen, as if she had blossomed into a woman right in front of his eyes. And even though she had not changed physically, something about her was completely different. Maybe it was just the new clothes and wearing her hair down? Whatever it was, he had to stop it ambushing him like this, it wasn't right at all. He took another large bit of pie, studying his plate as he chewed.

'Jay,' her tone was insistent, almost commanding. 'You have to tell me what is going on.'

Swallowing the last piece of pie, he let his eyes wander back to her. Fuck, she was beautiful, part of him would do anything that she asked right now.

'Jay, tell me!'

The inside of his head was a crashing kaleidoscope that needed straightening out before he opened his mouth. What should he say? A sigh pushed its way through him, it was going to have to be the truth.

'I'm in deep shit, Megan.'

It was hard to look at her, not because of those weird feelings, but because seeing his reality reflected in her face would be unbearable.

'I didn't tell you this when we left,' it took force to get the words out, 'But I didn't come over on my passport. The Uni still have it. They refused me permission to go to the conference and after that I couldn't risk them asking questions about where I was going and why. They thought I was in the Peak District. So I'm officially AWOL.'

Megan gasped and his eyes instinctively flew to her face, he dragged them away, pinning them to the floor. A dark well pulled at his guts, threatening to overwhelm him, but what choice did he have? He was going to have to tell her everything regardless of what she would think.

'It's worse than that, the police have been to my parent's house asking questions. Someone at Uni got hold of a picture of me on the demo and handed it in. So I'm wanted for that and for having disappeared from the course and left the country in breach of all the national security orders I signed, *and* for taking someone else's passport.'

That was it, everything that had felt so unspeakable shared in just a few short sentences, the horror story he had been keeping in, desperately believing he could fix it and get back to Liverpool before she even realised anything was wrong. But the time when that was possible had since long passed.

'Oh my God, Jay, what have you done?'

Her voice pitched in a rush of words. 'This could ruin your life. Why didn't you tell me? I would never have let you risk all that to bring me here!'

'It wasn't just for you, Megan.'

The truth was it hadn't been about her at all to begin with, it was just that he hadn't found a way to get rid of her and he had somehow ended up helping her. Although, it did feel like the natural choice now, much more than the version of him that had sat outside the police station planning to turn her in.

Another sigh pushed its way through his chest. 'I'd seen too much: Silvie dying, all the people in Bootle Cares, *you* could have died, what happened to the guys from the demo. I wanted to do something to try and at least make some of it right – and I promised Silvie.'

It had started off about him, then it had moved to Silvie, and now it seemed to be about Megan, too. The kaleidoscope turned and everything inside his head was chaos again.

Megan swallowed, the stupid part of her would have loved him to have risked everything for her, but that was just the remnants of her ridiculous fantasy and nothing to do with reality. All that bound them together was death – and now this.

'But how did you get someone else's passport?'

'Please don't be angry with me if I tell you.'

'I won't,' she promised, trying to sound calmer than she felt.

'I sort of stole it.'

It took all her will power not to swear at him.

'What do you mean?'

'I told an undergrad that I was looking for a research assistant for my final project and he would have to submit his passport for a background check.'

'Oh God, Jay.'

What else could she say? This was so much worse than anything she had imagined, it was too much. She pressed her face into her hands so she didn't have to look at him, why did she promise not to be angry? Part of her wanted to shout at him for being such an idiot, for being such an arrogant, entitled prick who thought the world moulded around him and he could do whatever he wanted without consequence – perfect material for a government job! He had completely fucked everything up. Just when it seemed like she was free, she could study, write, have the life she always dreamed of and he would go back to England and she could finally consign him to the past. But, instead, he had turned everything upside down and now he was a criminal stuck in Dublin with no way to leave.

Jay put his plate on the table and hugged his knees to

his chest. He looked small and vulnerable, like an orphaned little boy and her heart softened. It wasn't his fault he lived by those presumptions about the world, he was raised like that, he was supposed to be like that, and he had gambled all of his privilege and lost everything. And, despite what he said, it *was* partly about her. If he hadn't been so determined she should go to Silvie's funeral then she would be dead, and even after that he could have turned her in but hadn't. And no-one had made him go on that demo, he had done it because he cared. She moved over to the sofa and slipped onto the seat beside him, wrapping her arms round him. He leaned into her and started to cry.

'I'm sorry,' he whispered.

'It's all right.'

All right was the opposite of what it was, but she couldn't be angry with him anymore, especially not when he was all opened up and defenceless like this. She rocked him gently and her eyes moistened. Whatever it took, she would help him, she would find a way to sort this out. They were bonded together in a way that was much deeper than all of the silly romances she had once dreamt up.

'You should stay here tonight,' she said, and then, feeling his head move against her body, added, 'You can sleep on the sofa. We can figure something out in the morning.'

He looked up at her with tear-soaked eyes. 'I can't stay with you. If they find me, they will find you as well.'

'They can't do anything to me. I have citizenship

here. Anyway, they won't know you are here now, will they?'

Jay shook his head.

A thought flashed across her mind.

'You don't have your English phone with you, do you?'

'No. I ditched it after my parents got in touch. I broke it into pieces and put it in different bins around the city, so I guess it's safe for me to be here for one night.'

She fetched pillows and a duvet from the cupboard in the hallway and left Jay to wrestle them into the covers and make up a bed on the sofa. Then, finally alone in her own room, she sat on her bed and tried to organise everything in her mind. But it was too much, he had turned the world turned upside down, and it would take so much longer than one night for her to figure out how to re-right it again. Eventually, limbs heavy with tiredness she undressed and slid under the covers, willing her mind to quieten into sleep.

Chapter 34

The sounds of Megan moving around in the kitchen and the thick aroma of fresh coffee pulled Jay out of his first full night of sleep since he left the hotel. Blinking open his eyes he peered out from the corner of the duvet, she was piling a tray with all kinds of food, and his stomach rumbled in response.

As if she could feel him watching her, she turned. 'Morning,' she smiled.

Her hair was pulled up in a high ponytail on top of her head that swung behind her as she moved and silver studs winked in each ear. She seemed to be wearing some kind of sports clothes, whatever it was it was tight and black and he couldn't help looking at her body.

'What time is it?' he averted his eyes.

'It's a bit after ten. You were sleeping like a baby so I left you to it. I'm just back from the gym.'

He sat up, pulling the duvet around his chin, still blinking, as if that would pull the world back into recognisable focus. What kind of gym would she go to? And what she would do there?

She wheeled towards the table by the sofa with the

tray balanced on her lap. There were bowls of steaming porridge, fruit, and croissants like the ones she used to make in Liverpool. She turned back to the kitchenette and poured coffee into two mugs. For the first time he saw her hesitate, the tray was on the table and she obviously couldn't carry a mug in each hand and move her wheels at the same time. She put one down, about to bring them over one at a time.

He leapt up, glad to be able to help. 'I'll get them.'

Half way to the kitchen unit he realised he was just in his shorts. He froze, his eyes flicking to her, she turned and busied herself with the tray of food. Self-consciousness still tingled in his arms as he placed the mugs on the table and dived back under the duvet, pulling it up to his armpits. When he was settled she passed him a bowl of porridge followed by a banana for him to chop on top while she added the same to her bowl.

'Mmm, this is good,' he murmured between mouthfuls.

'It's banana, berry, and cacao,' she replied. 'I'm glad you like it.'

'You make such good food,' he smiled.

'Yeah, who knew?' she smiled back. 'I'm a woman of many talents.'

'That's for sure!' he replied, and before he could stop himself his eyes slid down the length of her body, *and the rest*, he thought.

Megan's phone pinged, she picked it up and smiled, her eyes twinkling as she tapped a quick response. Who could she be messaging? And who would she be so pleased to hear from? He opened his mouth to ask and then thought better of it. It felt too awkward to ask outright and, besides, he had to get used to the fact that she had a whole new life here already, she was at Uni, writing for the *Irish Times*, she even went to the gym and obviously had friends he didn't know about. It was hard to believe she was the same person he had met at Bootle Cares. How had they got from there to here with him severed from his old life, watching from a distant shore as everything he knew was washed away from him?

As if reading his thoughts she looked up and met his eyes.

'I haven't forgotten,' she said. 'We have some serious talking to do. But finish eating first while I get changed.'

She wheeled out of the room and returned an instant later with a big orange towel folded on her lap.

She threw it in his direction, laughing. 'Catch! You might want this!'

Her voice was just audible from her room as he showered, dressed, and tidied up the sofa. She was talking in a light sing-song tone he hadn't heard before, and the same intense curiosity tugged at him, who would she talk to like that? It felt wrong to be shut out like this, hovering on the periphery of her life, where she had everything to live for and he had nothing left. He moved across the room and opened the balcony door so he didn't have to hear anymore. Stepping outside into the tepid summer air, he took a deep breath and gazed across at the peaks of Christchurch Cathedral and pictured the churning brown river below. What would it have been like to be here in completely different circumstances?

He turned around, Megan was in the kitchen watching him. She had changed into an aubergine colour dress with long sleeves and a scooped neckline that hugged her body as closely as the sportswear, and her hair was coiled over her left shoulder. It was impossible not to look at her.

'You look nice,' the words tumbled out before he could think better of it.

She looked at him strangely for a moment and then smiled. 'Thanks, do you want some more coffee?'

Chapter 35

Megan took the tram to Abbey Street and then wheeled down to the main entrance of Trinity. It was quicker to take the Pearse St entrance but she enjoyed the grandeur of the front arch. She followed the smoothed pathway to the Campanile and then turned right and skirted the Old Library, Trinity felt like a living museum and she never tired of taking it all in. She continued past New Square and then cut through College Park and tuned left towards the less elegant part of the campus and the old railway arches that housed the cycling club.

How long was it now since the first time she had been there? It must only be a couple of weeks but it already felt so much a part of her life – and so did Aman. A warm tingle spread through her body at the thought of him, it was all so new, but it felt so good.

She had been on route to the library when he had first waylaid her, stepping forward from a small group and offering her a leaflet.

'Have you thought about joining the cycling club?' he asked in a soft Dublin accent.

He was tall with rich dark skin and hair knotted into

fine black dreadlocks that touched his shoulders.

Was he was mocking her, pitying her for her wheelchair? She met his eyes, they were warm and sincere.

He smiled gently. 'Handcycling, with your wheelchair, we have some handcycles you can borrow.'

It was impossible not to smile in return, he was extremely handsome, tall and lean with broad shoulders, sharp cheekbones and a wide sensual mouth.

'I'm Aman,' he said. 'You're Megan, aren't you? You're in my politics class.'

His eyes sparkled at her.

She could feel her body responding before her mind had caught up and she felt an electric fizz of delight that he already knew her name. The library could definitely wait.

'Yes, that's right,' she replied. 'But what is handcycling?'

'I can show you if you like?'

Megan looked at him again, *why not?* She was not going to get a more attractive offer any time soon.

Aman exchanged a few words with the rest of the group, returning his bundle of leaflets, and then set off with Megan through the centre of the campus.

'You're from England, aren't you?' he asked.

Megan nodded and sighed.

'I'm so sorry,' he said, his smile replaced with a soft frown. 'I read some of your stuff in the *Irish Times*. I can't imagine living somewhere like that, it must have been terrible.'

'It was,' she said, tears springing to her eyes. 'It was brutal and cruel,' her voice wobbled, 'I lost everyone I loved.'

Apart from Jay, a little voice whispered at the back of her mind.

'I'm glad you made it here,' Aman replied, gently touching her shoulder.

Swallowing her tears, she smiled up at him; he was lovely.

They cut through the sports field and turned left so they were nearly at the Pearse Street gate. Aman moved easily at her side, every now and then indicating the direction they should turn and smiling across at her with an intensity that brought a flush of heat to her skin. He led her to the old railway arches where a large door had been slid open to reveal a jumbled collection of bicycles, cargo bikes, and an array of objects that Megan did not recognise. There were a couple of people inside looking at some of the bikes. Aman turned left inside the door and, clearing a few bits of debris aside with his feet, led her to the near corner.

'Here are the handcycles,' he gestured. 'We've got four at the moment, one of them should definitely fit your chair.'

Megan looked at the strange contraptions, still no wiser about what she was supposed to do with them. They all had a single wheel and were either balancing on two spindly legs or a central stand. The chain she could identify from a regular bike, but these chains followed a long stem and met two hand pedals which were almost the height of her chin.

'Let me show you,' Aman said, dragging a battered looking wheelchair out from behind a cupboard.

He sat down in it and wheeled himself over to the handcycles. Megan stared, a whole new wave of feelings crashing through her. She had never seen someone who wasn't disabled sit into a wheelchair before, let alone be so totally at ease with moving around with it, yet Aman made it seem as natural as putting on a pair of shoes. He beckoned her over and she followed, blinking hard to clear her mind and focus on what he was showing her. But it was impossible not to keep glancing back at him, he was like no-one else she had ever met and the way he smiled at her, well, nobody had ever looked at her like that before, either.

Aman rolled his wheelchair up to one of the machines and tightened two clamps around the front bars of the wheelchair, taking care to show her each step of the process. He pushed two catches in place and then lifted the whole contraption until she heard a click.

'That's the sound that tells you you are connected up correctly,' he told her.

The front castors of the wheelchair and the legs of the handcycle were raised off the ground, and the large wheels of the chair and the wheel of the handcycle now formed a hand peddled tricycle.

Megan opened her mouth but didn't have any words.

Aman grinned, 'Come and see.'

He turned in a wide arc and headed out the door. She wheeled after him and he rode figures of eight in front of her peddling ferociously with his hands and smiling at her all the while.

'You want to try?' he called.

Megan laughed, finding her voice at last. 'Yes, yes I do!'

The moment her hands turned the pedals she was in love. It was as if she could fly, the power and speed with which she could move was intoxicating.

'My brother has one of these,' Aman called to her as they pedalled circuits of the sports field. 'I used to drive him mad wanting to go for a spin on it!'

She kept cycling until her arms ached so much that she had no choice but to stop.

'Not bad for a first attempt!' Aman beamed at her, seeming to relish her pleasure almost as much as she did – and she couldn't help smiling back, lapping-up every drop of his attention.

She didn't go to the library that day, or the next, instead she joined the cycling club and returned every day to relive the exhilaration of flying along the ground. She couldn't stop thinking about Aman, either. However much she told herself he was probably only being nice to her because his brother was disabled too, the fizzle in her stomach every time she remembered the way he looked at her told her something different. Then he messaged her and asked her if she wanted to go for a cycle at the weekend and the fizzle turned into a volcano.

Now in the sightline of the cycle club, she felt a little

burst of hope that he might be there today. But as soon as she turned inside the wide door it was obvious it was deserted aside from Annie, one of the mechanics, who was squatting elbow deep in cycle parts before an upturned tricycle. She smiled as soon as she saw Megan.

'They're all in,' she inclined her head towards the handcycles. 'You can take your pick.'

'Thanks, on your own today?'

Annie smiled knowingly and Megan felt herself flush, was she being that transparent?

'Yes, just me – and two tricycles with knackered gears.'

Thankfully Annie returned her attention to the tricycle, so Megan didn't have cover for being so obvious. She picked the blue handcycle with a centre stem and the larger front wheel – she had discovered it was good for speed and light to handle.

'Just leave your card on the counter and we can settle up when you get back,' Annie called over.

'Thanks,' Megan replied, flicking her membership card onto the cluttered wooden desk as she turned out of the building. 'See you later!'

The sun split through the clouds, bathing her in blinding light and transporting her back to the first Saturday she had gone to meet Aman at the arches and found him waiting beside an old cargo trike.

'I brought a picnic,' he smiled.

'Thank you,' she faltered, stomach fluttering already, he had grown even more attractive in the intervening days, and he was so considerate.

'That's very thoughtful.'

Never had words felt so inadequate. Their eyes locked and Megan's heart quickened in the silence between them. She turned away and busied herself with a handcycle.

They rode across the campus and through the main gate ignoring the "No Cycling" signs at the archway.

'Well you can hardly dismount and push your handcycle can you?' Aman pointed out.

'No,' Megan laughed.

Aman had attitude, Pavel would have liked him.

Aman led her right onto Westmorland and then left along the quays. There was a wide cycle lane and one more lane for the rest of the traffic. What had once been third lane was now taken up by the flood defences: rusting wedges of iron, nearly two meters high, bolted together to hold back the tidal surges. It looked nothing like the pictures of the Liffey in the Old Library which showed stone parapets and quaint arc of the Ha'penny bridge. But it seemed that even here, where the melt predictions had been carefully monitored, beauty was still a luxury too far in the face of the scale of the disaster.

After Heuston they turned up the incline towards the Phoenix Park and Megan nudged up the e-assist. Aman was cycling leisurely, pointing out landmarks here and there and smiling over at her as if he had just won a million dollars. He led her through the park until they came to a wooded area where sunlight dappled on the grass and deer grazed in between the trees.

'Time for a break?' he suggested.

'Yes, why not?' she smiled, she could have cycled further, but cycling wasn't her only interest.

Whilst she detached her handcycle, Aman spread a thick blanket on the ground and started unloading the contents of his carrier. He had a flask and cups, stuffed injera wraps he had made himself, fruit, and a sticky rice pudding. Megan eased herself out of her chair and onto the blanket beside him. It felt like she had been catapulted out of a nightmare and into a fairytale and at any moment she might wake up and find herself back in Bootle Cares or the tiny room in Jay's flat.

They ate and chatted about their studies and the degree courses they were going to apply for. Aman told her a little more about his brother. He was doing a PhD in Glasgow and it was him who had finally persuaded Aman to stop messing about and go to university.

'He was right,' Aman said, suddenly serious and his eyes glued to hers. 'Starting the access course is the best thing I have ever done.'

He let his words hang in the air, allowing their full meaning to percolate.

After a long pause he added, 'I really want to kiss you, Megan.'

Megan could feel herself flushing, she looked down and then back at Aman, ashamed.

'You look scared,' his face was worried.

She must be bright red, she must look so stupid. She wanted to kiss him, her tummy was tumbling with anticipation, but her inexperience was crushing.

'I've never kissed anyone before,' she managed to

whisper, not meeting his eyes.

Aman's face softened. 'Really?! But you are so beautiful!'

He reached forward and gently tipped her chin upwards so that she had no choice but to meet his gaze.

'That makes me want to kiss you even more.'

He smiled tenderly and moved a little closer to her. He took her hand and kissed the back of it.

Megan giggled.

'That's better,' he said and turned her hand over and kissed her palm, gazing up at her through thick black lashes.

His lips felt delicious against her skin. She reached up and touched his cheek, drawing his face a little closer to hers. He held her eyes and ran his hand slowly up her arm to the back of her neck, making electricity where his fingers touched her skin. He leaned towards her and brought his mouth gently to her lips and then moved away, his eyes still fixed on hers. She leaned forward and brought her mouth to his, very he slowly returned her kiss until, all of a sudden, she knew exactly what to do.

Chapter 36

A warm tingle spread through Megan's body as she remembered their first kiss, it was intoxicating. A pedestrian jumped out of her path and she squeezed the breaks, smiling an apology, but the man walked on, eyes already returned to the screen in front of him. She had not been paying attention, she had to focus, her mission today was to see for herself what Jay had told her, and Aman, well, she was seeing him tomorrow anyway.

She exited Trinity at the Pearse Street gate and turned onto Pearse Street itself. The cycle lane was a little narrower here, but traffic was scarce and mostly electric delivery vans. Few people used cars in the cities, the link between car ownership and climate breakdown made it an anathema – nobody wanted to be that conspicuously a part of the problem: a car was something to be avoided rather than aspired to, and people borrowed rather than owned them.

As she reached the junction with Maken Street curiosity tugged at her. She could cross the river on the new bridge to view the flood defences they had been learning about in the Contemporary History module. The thrill of horror she had felt learning about the decision to abandon the East Wall, the quays developments, the eastern rim of Rings End and all of Fairfield Park tempted her to divert her path. Building the flood defence at the North Strand Road had ensured the port could be refigured and still operate, but it also meant all of those dwellings as well as the port tunnel, that was not even thirty years old, had been sacrificed to the water. That was the trade-off for a tidal barrage which would save the Custom House and the remainder of Dublin, well, for a few more years at least. But it had cost a historic part of the city along with the events arena and the apartment blocks that had sprang up in the docklands during the late twentieth century boom-time.

What must it have been like for the people that lived in the little old cottages and the flashy new apartments to be told their homes would submerged and Dublin rebuilt westwards? Would the offer of a brand new zero-energy dwelling compensate for watching your home disappear under the rising tide? It wasn't a choice anyway. Most of the city's eastern edge was being relocated as the sea level kept on rising.

Suddenly she was back at the roadblock, the day after Silvie's funeral, staring at the filthy water that had taken the last of the people she loved. Of course she wouldn't turn up along the bridge, even though no-one had died it was still cruel to spectate on other people's upended lives. Besides, there was something much more important she had to do today – she had to go and see for herself what Jay had told her. It was impossible to even begin to think coherently about making a plan until she had seen it for herself. It wasn't that she didn't believe him, it was just very hard to visualise him squatting with a bunch of religious nutters in the abandoned houses along the Sandymount sea defence.

Cycling over the river Dodder towards Irish Town Road, she risked a glance at the water below – for a small river it looked very angry. What it must have been like in the decades past, when poisoned sea water was not such an threat and clean water such a scarce resource? The past, the present, the future – *her* future – it was hard to make it all fit together.

The road surface smoothed beneath her wheels and inclined upwards, requiring an extra notch of e-assist. This must be the new section of road that had been rebuilt to accommodate the defences. As she crested the hill the sight brought her to a halt, nothing could have prepared her for this. Stretching ahead and to her left as far as she could see was the Sandymount sea defence. It was even bigger and uglier than the one along the quays, but constructed from the same rusting metal wedges. Even so, it looked desperately fragile, like a paper cup filled to the brim and just about to wilt under the pressure of the water. She was afraid to get any closer, the tide was in and the water seemed ready to spill over at any point. Should she just turn back? No, she couldn't do that, Jay was staying in a house not far from here, she had to continue. And surely the road would be closed if there was any real risk? Besides, if the threat was much bigger than a few splashes or puddles then perhaps being at the forefront would be a blessing.

Nudging down the e-assist she turned onto Sandymount Road and then Sea Fort Avenue – an ironic choice of name for the once prestigious street of houses that now appeared mostly abandoned and utterly at the mercy of the water. The next turn brought her right up against the sea defences on Strand Road, and they were no more reassuring close-up than from a distance: rusting metal sealed together with concrete and, hopefully, but not obviously, pinned to strong foundations. In places the concrete was cracked and damp, and in others tiny slithers of water spilled through. Fear and fascination propelled her forwards, her eyes constantly finding spots where the barriers appeared to have been patched up or reinforced, but with materials that seemed far too rudimentary for such a vital function.

Then, as she reached the Martello Tower, she saw them: a group of about twenty men and women all dressed in pale clothes gathered by the wall. She slowed, this must be the maniacs Jay had told her about. As she got closer she could see they were all wearing a white tabard with some kind of colourful logo over regular clothes that had been washed into various shades of off-white. When she was close enough to hear what they were saying, she realised one of the men was striking the flood defence with a small hammer. Another man had his hands raised to the sky and apparently was praying.

'Almighty God, deliver your Brethren from the sin that has polluted this land. Send your cleansing waters over us and we will live forever in purity.'

Why weren't the gardaí here? Those people were trying to make a hole in the sea defence! Megan stared in horror, they really were insane. Jay had told her the Brethren believed the flood was punishment for all the sin in the land – although whether they meant Ireland, the Celtic Union, or the whole world wasn't really clear. Either way, God was angry with Ireland for legalising same sex marriage and abortion decades previously, and the waters had been sent to purify them of their sins. The tides should be allowed to wash the land clean and only the righteous would survive.

'They're bonkers,' Jay had said. 'But harmless, really, actually a lot of them are quite nice. Generous.'

'Not if you're gay or have an unwanted pregnancy!' Megan had retorted, angry with him for his inability to think of anyone other than himself.

'True,' he said. 'But they are keeping me alive and safe at the moment and I have to appreciate that.'

It had been impossible to fully grasp his situation when they talked, and even seeing it now, it still didn't feel quite real. It was such a shock, she was used to Jay being young, rich, and privileged, moving about the world with an ease that made him oblivious to his own good fortune and everyone else's suffering. It was difficult to comprehend anything else, especially this new reality where he was an illegal immigrant, wanted for offenses that would send him to prison for a long time, and where his life – and his family's if they tried to help him – would be ruined forever.

She was right beside the group now, part of her

wanted to hover in morbid curiosity, but she was also afraid that if they noticed her they might take her for a sinner and who knows what they would do to her? They had had weirdos like that come round Bootle Cares from time to time. They claimed to be on some kind of mercy mission, but usually they pontificated about sins of the body and prayers of redemption as an excuse for touching them. Megan and Pavel always tried to stay close to each other and to Cathy when they were around, Megan was young and Cathy was generous and trusting and easy to take advantage of.

Megan skirted past the group, deciding it was best to ignore them, and to hope they did the same as she continued down the strand. The houses were a mix of late nineteenth and early twentieth century builds, designed for middle class comfort with the luxury of a sea-view. Now they were mostly empty with overgrown front gardens and broken windows. The occasional house still appeared to be occupied, the windows defended with grills and sandbags piled up against the garden walls – as if that would offer any protection against the weight of the water just a few metres away. Then she saw a group of houses that were different, the front gardens had all been joined together. About two thirds of the area was cultivated and the remainder held a jumble of cars and vans. The houses were painted white with an attempt at a colourful logo over the top: BGW, Brethren of God's Will, in uneven lettering and surrounded by a sparkling halo of coloured glass. A couple of the vans had the same logo on the sides and behind them Megan glimpsed the black Skoda. It brought her to an abrupt halt. The registration plates were gone, Jay had removed them as soon as he left the hotel, but it was still unmistakably the car that had brought them here. The bonnet was raised and there were tools scattered around, but no-one appeared to be working on it, they must all be at high-tide prayers at the sea wall. Might Jay be inside the house? And what would he be doing? It would be so easy to go and knock on the door and to make all of this finally and indisputably real; but it would also be dangerous. Even though the road appeared deserted, she could not be certain there was no-one around and she could not risk leading someone to him.

It was the only thing that was clear when they had talked: they would have to be careful about where and when they met. Now that Megan was clearly alive and publishing in Ireland, it would be all too easy to find her in Dublin and discover her with Jay close by. And even though she took meticulous care with what she wrote, revealing nothing about her escape or her journey, her arrival in Ireland corresponded with the time Jay had disappeared from England and it would not be too difficult to put them together, especially with Silvie in common. They agreed Jay needed to stay away from her flat and, from now on, they would meet in different locations around the city.

As Megan gazed at the houses and the battered Skoda her heart knotted. Jay's whole life had turned upside down in a way that would have seemed laughable just a few months before. She pulled herself away, it was not a good idea to linger here, drawing attention to the fact Jay might be inside or risking the Brethren returning and finding her there. She continued a little further in the same direction, reaching a small junction where the painted hump of a mini roundabout was still just about visible. Circling around to face back the way she had travelled, she tried to imagine the now-deserted road in the decades before, nose-to-tail with cars and the pride of those who lived here. She slowed again as she drew alongside the Brethren's houses and another rush of pain for what Jay's life had become flooded her.

A little further up the road the Brethren were still praying. Looking away, she glimpsed the derelict petrol station on her near side, she had been too engrossed in watching the prayers to notice it when she had approached. This must be the place where Jay had been sleeping in the car before the Brethren offered him shelter. Behind the overgrowth she could just make out the door he had forced and found a bathroom still with running water.

How had it come to that and he had not even told her? What had he been thinking? It was impossible not to feel angry with him. And then she thought of his abandoned flat in Merebank, the red Tesla in the carpark, and him with no way of getting his old life back. She would do everything in her power to help him. She would talk to Udaya at the asylum centre and find out what the application process would be like for him, being careful not to give too much away. The fact he was there because he had helped an Irish citizen to escape persecution might add levity to his application. Whatever it took she would find a way, if her own life could be so radically transformed in the space of a few short weeks surely it was possible for him, too.

Chapter 37

Jay was waiting for Megan in the tiny commemorative garden across the road from the main entrance to Trinity. He'd arrived early, keen to get away from Sandymount as soon as possible, and had read all the plaques at least twice, lingering for the longest amount of time over the notice which described how the garden had been opened in 2034, on the former site of the Henry Grattan statue. It was to commemorate the completion of the sea defences, just in time, right before the melt. What it had been like before then, living with the endless planning and calculating for what was to come or, in the case of England, the complete denial of it? How had people for so many decades collectively decided to do nothing? Why leave everything until it was too late? They must have believed they could fix it somehow. In all honesty, he would probably have felt like that too, convinced that everything would work out because it always had for him – until now.

Restless, he perched on the back of a bench with his feet on the seat and watched as students from various summer schools drifted out of the archway and onto the pavement on the other side of the road. Then she appeared, making her way along the smooth paving slabs laid in between the cobblestones. She was with a small group of two women and one man, all of different skin colour, she was by far the palest, just like Silvie always used to be. One of the women was also white, but she was very tanned, almost as dark as the woman beside her who looked Asian. The only male amongst them had the darkest skin of all and fine black dreadlocks that reached his shoulders. He had dark green drainpipe trousers with a baggy white shirt and was walking very close to Megan. He looked a bit like a poet or an artist. The four reached the pavement and the two women cut away towards Nassau Street. Megan stayed talking to the man. Jay was about to get up and go over to them when the man leaned down and kissed her. Jay blinked, he could not believe his eyes: that guy was kissing Megan, that couldn't be right, and yet she had her hand on his cheek and their mouths were pressed together and there was no mistaking what they were doing.

Disbelief pounded through his limbs, he felt like grabbing the nearest passer-by and shouting, "That man is kissing Megan!" As if saying it out loud would make them stop, but they continued, oblivious to everything else around them.

When they finally parted the man turned in the direction of Nassau Street and Megan watched him walk away with a smile deep enough to drown in. Still immobilised, he struggled to make sense of it. It was such a shock, he had never imagined a man would be interested in Megan like that. But why? And why did it make him feel so burnt inside? He shouldn't really be that shocked someone would want to kiss her – after all, she was attractive and resourceful, she was smart and funny too and more compassionate than anyone he had ever met. But he thought only he could see that, and even then it was surely the ghost of Silvie and not something anyone else would notice. Might they even be sleeping together? His stomach lurched, the thought of that pseudo poet, or any other guy, fucking Megan filled him with rage. A protective anger even if it scorched with the heat of jealousy.

Megan was moving now, turning towards Pearse Street to use the crossing. She would have to cross again at College Green to get to the memorial park. As she neared the first crossing, a small blue van mounted the pavement and screeched to a halt, narrowly missing her. Everything was in slow-motion, three men leapt out and surrounded Megan, one of them raising his hand to her breastbone and pushing her backwards so her chair tipped over. She screamed and flailed as she fell, but she was on the floor and the other two men caught her arms and dragged her out of her chair. She struggled against them and one of them punched her in the face, completely overpowering her. People on the pavement were staring and shouting but no-one was doing anything. Finally, a burst of rage fired Jay out of his paralysis and he sprang across the road, yelling at the men. A car slammed to a halt just millimetres from him and he vaulted the bonnet. Swinging his fist as hard as he could he hit the nearest of the men in the side of the head and threw himself towards Megan to try and protect her. A punch with the force of a cannon ball drove into his stomach and sent him flying backwards towards the road. A large pair of hands grabbed him and propped him out of harm's way against a stationary car.

'Alright son, what's all this about?'

Bent double and gasping for air he forced himself to respond, it was the gardaí.

'Help her,' he wheezed.

Two more gardaí got out of the car, tasers drawn. For a moment, Jay thought they were about to attack him, but the three men were now backing off and the garda who had caught Jay was now helping Megan back into her chair. He was huge, he looked like he could have picked each of the men up in one hand and slung them over the iron railings of the campus perimeter. Jay staggered towards Megan and knelt down beside her, clutching his stomach and trying to catch his breath. She looked terrified, her face was red and grazed and she was also gasping for air. He took her hand, she was trembling and there was shouting all around them.

'You're not in England now!' one of the gardaí yelled. 'You can't just come here and drag young women off the streets!'

'I'm afraid we can,' one of the men retorted. 'This is not a criminal matter and therefore not in your jurisdiction. We are detaining her under the Mental Health Act. She has come here and claimed asylum under false pretences and is in urgent need of psychiatric treatment.'

Jay and Megan looked at each other, they were trying to take her back. They had to get away, but a crowd had gathered around them that would be impossible to pass through.

A siren closed in and a garda van pulled up. Four more gardaí jumped out, two men and two women. Jay didn't know who he was most afraid of, the three men with the van or the now seven gardaí. The shouting continued and one of the women gardaí moved over to them.

'Please,' Megan gasped. 'I have citizenship here, they can't take me.'

'Do you have ID?'

Megan dropped Jay's hand a rummaged in the pouch under her chair.

'Here,' she said, pulling out her official ID card.

The garda inspected it. 'Thank you, miss, and who is this?' she asked, indicating Jay.

'He's my PCA,' Megan replied without missing a beat. 'He was meeting me after my last class.'

The garda regarded Jay derisively. It was easy to see how pathetic he must appear, kneeling on the floor and gasping for breath after just one punch and the garda looked like she would no-more believe he was Megan's carer than he was the second coming of Christ.

'Okay,' she said after a pause. 'Let's get you home.'

Jay's instinct was to get away from the gardaí with the same urgency as the guys with the van. But Megan assented and he kept his mouth shut – if the garda heard his English accent she might ask for his ID and then he would be in deep shit.

Thankfully, she didn't say anything more but went over and spoke to the garda who had been driving the car. After a brief conversation the pair of them returned and helped Megan, who was still shaking, into the back seat of the car, putting her chair in the boot while Jay climbed in the other side. Megan told them her address and the driver started the engine. The other gardaí were still arguing with the men on the pavement and the crowd had spilled out into the road. The driver blared the siren and the crowd quickly moved back onto the pavement. Jay could see him glancing back at Megan in the rear-view mirror and he took her hand protectively, even though he had much more reason to be scared of the gardaí than she did.

'Are you Megan Connolly?' the driver asked eventually.

Megan nodded with a slight smile. 'Yes, that's me,' she replied.

'Ah, no wonder the bastards are trying to take you away,' he smiled. 'I've read your stuff. They must be mightily pissed off with you!'

'Thanks, I think,' Megan faltered.

'Seriously, though,' the garda continued, 'It's not the first time we've seen something like this and it probably won't be the last. They do sometimes come and try and snatch people who have got asylum over here – especially the ones with a story to tell that they would rather people didn't know about. There's not a lot we can do in terms of trying to prosecute them because unlike Scotland and Wales we don't have any extradition or jurisdiction treaties with England, and of course the bastards they send over come from high enough up to be immune to anything we might try to do.'

He sighed, 'So you need to be careful. We can give you a panic button and a couple of emergency numbers, but you really shouldn't be out and about on your own.'

For the first time he looked squarely at Jay. 'And you need to do a better job of taking care of her, mate.'

Jay nodded. 'Sure,' he mumbled trying to feign a Dublin accent.

Megan glanced sideways at him.

'It's not his fault,' she said, and then before she could continue the garda cut in.

'No, no, I wasn't saying it was. You both need to be careful, that's all.'

Chapter 38

As soon as the gardaí left, Megan went into her bedroom, curled up on her bed and burst into tears. Jay hesitated, unsure whether or not he should follow her, but it was impossible to leave her on her own sobbing like that. He perched on the edge of her bed and gently stroked her back, but she didn't even seem to know he was there. Instinct told him he should hold her so, pushing aside a wave of doubt, he lay down on the bed and curled himself around her like a protective shell and held her until she cried herself to sleep. When it was evident she was finally sleeping deeply, he gently eased his body away, folding the duvet around her and tiptoed into the other room. Taking a glass of water from the sink he moved over to the balcony and opened the door. He took a slug from the glass and leaned on the railings looking out across the city – another ruined dream.

The sky was turning dark, he should definitely be getting back to Sandymount, although the thought of travelling alone across the city filled him with dread. More importantly, even though it was not a good idea for him to be at Megan's flat, he couldn't leave her on her own. He turned back to the warmth inside, closing the door behind him. There were sounds of Megan moving around in the other room.

'Sorry,' she said, appearing in the doorway.

She had changed into pyjamas and pulled her long, faded cardigan around her. It was one of the few remaining things from her days at Bootle Cares. It was amazing how different she looked now compared to back then even in the same old cardigan.

'I didn't mean to go to sleep and ignore you,' she apologised again.

He looked at her face, it was red and swollen where they had hit her and a bruise was throbbing into place.

'It looks like they really hurt you,' he said moving over to her.

He hovered, wanting to touch her face, to stroke her uninjured cheek, but held back.

'Maybe you should see a doctor?'

'No, I'm fine, I've had worse.'

What did she mean by that? Was she saying she had been hit before? By whom? When? Then he remembered the time he had seen Cathy being restrained at Bootle Cares. He and Silvie had been leaving after visiting Megan. It was a Sunday afternoon and Cathy had been upset and shouting about something. Four large care staff appeared from nowhere and barrelled into her, pinned her to the ground and sedated her. But Jay was sure he saw one of them hit her first, punching her in the face with a sadistic relish that turned his stomach. He and

Silvie had stood there uselessly, not quite believing what they were witnessing and not sure what to do. He looked at Megan and hoped they had never done anything like that to her.

'Are *you* okay?' she asked.

'Yes, I was just a bit winded that's all.'

He couldn't say he had had worse, no-one had ever hit him like that before. Megan went over to the freezer and pulled out a pizza and transferred it to the oven.

'Will you stay with me tonight?' she asked, looking straight at him.

Her eyes were so sad his heart hurt.

'Yes, of course,' he said, thankful he could provide something she needed.

But later on, after they had eaten, when he went to get the duvet out of the cupboard in the hall, she stopped him.

'Will you stay in my room?' she asked. 'I don't want to be on my own.'

His face must have betrayed him because she added quickly, 'I mean just as a friend, so I feel safe.'

'I know,' he said too fast, totally failing to sound as if the thought of anything else had never crossed his mind.

Without thinking, he blurted, 'I know you have a boyfriend,' instantly regretting the implication that was the only reason she wouldn't sleep with him.

He rushed on in a panic. 'I saw you together just before—'

He could feel himself flushing, he was making a complete dick of himself. Megan looked at him but he couldn't read her expression.

'Oh,' she said and went into the bathroom.

After she had finished, Jay took his time in the bathroom. Megan had laid out towels and toothbrush for him and when he entered her bedroom she was already under the duvet, her old cardigan discarded on the floor. Self-consciously he stripped down to his shorts and undershirt, climbed into the far side of the bed and lay awkwardly at the edge.

She turned to face him. 'Jay, can I have a hug?'

He shuffled towards her and lifted his arms so she could fit herself around him. He cautiously lowered his arms around her, acutely aware of only the thin fabric that separated their bodies and the warm sweet smell of her skin.

'Thanks,' she whispered.

Slowly they began to relax, their bodies softening into each other. Jay stroked her hair and rested the side of his face against the top of her head, glad it was him she had asked to stay and not her boyfriend.

'I'm too scared to be on my own tonight,' she whispered into his shoulder. 'What happened today reminds me too much of Bootle Cares.'

Then she took a deep breath and told him about Ben.

She probably wasn't aware of the tears that slid down his cheeks and onto the pillow as she recounted what that bastard had done to her. It was unbearable to think about someone hurting her like that or to imagine the living horror of it: Megan trapped in that hellhole whilst unspeakable things were done to her. Jay held her tight, she seemed so fragile but also the strongest person he had ever known. In his tired heart he promised he would protect her, he would be the brother she never had, the brother Silvie would have wanted him to be.

Chapter 39

Jay meandered back to the garden behind the museum building where Megan had suggested they meet. It was shaded and likely to be deserted on a weekend morning and, even if not, the grounds of Trinity were pretty safe. As usual, he had arrived early and, after making sure he had the correct meeting place, had wandered round the campus trying to absorb some of Megan's new realm.

It was another hot, dry day and he squatted in the shade of a skeletal cherry blossom – a perpetual reminder that the old adages about Ireland's constant rain were redundant, along with the moniker of The Emerald Isle. It was now dusty brown rather than green, crops were struggling and another water shortage loomed. The Brethren were frenetically working on their irrigation system made up of condensation vats and seawater purified in a temperamental solar rig-up. But most of the population still seemed to enjoy the sun, not yet having fully adjusted to it no longer being the luxury that previous generations had flown abroad in search of every summer.

On first glimpse of Megan approaching he stepped

out into the sunlight so he was in clear view – not pleased her boyfriend walking was alongside her, or what them arriving together at that time of the morning implied. They were holding hands in a way that looked easy despite a significant height difference between them, Megan wheeling herself with her free hand, smiling up at him as they chatted. What a strange tableaux they presented – jarringly out of the ordinary and yet somehow totally natural. It set his stomach churning with so many different feelings that when she reached his side and hugged him he held on to her, delaying the moment of being introduced to her boyfriend as much as possible. Aman beamed and looked like he wanted to pull Jay into a hug too, but Jay extended his arm offering a formal handshake instead, pulling himself up to his full height. Aman was still a good half a head taller and Jay wished more than anything he wasn't there.

Aman smiled warmly. 'Megan has told me so much about you, it's great to finally meet you.'

Aman looked like he might try the hug again, but he hesitated in the lack of reciprocation. 'I'm really grateful for everything you have done for Megan.'

Aman looked to Megan and then back at Jay as if Jay had brought her over to Ireland especially for him.

'I really wanted you two to meet each other,' Megan radiated happiness.

'Um, yes,' Jay nodded, trying to feign the enthusiasm the two of them clearly felt.

'Right, well, now we have I had better leave you two to it,' Aman conceded.

Could Aman sense the forcedness of his response – and what else might he be able to feel?

Looking at Megan, Aman added, 'You're sure you'll be okay?'

'Of course she'll be okay with me!' Jay retorted, not concealing the sting of the slight, after all, he was the one who had got her here.

'I know,' Aman gave Jay conciliatory glance and then kissed Megan full on the mouth, right in front of him, barely giving him time to look away.

'He seems really nice,' Jay said as naturally as he could as Aman strode away.

He wanted to ask how long she had been seeing him, how they met, how long they had been sleeping together – but he was not her dad or some kind of keeper.

'I think so,' Megan smiled in the direction of Aman's retreating back. 'He's on my course, but we met properly because of the cycling club.'

Keeping his mouth shut had paid off, she had told him most of what he wanted to know anyway and, if he thought about it later, he would be able to work out how many weeks they had been together from the time she first told him about the handcycle. And, if he thought about it even more, he could probably work out from that how long they had been sleeping together too – but that suddenly felt very creepy and he switched topic.

'Will we stay here or go for a wander?' he asked, indicating the retreating shade as the sun peered over the buildings.

'Let's go and get coffee somewhere shady, my treat,'

Megan smiled.

Megan did her best to make it seem casual, natural she would buy him things, but that did not soften the barb. And it wasn't just her, it was the Brethren too. All of his basic needs were now provided for by a disabled woman who was four years his junior and a cultish group of squatters. It was little consolation he had helped Megan to begin with, or that his relationship with the Brethren was more or less reciprocal: in addition to his board and lodging they provided him with a daily schedule of tasks to ensure he earned his keep.

'The devil makes work for idle hands,' Brother Paul had informed him.

Paul seemed to call most of the shots, including leading the high-tide prayers that Jay had so far managed to avoid. Paul also saw to it that he was provided with a regulation grey apron to wear whilst he worked on his assigned tasks but, thankfully, had not yet insisted on him wearing white – an incongruous choice of colour for a group which spent most of their time in manual labour attempting to be self-sufficient.

He moved alongside Megan, accustomed to walking with her like this now, even though it had taken a while to get used to. The image of Aman holding her hand flashed into his mind, what would that feel like? It had never even occurred to him it would be possible, let alone he would ever see her hand-in-hand with someone.

Her voice trailed off, he hadn't heard anything she had said.

'Sorry, what was that?'

It shouldn't make him feel so weird, Megan and Aman, but he couldn't help it.

'This way,' she nodded, leading him through the front arch. 'I have somewhere new to show you.'

She studied him, 'Are you okay?'

'Fine,' he faltered. 'Just a bit tired.'

'The Brethren have been working me hard,' he added in explanation. 'In the garden.'

He wasn't going to tell her it turned out he was pretty useless at all of the men's jobs like building and maintenance, so he was mostly relegated to working inside the houses with the women, and only occasionally allowed to help outside with the garden and even then under strict supervision. The garden was the only place where men and women worked alongside each other. It was as if The Brethren couldn't decide if the garden was outside and therefore men's work, or related to food and therefore a female role, so for the time being it remained mixed.

In all honesty, he preferred working with the women, even if the men saw it as emasculating. The women were generally more open and less dogmatic and easier to get on with. One of the women, Aoife, had been a teacher in a decent school before she joined the Brethren and she often chatted to him in quite a normal way whilst he scrubbed the floors or helped her picking the weeds out of the vegetable patch.

'What are you growing?' Megan asked

'Mostly vegetables, and some herbs they use for medicine.'

That was the most he knew about it, he still couldn't distinguish the plants they had sown from the weeds they were supposed to be pulling out and Aoife kept a close eye on him.

Peter, the mechanic, was kind and patient with him too – and he clearly had some kind of special dispensation that allowed him to wear dark overalls when he was working on the cars. Peter had initially tried to teach him a little about mechanics when he began converting the Skoda so it could run on both bio-fuel and regular vegetable oil, but Jay did not have the aptitude for it, he was used to electric cars that didn't rely on something as dirty and complex as a combustion engine. Even when he was working on the cars, Peter seemed a little out of place with the Brethren, a gentle soul, not really suited for a life declaiming sin and inviting catastrophe.

Megan led them through the front gates of Trinity and past the memorial garden where their previous ill-fated attempt to meet up had begun.

'Are you okay,' he asked.

His resentment of Aman now felt petty and out of place, she had been told she must be careful and shouldn't be alone.

'Mhm,' she nodded. 'It was a little strange the first time I was back here, but I have to get used to it, I'm not going to stop going to Uni!'

'And Aman is usually with me or meets me off the tram,' she added.

'That's good.'

It *was* good, but it didn't feel it.

They continued on Dame Street and turned left into the castle grounds where a smooth pathway had been laid in between the cobbles which led them over Ship Street and into the castle garden. There were benches scattered around and it was easy to find somewhere they could talk without being overheard. Megan picked a bench that was shaded by a tree and settled herself while Jay went inside the old coach house for coffees with a twenty she had given him. Taking money from her was uncomfortable, but the alternative was to make her wheel herself all the way inside just for the sake of his pride, the path was too uneven for her to have any hope of carrying the drinks back herself without spilling most of them.

He joined a short queue of people and gazed around the cool brick interior, catching his reflection in the mirror behind the counter. What did people see when they looked at him now? Could they see past his expensive clothes, did they know he was a squatter, here illegally? And what would they do if they did? He knew how he used to feel about people like that – judging them for their situation, certain those who lived in the shadows deserved what they got and they had either chosen that life or fallen into it because of who they were. It had always seemed obvious there must be some kind of darkness, something sinister or malevolent inside them that had led them that way. Yet he was the same person he had always been, he had not meant to do anything bad, he had been trying to do the opposite, to make something right, and yet here he was.

The woman behind the counter smiled at him. 'What can I get you?'

'Two oat lattes, please,' his voice was flat and he wasn't smiling.

Just in time he caught her eye and offered her an appreciative smile. She instantly responded in kind, sending a brief warm bubble of reassurance though his belly.

Megan was sitting turned half sideways on the bench with her legs tucked up to one side as he placed the tray beside her.

'Thanks, Jay,' she smiled, sliding the change from the corner of the tray into her purse.

Jay sat down the other side of the tray and lifted his coffee in reply.

'So,' she began. 'I have been talking to Udaya, my case worker.'

'Don't worry,' she rushed on before he could interject a stream of anxiety. 'I told her it was hypothetical, I mean I think she knows it's not entirely, but she is happy to play along and I haven't said enough for her to really figure out what is going on.'

Megan attempted a reassuring smile and then took a deep breath and the smile wavered.

'In order to claim asylum you need to show you are being persecuted or that you are at risk of persecution if you go back to England. I think the demo and the fact you brought me here could be enough, especially because we know the police are looking for you. I can't ask too directly about your situation in case that starts to make it too obvious, but from what Udaya said I think you have a chance of qualifying for asylum.'

That did not feel very likely from where he was sitting. Even though he knew what he would face if he returned to England, it seemed absurd to suggest he could claim asylum. Was ten years imprisonment with hard labour for crimes he had chosen to commit sufficient grounds for another country to take him in? He had done it all of his own free will.

'Do you really think that's enough?'

Nothing in his life could remotely resemble persecution, not even the demo, he chose it all, just like he chose to steal a passport and smuggle her out of England, surely that was not what she meant.

'Everything that happened was my choice, I wasn't threatened or forced or anything. I'd had a very lucky life, I'd never been persecuted for anything.'

A series of expressions crossed Megan's face. She looked both pleased and disappointed. Maybe pleased that he didn't seem so much like the selfish, entitled prick she had once thought, but disappointed by the obvious flimsiness of her plan.

'Well,' she said slowly. 'The only other thing you could try is a straightforward immigration application, but you don't have your passport or any work lined up here.'

It seemed like every way he turned he was confronted with a brick wall. Asylum, however unlikely, was probably his only chance – that or going back to England and turning himself in. And he could not do that to his family, he couldn't it to himself, either. He could not survive ten years in an English prison. He sighed, claiming asylum was a fragile hope but it was all he had.

'So what would I need to do if I was going to go ahead with the asylum claim? Is it the same as you?'

'Not quite, you will need to present at a garda station and they will refer you to one of the foreigners' asylum centres.'

Megan winced as she said it, she could probably hear that it didn't sound much more appealing than turning himself in to the English authorities.

How was this his life now? It had once been so perfect. A pang of loss for Silvie stabbed his heart, misting his eyes and he took a long draw of breath.

'You know, sometimes this feels like a very long, bad dream and soon I'm going to wake up next to Silvie and none of this will have happened.'

It felt like decades since his life had been that simple.

Megan reached over and took his hand. 'I know, sometimes I feel like you and Silvie have paid the price for my freedom. Like there is some horrible trade-off that means other people have to suffer for someone else to have their liberty.'

'Well that's true in a way, isn't it?'

Megan looked at him, not hiding her surprise.

'Freedom and prosperity for some are always built on the suffering and oppression of others.'

That was definitely Silvie talking, he imagined her with them now, what she would say and what she would think of him and everything he had done. If he had sacrificed his own freedom for Megan then at least there was no doubt he had lived up to his promise, he had proved himself in a way he never had done when she was alive. But at what cost? Did he really have to destroy everything he had in the pursuit of Megan's freedom? And if he could rewind it all and start again, would he act differently knowing where it would lead him?

That was an impossible question, he didn't want to have to make a choice between Megan's life and his own. And there was no point agonising over what he could have done differently that would have resulted in the same outcome for Megan but without the consequences for him. He was just tormenting himself trying to imagine some way he could have rebalanced the scales in both of their favour, it was far too late for that now.

He could feel Megan's eyes on him as he stared out across the gardens. Turning to face her, he immediately knew the answer. Of course he would do exactly the same all over again, he could not have left her to that life of hell in England, she was worth it whatever it cost him.

'Okay,' he said. 'I guess I have to give it a try.'

Relief spread across her face.

'I'll do everything I can to help, just tell me anything you need. I really want to make this work.'

'I will,' he said. 'I need a couple of days to get my head around it and organise my things and then I'll go and turn myself in.'

Megan squeezed his hand, he placed his other hand on top of hers, if only they could stay like this forever.

Chapter 40

The scent of still-warm cinnamon rolls wafting from the top of her rucksack, baked especially for her picnic with Aman, wasn't doing anything to abate the worries about Jay. If anything it was making it worse, pulling her back to the kitchen in Merebank that he may never see again.

It was already two days since he had brought most of his belongings to her flat, leaving a scant supply with the Brethren who were keeping his room on hand, and she had heard nothing from him. Might he have changed his mind and decided not to go through with it? He had been reluctant in the first place and presumably that's why the Brethren were keeping his room available, hoping he would change his mind and stay with them. They didn't really think he would convert to their way of life, did they? Jay insisted they were just being hospitable and they would continue to welcome him back whatever he believed. But that didn't seem very plausible, it was much more likely they wanted to keep him in a debt of obligation that they could call in when it suited them. He was already cleaning for them and working in the garden and they had been making modifications to the Skoda which seemed to be for their benefit rather than his.

They had cycled half way through Pheonix Park already, the warm evening breeze stroking her skin dry of perspiration. Aman was riding behind her, letting her set the pace as they wove between the other cyclists that were faceless silhouettes on the periphery of her thoughts. Pulling herself back into the present she glanced behind her. Aman immediately caught her eye and smiled broadly sending a ricochet of delight through her heart, quickly followed by a twinge of guilt. If only everything could be alright for Jay in the same way it was for her, it wasn't right that his life was ruined while hers was transformed. If only it was as simple as they had planned, not this catastrophic mess. Why had he been so stupid as to take someone else's passport? Or had they both been stupid to believe it could ever really be as straightforward as they had planned? But in truth it was always going to be more complicated than that, passport aside, there were pictures of Jay at the demo and that meant there would not have been an easy passage for him even if he had got back to England. Participating in a demo alone would have cost him his MSc and earnt him some jail time.

She turned off the main path towards the Farmleigh farm that had been returned to its original purpose after decades of functioning only as a tourist attraction. The gates were closed this late in the afternoon, but the trees on the perimeter and the wildflowers spilling through fencing – as well as the easy proximity to the path – made it a nice place to stop.

Aman paused while they were unpacking her bag, kneeling on the blanket directly in front of her as if he could read her thoughts from her face.

'He likes you,' he half smiled, his eyes focused intently on hers.

'I know, he's like a brother to me,' she replied. 'We've been through a lot together and things are very difficult for him at the moment.'

Aman knew a little, but she was careful what she said. It wasn't that she didn't trust him, it just felt like the less people knew the full truth of what Jay had done the safer.

'It's more than that, he *really* likes you,' Aman replied.

A sparkle of delight ignited in the pit of her belly but was quickly submerged by another wave of guilt.

'I remind him of Silvie, that's all.'

Aman did not look convinced. 'Have you two ever been together?'

'What? No, you know we haven't!'

Aman knew he was her first, surely he couldn't doubt that?

She sighed. 'He tried to kiss me once, just after Silvie died, but that was ages ago and only because I reminded him of her. I'm telling you, that's all it is.'

'That's not what it looks like to me,' Aman said firmly, and then, 'Do you like him?'

His expression was intense but soft. He wanted answers from her but there didn't seem to be any hostility in his eyes.

Megan inhaled deeply. 'I used to, a long time ago, in England.'

She exhaled, all that longing and fantasising was over now, wasn't it? She was with Aman and she had never experienced anything like this – it was like everything Pavel promised her coming true.

She reached forwards and touched his cheek. 'I like *you*.'

'Well he likes you, I can tell,' Aman smiled, the intensity slowly diminishing from his eyes.

'Stop saying that!' Megan chided, laughing. 'Are you jealous?'

She meant the question as a joke but he responded thoughtfully.

'No, I don't think so. Not jealous, curious.'

Then his demeanour changed and he laughed. 'I mean after everything he's done for you, I'm sure he must feel entitled to at least one thank you shag!'

Megan laughed and punched him lightly on the shoulder. 'Speak for yourself! He's not like that!'

Aman caught her wrists playfully and drew her towards him. He kissed her mouth and said, 'Well I'll make sure I show you some proper gratitude later.'

It was not yet fully dark and the oblong of sky in the sloping window above his single mattress was turning from mauve to inky blue. Jay had escaped up to his room straight after dinner, feigning a headache as an excuse for his constant blinking and watery eyes.

Tomorrow he was going to have to do it, but even this small, sparsely furnished room on the top floor of a maniacs' commune had a strong gravitational pull. It was the finality of it. Once he went to the garda station there was no going back, no way to deny what he had done or the devastating impact on his parents. After everything they had done for him, he had utterly betrayed them. There was no getting away from how terrible it looked: the youngest son of the former Northwest Police Chief and Regional Administrator being wanted for questioning in relation to national security offences. They must be so angry and ashamed, and whatever happened to him, or them, he had shattered their hard-earned retirement and left their lives in ruins. They would never forgive him.

The tears he had kept at bay all day finally pushed their way onto his cheeks. For the first time in his life he was utterly powerless: he had nothing and he was nothing. An ache of longing pushed more tears from his eyes, longing for a secure place in the world, of being loved – all the things he once took for granted. He had never felt so alone or so unwanted in his whole life.

Chapter 41

Megan took the tram to Busáras and then crossed onto Frenchman's Lane. Initially she had smiled at the asylum-seekers hostel being on a road named after a foreigner, but as she approached the foreboding grey building any remnants of mirth drained from her body. Rows of bunkbeds, stacked three or four high, were pressed up against barred windows and the heavy front door was rimmed with security cameras. It had once been a tourist hostel and before that an industrial building repurposed to create a venue that was novel and edgy. But, like most of the tourist sector, the hostel had to reformulate itself for the post-melt world. Cheap flights and globe-trotting tourists were a thing of the past, but huge swathes of the global south were on the move as they fled from the worst impacts of the climate disaster and the violent upheavals that followed hand in glove.

Now, the visage of asylum-seekers, including Jay, crammed into an old warehouse made her shudder. He had already told her about a warning from a bunkmate to keep everything important with him at all times — especially when there was a dorm-search, when even the lockers with their clothes in got turned over, and there was no guarantee that a nice pair of running shoes or an expensive shirt would still be there afterwards. At least most of his things were at her place, but how would he cope in this brutal, prison-like hostel packed with desperate strangers who had escaped from who knows what and where?

Jay must have been watching for her because he exited the main door before she rang the bell. He leant down and hugged her and she held him tight, trying to absorb some of his anguish and assuage some of her guilt for having brought him here. Even though she would have never agreed to the escape plan if she had known he would use someone else's passport, it was still undeniable that ultimately he was there because of her and, on top of that, she had persuaded him to try and seek asylum.

'Let's go somewhere nice,' she said, as if that might offer some consolation, leading him towards the tram stop on O'Connell Street. 'I got you this,' she handed him a travel card.

'Thank you,' he turned it over in his hands without really looking at it.

He seemed preoccupied, but as she studied him he met her gaze. He was pensive, but not distant in the way he had been when he was lying to her, he seemed thoughtful rather than guarded.

'Make it somewhere quiet,' he told her. 'There's something I want to talk to you about.'

They boarded the tram and Jay stood beside her in the wheelchair space with one hand wrapped around the pole and the other dangling against his thigh. His experience of the asylum system was already so different to hers, her Irish heritage had smoothed her path, providing instant legitimacy and rendering the process little more than a formality. For Jay, it was the opposite: slow, uncertain, and full of suspicion. She had taken it all for granted, not noticing how lucky she was, in exactly the same way that nettled her when Jay did the same. There was such an air of trepidation about him as he stood beside her that she wanted to reach out and take his hand, but she stopped herself. Would that be a strange thing to do, what would he think? Sometimes being around Jay was still confusing even though she really cared for Aman. It must just be that she felt responsible for him now, like a big sister, as if their roles had reversed.

They left the tram at Ranelagh, an old middle-class suburb with a main street packed with bars, cafes, and restaurants which seemed to have been untouched by the upheaval that had transformed so much of the world. Megan led them to cafe that she knew had a shaded courtyard garden and ordered coffees at the counter before they settled themselves into a quiet corner.

'I had another interview at the Asylum and Immigration Centre yesterday,' he told her as soon as the coffees arrived.

'They have made me an offer.'

Megan's heart leapt, at last things might be turning around and something other than destitution or imprisonment was possible. The whole process was so hard and he hadn't even chosen this. How desperate must those poor souls be who risked incomprehensibly dangerous journeys half way across the world only to face this? Jay had told her about a man from Libya who had befriended him at the hostel, Hassan. His family had been killed for their pro-democracy work and Hassan knew he would be next. He had travelled on foot, he had sailed in leaking dinghies, he had been beaten, robbed and attacked all in the desperate hope of safety and a better life only to find himself trapped in a system that seemed to be more about closing doors than offering safety.

She reached over and squeezed Jay's arm. 'Is it good?'

He took a deep breath. 'It's mixed,' he replied. 'It turns out they are definitely not interested in the fact that I got here helping you to escape, they said I should have claimed asylum when we first arrived if I wanted that taken into account.'

If only they had known that then, but how could they? She had not even been aware he had travelled on a stolen passport, and he had still truly believed he would get back to England. But if she had known sooner could she have done something to help? Perhaps she could have claimed Jay was her PCA, like she had told the gardaí. Although, the thought of Jay acting as her carer even for make-believe turned her stomach, and it was far too late for that now anyway.

Jay looked at her with small glimmer of light in his eyes. 'They *are* interested in something else,' he held her gaze. 'They want to know about the Military Bio-engineering programme. They seem to be concerned that some kind of biological weaponry is being developed, possibly a virus that could be spread around the CU.' He shrugged and looked away. 'I'm sure I don't know very much that is actually of interest to them, and I certainly don't know anything that dramatic.' He looked back at her. 'But they don't seem too worried about what I think, they just want access to all the material I have.'

He shrugged again. 'I guess they have never had the chance to get hold of any of that kind of stuff before.'

The security level of his course had always been a bit mysterious to her and even though she knew the Uni held his passport and biometric data she had no idea if that was normal or not.

He took another deep breath. 'So, they have offered me a deal. If I hand over all my tech and everything from the course, I get fast-tracked citizenship, possibly within a few weeks.'

Megan gasped, there was a way to make it work!

Jay gave a half smile in acknowledgment of her sudden hope, but he still looked afraid.

'It's very tempting. But if I go through with it there really is no going back. Ever.'

He swallowed, steadying himself. 'I will be classed as a terrorist as soon as the English authorities figure out what I have done, and whatever about ten years with hard-labour for everything else, terrorism is the end of the line.'

Megan exhaled, her hope crushed. 'Jay, I'm so sorry it has come to this, I feel terrible.'

Her pity stung like a slap, the last thing he wanted was her feeling sorry for him.

'I did it, Megan, so please stop saying sorry, you didn't know anything about it!'

It came out harsher than he had intended.

'Sorry,' he added. 'I didn't mean it like that, I just don't want you to feel guilty.'

It was humiliating to think of her pitying him; he was a man, not a charity case. Imagine if she saw him now the way he had seen her when Silvie had first taken him to Bootle Cares. That would be the worst possible punishment, even though he couldn't imagine thinking that way about her now.

The silence thickened between them and he realised he was staring at his hands knotting around themselves on the table. He looked up, she still looked crestfallen, he had really hurt her.

'I'm sorry,' he said again, moving to take one of her hands between his. 'I didn't mean to have a go at you, I just don't want you to feel shit on top of everything else.'

The woundedness in her eyes forced a sigh from deep inside his chest.

'Except now I have made you feel really shitty. I'm sorry, Megan.'

Her face slowly relaxed into a smile.

'How about we agree to both stop saying sorry?'

She added her free hand to the bundle.

'Okay, unless of course you do something really terrible!' he joked, pushing the pain away and releasing her hand so he could take both of them in his.

She let him hold her hand for a moment and then broke away and sipped her coffee, switching to practical mode. 'What do you think you should do, deep down? What was your initial feeling when they offered it to you?'

He let his mind return to the dingy interview room with the small metal table and chairs bolted to the floor and the camera trained on his every movement. The plump middle-aged official in his slightly too small grey European-style suit and his silent, uniformed companion were as visceral now as if they were right in front of him.

'I felt relief first of all, and then fear.'

'Tell me about the relief,' Megan probed.

'It was like he handed me a lifeline. I have something they want, something that can get me out of this mess. Because the reality is, even if I manged to get back to England tomorrow, I'd be looking at a significant jail term, and that's if I'm lucky.' He shook his head. 'I don't know what my family would do, but most likely they would have to disown me, so really I have already lost everything.'

As he said it he realised that had been Megan's life since Silvie's death and the flood. She had been stateless and homeless and at risk of institutionalisation just as he was now and yet she had borne it with much more calm and dignity than he was managing. She was watching him, waiting to see if he was going to say anything else. How did she get to be so strong?

When it was clear he wasn't going to say any more she asked, 'So what about the fear?'

'The fear is that this is the final nail in the coffin for any life for me in England. I would be effectively choosing to make myself a terrorist. That is so much worse than everything else put together. It would destroy my family and I would never see them again. It really is throwing my whole life away and starting again with nothing.'

Leaning forward, he pressed the heels of his hands against his eyes, willing himself not to cry. Megan must have felt his pain because she placed her hand between his shoulder blades and gently rubbed his back in the same way he used to comfort her.

He sighed and sat back up. 'It just seems incomprehensible that I would choose to do something that would make me a terrorist.'

He looked at her, willing her to understand what he was facing and how unreal it felt, he wanted her understanding, not her pity.

'And then, what if I go through with it and they change their minds and decide what I have given them isn't enough to warrant citizenship? Then I'd be a terrorist in the eyes of England and no hope of being legal here.'

Was this really possible? Had others had such a dramatic and unlikely descent as him? All those stories from long ago that he had disbelieved about migrants who were doctors, lawyers, or journalists in their home countries, losing everything, could they have been true? And how had people coped with such devastation *and* the cruelty of it? To think of it all as an accident of circumstance made it too hard to bear. And yet that's what Megan's life showed him every day: if she had been born just a couple of hundred miles westwards in Ireland her entire existence would have been completely unrecognisable.

Megan looked at him. 'Did they give you time to think about it? Or do you have to decide straight away?'

'He gave me a week. I have another appointment scheduled in six days and they want a decision then. He implied that if it's not the right one from their point of view then my asylum application will be at the back of a very long queue.'

'They don't make it easy,' she sighed.

He had been staring into his coffee cup while he spoke, but he looked directly into her eyes. 'What do you think I should do?'

Before she had the chance to protest that it should be his decision, he raised his hand.

'Just tell me,' he insisted.

She swallowed. 'I think you should do it,' she said quickly, not even trying to dress it up with judicious caution. 'At least you will belong somewhere then, even if it's not your first choice of where you want to be.'

She returned her hand to his back. 'You know I'm here for you in whatever way I can be, don't you? I will do whatever I can to make this work out for you and we will always be friends.'

'Thank you,' he took a deep breath and pulled her into a hug.

A wave of sadness washed through him threatening

more tears and he blinked frantically into her hair, he couldn't start sobbing here. Megan had seen him cry before, but that was in private, not somewhere like this – the kind of place he used to feel comfortable: smart and cool, pretending to be casual but with a distinct air of class about it. Recently he had started to feel very conspicuous everywhere he went. Swallowing down his tears he released the hug and checked the time on his CU phone, his watch was at her flat, it was expensive and wouldn't last long at the hostel.

'I should start heading back soon.'

They were only allowed out for a couple of hours at a time and signing in and out was essential.

'I'll come back with you,' Megan offered.

Was that more pity?

'You don't have to do that.'

'I want to, I like spending time with you.'

He smiled, grateful.

'Obviously this is not my ideal choice of how to spend time with a friend, but we'll just have to make do,' she smiled in return.

Chapter 42

Jay was in the near-deserted canteen with Hassan when a commotion broke out at the front door, there was shouting and something shattering. Instinctively, Jay began to back towards the fire exit and Hassan moved with him, gripping his arm. Adrenaline was pounding through his limbs, it was English voices he could hear, English men shouting.

'Shit, I've got to go!' he gasped, but Hassan tightened his grip, holding him back.

'No,' he hissed. 'You're not leaving.'

'Let me go!' Jay cried trying to shake free.

'In here! Tell them he's in here!' Hassan yelled towards the last remaining stragglers in the canteen.

Jay gasped and swung his free arm to hit Hassan, but Hassan was too quick for him and landed a blow to his face. Despite the shock of the pain, Jay struggled and managed to hit him back. They tussled and fell to the floor, Hassan kneeling on top of him, pinning him down with the weight of his body and striking him in the face.

'English bastard!' he spat.

'What?'

He was so dumfounded he stopped struggling for a moment, and then it dawned on him. Hassan had not been befriending him, he had been getting information. That was why he was so obsessed with the English news and hearing all about England. And even though he had been careful, Hassan had still figured out who he was and turned him in. Just because the Irish looked at the English government with scorn and felt sympathy for its citizens didn't mean that people from other parts of the world did, especially where there were long memories of British interventions.

'You get to go to jail, and I get an English passport,' Hassan sneered.

'What?! You fucking idiot! You stupid bastard! Do you have any idea what you have done?' Jay screamed into his face.

A surge of rage and fear powered him off the floor, throwing Hassan from him. He crashed out of the fire doors and leapt over the wall at the back of the building, falling awkwardly. Forcing himself up, he fled along the side of the next building, staggering from the fall. A gate loomed in front of him, blocking his path, using all the power in his aching body he flung himself over the top and found himself on a road leading under the railway bridge. Heart pounding, he kept running despite the pain in his ankle, speeding up the next lane before he realised it was a dead end. It was too risky to turn back, so he hurled himself at the lowest point of the wall, just managing to scramble over the top and drop onto a row of recycling bins on the other side. There was another wall ahead, but this was low and he cleared it easily, finding himself on Talbot Street. In a second he orientated himself and started sprinting towards O'Connell St, glancing left and right as he reached the pavement edge. There was a tram at the post office and he sprang across the road and pushed himself on board just as the doors were closing. Flopping into the nearest seat, gasping for breath, he was attracting a lot of attention. People were staring at him and his was smarting where Hassan had hit him. He bought his hand to his mouth, there was blood on his fingertips. He quickly unbuttoned his shirt, glad of his undershirt, and wiped his face on the fabric, wincing where it contacted the wounds. The looks from the passengers made clear it wasn't any more socially acceptable to wipe his bloody face on his shirt than it was to sit there bleeding. He returned the shirt to his face for a moment of reprieve from the staring eyes and allowed a few silent tears of shocked betrayal to slip free. Then he took a deep breath to pull himself together. There were already bruises throbbing into place on his ribs where Hassan had knelt on him and he rotated his ankles to test for damage. Although Hassan had hurt him, it felt like nothing more than cuts and bruises. And thankfully his phone, his travel card, his small amount of cash the key to the BGW house had all survived in his pockets. It was hard to believe what Hassan had done. And for what? What kind of life did he think he was going to have in England?

The tram eased against the platform at Ranelagh and he alighted checking that no one was paying particular attention to him anymore before jogging up the canal towards Sandymount. There was still enough adrenalin in his body to keep him moving in spite of the pain. Even so, he was trotting rather than sprinting now, his bloodstained shirt trailing out from his waist. He checked behind him every few metres and each time he turned onto a different street, but he was on his own. A wash of relief spread through him as the Martello tower came into view and then the white painted BGW houses shortly afterwards. Pausing for a moment to catch his breath with his hands resting on his knees, he checked the street twice and then straightened up and walked up the driveway and let himself in to house three. As the door closed behind him, a deep sigh of relief pushed its way out of his lungs, he was safe – he had never said anything to Hassan about the Brethren so there was no way they would find him here. As he moved towards the stairs, Aoife popped her head out from the kitchen and her smile changed to confusion and then concern.

'Jay,' she breathed. 'What happened? Are you alright?'

She moved towards him, touching his cheek with one hand and taking his wrist in the other.

'Come here and let me clean you up.'

He let her lead him into the kitchen and bathe his face, her fussing over him was nice, it made him feel cared for.

When she had finished bathing his bruised and broken skin, she rested her palm against his cheek and looked deep into his eyes.

'Tell me what happened.'

If it wasn't for where he was, and the fact she was probably nearly forty, he would have been certain she was coming on to him. He had sometimes wondered what kind of bed-hopping went on among the Brethren. There were a handful of couples who had been together since before they joined, but the majority seemed to be single. Perhaps there was some kind of unspoken agreement that everyone ignored what went on behind closed doors as long as it was discreet. Because, despite all their preaching about sin, he did not believe they were all celibate, certainly not the with the way Aoife was looking at him.

'You can tell me anything, Jay,' she coaxed.

As he relayed his story he expected her to be worried about the English following him there and wreaking havoc in the Brethren's domain, but she was stoic.

'They can't do anything to us, Jay, God decides our destiny, and we know that whatever He chooses the correct path for us.'

The contrast between Aoife's gentle ordinariness and the bonkers ideas that came out of her mouth was jarring, but he knew better than to argue, so he nodded and smiled through his swollen lip, at least he was safe.

Aoife scuttled round the kitchen, brewing a healing infusion that smelled a bit like damp socks, and taking his shirt to soak in another potion that would get rid of the bloodstains. It seemed she would have been content to fuss over him for the rest of the evening, but all he really wanted to do now was go upstairs, shut the door and lie down on his own. Finally, she told him it was nearly time for high tide prayers and he insisted she should join the others.

As he opened the attic room door, the scent of floorboards warmed by the heat of the afternoon sun enveloped him in a woody hug and he lowered himself onto the mattress. Then he remembered Megan and bolted upright, grabbing his phone. How had he not thought of her before? No doubt the English knew where she was and would assume he had gone to her.

'*Megan be careful tonight, they came for me at the hostel,*' he tapped. '*I'm safe but they might look for me at your place.*'

He swallowed, he didn't want to type the next line but he had to.

'*You shouldn't be on your own, get Aman to stay with you and make sure the gardaí know you are at risk.*'

The last of his energy departed with the message and he flopped back onto the bed, his fingers still lightly circling the phone, knuckles sore from throwing punches. It buzzed in reply.

'*Jay, are you okay? Can I see you? Don't worry about me, Aman is already here and he will stay with me tonight. I'm worried about you.*'

Jay's heart swelled and then shrunk as if it had been punctured. Why was the right thing to do always so hard?

'*I'm glad he's already there,*' he lied. '*We should wait a while to make sure it's safe before we meet up again.*'

The next morning he was barely awake before Aoife was knocking on his bedroom door and fussing around him, trying to attend to his every need like he was a hero returned from battle. Every time he moved it felt like he aggravated a bruise or a lesion, but he knew better than to let his body seize up. He stretched gingerly and made his way downstairs to the kitchen – there was one thing she could definitely do for him today.

'I'm no hairdresser!' she kept repeating, when he told her he wanted a haircut.

But from the look on her face when he insisted, it felt more like she didn't want to change the way he looked.

'Please, Aoife,' he coaxed. 'I need to do everything I can to be safe and that includes trying to make myself look as different as possible.'

'Okay,' she finally relented with a sigh and went to fetch some scissors.

She draped an off-white towel around his shoulders and snipped tentatively, running her fingers through his hair as she worked. Very gently, she tilted his head in different directions, taking care to do her very best. Other than Megan, she was the first person who had touched him in a long time and her tenderness made his skin tingle.

'What made you leave teaching and join the Brethren?' he asked drawn into the intimacy of the moment.

Aoife sighed heavily.

'Sorry if it's too personal, I didn't mean to pry,' he backtracked, speaking at his thighs, his head bent forward while she cut around his collar.

She stopped snipping and rested her hand on his shoulder for a moment, seeming to consider whether or not she wanted to tell her story. She sighed again and then resumed snipping.

'I was supporting my husband,' she said. 'I was deputy head, so I was earning a good salary. He wanted to go back to university and study marine engineering and I was happy to be the breadwinner. I even took on some tutoring with some of the sixth formers so we had enough money for him to be able to go on fieldtrips to the Mediterranean and Adriatic.'

Aoife sighed again and tilted Jay's head back into an upright position. She put the scissors on the table and held out strands of hair from either side of his head to check the symmetry. She picked up the scissors again and snipped carefully at one side and took a deep breath.

'He was sleeping with one of the girls I was tutoring.' She paused. 'I couldn't go back to work. I couldn't stay with him. I just left. I was so humiliated. I stayed in a guest house for a bit. Mary from house two used to do a bit of cleaning there to bring in some money and she persuaded me to come here. It was such a relief to find shelter away from all the judging eyes.'

He felt her stand a little straighter behind him.

'And there is a simple way of life here with clear moral standards. I don't know what would have become of me if it wasn't for the Brethren.'

'God I'm so sorry,' was all he could find to say.

That had not been what he was expecting at all, he had imagined some kind of fanciful mystical conversion not a betrayal with a schoolgirl by a cheating husband. Then it dawned on him he had just blasphemed in front of her.

'Shit, sorry, I didn't mean to curse – or swear,' he added realising he had simply exchanged one profanity for another.

Aoife giggled. 'Don't worry about it. A lot worse came out of my mouth at the time!'

She was silent for a moment. Then, relieved to change the subject back to Jay added, 'Okay, I think I'm done, have a look in the hall mirror and see if you like it.'

He got up and went over to the mirror with the towel still draped around his shoulders. The reflection staring back at him was a shock, with his battered face and shorter hair he looked like a criminal, barely recognisable to himself, let alone anyone else.

'It's fine, thank you.'

'You don't like it, you think I've made a mess,' it was hard to know if it was a question or a statement.

'Liking it is not really the point,' he sighed. 'I just need to look different and you've managed that fine.'

Her reflection appeared behind him in the mirror and she reached up and took a newly shortened lock from behind his ear and curled it around her fingers. She looked like she might cry.

'It's great,' he reassured her, turning and resting his hand on her shoulder. 'Thank you.'

She blinked and smiled and then hurried off to the kitchen promising another herbal poultice for his bruises.

Jay removed the towel from his shoulders and shook it outside the back door, feeling guilty. He shouldn't have invited a confidence from her, she was still clearly very affected by it. Worse than that, he had created an intimacy between them that he was going to have to carefully extricate himself from. Weird beliefs aside, he liked her and he neither wanted to upset her nor give the impression he was bonding with her – things were messy and complicated enough as it was.

Chapter 43

'What do you know about Silvie Connolly?'

It was a stab in the heart.

'She's dead,' Jay choked.

Tears clawed at his throat and he looked away. The camera in the far corner winked at him, every minutiae of every response was yet more evidence to add to the retina scan and fingerprints they had taken after they searched him that morning.

He took a deep breath and tried to compose himself, studying the two men in front of him. Was it some kind of trick? They had spent the first hour asking him mundane questions about his life they must already know the answers to, and what had Silvie got to do with any of it? Could it be a tactic to try and break him down? But there was no need, he had given them everything he had, he would answer all of their questions. His heart sped up, they didn't think he had killed her did they? Or why he didn't want to go back to England? Tears of horror sprung to his eyes, he swallowed, knotting his hands on the table in front of him and then stopped, afraid that was only making him look more guilty.

The interrogators exchanged glances, they had told him their names at the beginning but it might as well have been Adam and Eve for all he could remember.

'And her role in the PLI?'

Yet another change of direction, it was hard to keep up, especially when he hadn't even figured out the last thing they asked before they moved onto something else.

'What's that?'

The men looked at each other again as if they were confirming everything by telepathy.

The smaller one spoke, 'The People's Liberation Initiative.'

'Never heard of it,' he looked from one to the other for an answer. 'What's that got to with Si—'

The realisation slammed into him before he could even finish the sentence. The room tipped on its axis, sending him spinning backwards through time, gasping for air as hard as if they had hit him. *No, she can't have. That means she would have been lying to me all the time we were together. She can't have, we loved each other.*

An avalanche of tears pushed through him, he couldn't speak, he couldn't even hear if they were asking him more questions, he just sobbed into his hands. Another piece of his life, another rock of who he was and what he knew was gone, he didn't even have his memories anymore.

Lying on the mattress in house three he tried to rationalise away the weight in his chest. It couldn't be true, could it? The interrogators had neither confirmed nor denied anything, they had simply provided him with some paper towels to dry his face and told him to come back to continue the interview the next day.

Silvie couldn't have kept something like that from him, could she? She had been to his parents' house, for goodness sake. Besides, if she was part of some illegal organisation why had she applied to the MSc in Military Bio-engineering – a security-listed course which required her passport and a DNA swab? No one in a subversive organisation was going to do that.

Results day flashed into his mind: he could see Silvie's face as clearly as if she was there in the house with him. She was smiling for him as he clicked between his final results, passes in everything, and his acceptance on the MSc. There was a shadow behind the smile, but that was only to be expected, despite a clean slate of distinctions her application had been declined.

'I'm sorry,' he had consoled her. 'You deserve it just as much as me.'

But they both knew the seminar recordings would put pay to any hope she had of being accepted – so why had she applied at all?

'It's okay,' she had reassured him. 'I still have the teaching post-grad to hear back from.'

And she had sailed though that and been placed in a pretty good school, which was hardly going to happen if she was a member of an illegal organisation, was it? But then why had she wasted a whole year of her life on the assessment and screening process for a course that was never going to admit her? He hadn't thought much about it at the time, he had been flushed with love and enchanted by the prospect of spending two years studying alongside her. So he had simply assumed that, despite all her questioning, ultimately she wasn't that different and she would do whatever it took to secure her future just like everyone else. Could she really have had another agenda altogether?

It made his head hurt and he desperately needed sleep. He tried to focus on the "safe house" he had been promised in return for all his tech, and the prospect of being alone there in a few days. The last thing he wanted sliding into his dreams was a version of Silvie that might make sense of the man with the Committee car.

Chapter 44

Scanning her surroundings, Megan saw a figure moving diagonally across St Stevens Green towards her and a charge of recognition pulled taught between them, her body recognising him before her mind caught up. He was wearing large, dark glasses, his hair was shorter, falling into curls at his ears and collar without the length to flatten it into waves and he was growing a beard. The stride was more restrained than usual, but it was definitely Jay. As he got closer she waved and he increased his pace, traces of bruising around his cheekbone and the cuts to his mouth still visible.

'You look different,' she said as he drew near.

'That's the general idea,' he replied flattening his mouth into a half smile and removing the glasses.

'Well just so long as you don't start wearing all-white and attending high-tide prayers,' she smiled.

'Don't worry, I'm not that far gone yet,' he smiled back.

It was a proper smile this time that reached his eyes and made him look like his former self despite the hair and the beard. He sat down on the bench beside her and she turned towards him tucking her feet up beside her, her knees brushing his thigh.

'That must have been really nasty,' she said touching his face by the bruises. 'Did you get someone to look at it?'

'Just Aoife, one of the Brethren. She cut my hair as well.'

He must have read the disapproval from her face.

'I'm okay, honestly.'

Then he opened his arms and they hugged.

'It's so good to see you, Jay," she breathed into his shoulder, wishing again that she could absorb some of his pain. 'I've been so worried about you.'

He held her tight, it felt like they could stay like that for a very long time, but he broke away from her and took a deep breath. 'I took the deal.'

Megan nodded, relieved to finally have it confirmed. He had messaged her nearly every day on the encrypted phone he had been given, but he was still guarded in what he said and she wasn't sure how much to ask. Now they were finally face-to-face she wanted every detail.

'They actually had more on the table than they had initially implied,' he continued. 'Including a safe house for me – well, a basement flat on the North Circular Road near Phoenix Park. It's got all kinds of security on it, reinforced doors and windows, alarms, a panic room—'

That was near where she and Aman cycled.

'Can I see it?' she interrupted.

A series of expressions crossed his face before he

answered.

'I don't think that's a very good idea. They could well be keeping tabs on you and that would lead them straight to me.'

Disappointment stung her.

'Besides, it's also down a lot of steps,' he added. 'It's one of the old red-brick houses that has been converted into flats, so it would be almost impossible for you to get in.'

'Sorry, I wasn't thinking.'

Why did it make her feel so bad?

'Does that mean you shouldn't come to my place, either?'

'I don't know,' he said slowly, as if it was painful getting the words out. 'I guess I shouldn't, not for a while anyway.'

Megan sighed, 'I was going to offer to make you dinner.' Then an idea struck her. 'I guess it will just have to be a picnic instead!'

'I'd really like that,' he smiled.

'Good,' she smiled. 'Me too.'

'But tell me what is happening with your case, what are they doing and how long will it take,' she pressed.

'They have my laptop and all my course work. They have copied everything off it and now they are taking it apart. They are going to interview me on all of it once they are satisfied they have found everything, so it's going to take a while. In the meantime they have just been asking me stuff about my life and why I came here.'

He turned and took a wallet from his back pocket

and opened it.

'And they have given me this.'

The wallet was stuffed with cash, was he was showing her how much money he had? Surely he didn't think that meant anything to her? But he drew out an embossed titanium card and handed it to her. She flipped it over in her fingers. It was an ID card. *Jason Bulmer*, it read. *Irish Residency Permit*. It included his date of birth and a picture of him with his hair newly cut, the scraggy beginnings of a beard and fresh injuries on his face. An unrestrained burst of laughter escaped from her. It was partly relief, and partly the incongruity of him looking so awful on such an important document.

'You look more like a convict than a legal resident,' she gasped.

He playfully snatched the card back from her. 'Hey, that's no way to speak to someone who has the legal right to reside in this country!' he laughed.

'I'm sorry,' Megan smiled bowing her head in mock gravity.

He reached forward and lifted her chin. 'Yes, show a little more respect please!'

They held each other's gaze, smiling, and for a second it felt like he was moving towards her. She blinked, but he was just smiling at her in his usual way.

'I won't get a passport and a full ID card until they are happy they have squeezed every last drop of information out of me.'

She definitely must have imagined whatever it was.

Then, to her surprise he added, 'I got you something.'

An unexpected somersault of delight tumbled through her stomach.

He reached into a small backpack and brought out a flat, oblong box and handed it to her. She had no idea what Jay might think to gift her, but she had a lovely warm glow inside. As soon as she opened the lid, tears sprang to her eyes. Inside was a slate picture frame containing the image of her, Pavel, and Silvie he had taken at Bootle Cares all that time ago. Lifting it from the box she held it against her heart, her eyes streaming while she breathed into pain and joy of it. Then, she laid it back into the box, staring at Silvie and Pavel, tracing their faces with her fingertip.

She turned to Jay and, taking his hands in hers, she leaned forward and kissed him on the cheek.

'Thank you,' she whispered. 'This means more than anything to me.'

Chapter 44

They tried again.

The three-word message from Megan sent chills down his spine.

Where are you? Are you okay? he replied, heart racing.

Sorry, I sent that before I had finished writing it. I'm fine now. I'm at James' hospital with Aman.

Jay got up to go straight there.

Don't try and come here, she had already guessed what he was doing. *They might try and take you.*

He sighed and slumped back down.

Are you alright? he asked again.

Yes. But it was different this time. I think they might have been trying to get me to find you.

It was unbearable to think of people hurting Megan because of him.

Another message pinged. *After all, you have probably pissed them off even more than I have at this stage!*

She was trying to lighten things but he needed the reassurance of her voice.

Can we talk?

I can't now, I'll call you later, when I'm back at home.

Are you going to stay at your flat tonight? Is that safe?

The gardaí are going to give me protection for a while and Aman will stay with me.

If only she could come and stay with him in the safe house, or he could stay at her flat, holding her to keep her safe like he had done before. His stomach knotted and he pushed the image out of his mind, they were protecting her, that was the most important thing.

Where are you? she asked.

I'm at the safe house.

Good, stay there and be extra careful.

He had still been spending a lot of time at house three in spite of the flat, telling himself it was probably safer there, after all the English might know about the safe houses, but they would never expect to find him at the sea defence with the Brethren. It saved him from admitting the homely draw of house three where there were always big pots of food being prepared, handcrafts on the walls, gardening and mending going on and how barren the safe house felt in comparison. It was nice enough, painted in soft off-white shades and supplied with mid-range contemporary furniture and appliances, but it felt cold and clinical after the home-made hotchpotch of the BGW houses, and being alone felt more and more uncomfortable. He had lived in such close proximity to other people for months now, firstly Megan, then the Brethren, and even the guys at hostel, and he didn't relish the prospect of long hours alone with his churning thoughts.

He hadn't told Megan about Silvie and the PLI. After

all, there was nothing definite to say: they had asked questions he didn't know the answers to – and they certainly weren't going to give him any answers. Besides, he didn't want to worry Megan with something that might not even be true. Deep down, he was also a little afraid she might already know something and, at the moment, she was all that was keeping him from drowning, and the last thing he wanted was for her to be another leaking boat.

But that morning, despite longing for distraction, he had needed to escape from the Brethren for a while. They were planning some special festival and kept trying to drag him into it. On top of that, Aoife had increasingly started finding reasons to come up and knock on his bedroom door. She would hover shyly in his space, waiting for him to invite her in, and he was running out of ways to gently manoeuvre her out again.

He paced the flat waiting for Megan to message saying he could call her, but time creaked slowly on. The waiting was becoming unbearable, so he changed into his running things and headed out for the park. It was evening, not his usual time, but he had to do something with all the pent-up anxiety other than circle the flat like a caged animal. He jogged into the park and trotted towards the tea rooms and the fish pond, not running at full pace, on top of his regular morning run he also had jogged most of the way from Sandymount to the flat on the North Circular Road and there wasn't much left in his legs.

He turned onto a path that skirted the grounds of

Áras an Uachtaráin, the presidential house, which was mostly shielded from view by trees and thick shrubbery which no doubt had some kind of security fence concealed within. As the path drew alongside the main thoroughfare, he became aware of a car driving along very slowly directly parallel to him. His heart accelerated and he increased his pace slightly and the car did the same, remaining level. Dropping to one knee and pretending to fix a shoelace, he peered upwards at the car. It was a sliver-grey Lexus with tinted windows, it continued to move very slowly along the road and then stopped. Taking a deep breath, he swapped knees and fiddled with his other shoe, priming himself to bolt at any moment. The passenger window rolled down and a middle-aged woman with a pasty face and dyed blonde hair leaned out and snapped some pictures on her phone. She was not pointing the phone directly at him, but he was sure he was in the periphery of the shot, he kept his head dipped forwards so the shadow of his hair obscured his face. Time froze; were the photos being compared with images from his English ID on some kind of terrorist database? Even though he looked different enough to a casual observer, any algorithm would instantly identify him. Was this the end? His only chance was sprinting back towards Áras an Uachtaráin, and hoping he could reach the main gate and the armed gardaí before the English authorities caught him.

Then, the window rolled back up and the car moved off at normal speed. Exhaling sweet relief, Jay rested his head on his knee, heart threatening to break through his chest wall. When the car was completely out of sight he got shakily to his feet and checked the park around him. There was hardly anyone about and no-one seemed to be paying him any attention. Grasping his opportunity, he turned and sprinted back to in the direction he had come, checking every few metres to see if the car reappeared or if anyone was watching him from the pavement, but it was all quiet. His hands were still trembling as he let himself back inside the flat, locked the door and slid the security bolts in place and double-checked them. He turned into the kitchen for a glass of water. From the window he could see up to street level, the pavement was empty, but still he was never more grateful for the barred widows and reinforced glass. He took a slug of water and then rolled the cool surface of the glass against his forehead. It was probably nothing, just a coincidence.

His phone buzzed.

Let's chat. It was Megan.

He called her instantly, but as soon as he said her name, she could tell something wasn't right.

'Jay, what's wrong?'

'Nothing, I just had a bit of a fright that's all.'

He told her what had happened.

'Please be careful, they are definitely up to something.'

The way she said "they" was oddly reminiscent of his first conversations with Silvie and the sinister "they" she had often referenced in an ominous tone. It had seemed slightly loopy then, a little bit like the Brethren now, and he had only indulged her in the beginning because he fancied her. But now "they" had taken on a whole new reality, both for him and for whatever secrets she had kept from him.

'Tell me what happened to you. Did they hurt you?'

Megan's safety was the most important thing right now.

'No, not really. They weren't rough this time, they gave me some kind of sedative, so I had to stay at the hospital to get tested and wait while it wore off.'

Megan inhaled and started from the beginning. 'It was this morning, I was getting off the tram at Abbey Street to go to uni, Aman was meeting me at the corner.'

Relief washed through him, if she was meeting Aman in the morning that meant he wasn't staying with her all the time, but the relief was quickly replaced with shame. How could his first thought be about how much time Aman was spending at her flat; how often he was sleeping with her? What kind of person was he?

Megan continued. 'It was busy when I got off, the pavement was crowded, and people were really close to me. I felt something sharp on my neck and went to brush it away and this woman had suddenly taken hold of my hand and I was dizzy. Then someone was pushing me in the opposite direction than I was supposed to be going. I tried to call out but I was just slurring, I couldn't say anything, I was all floppy. It was really scary.'

Jay exhaled, not even aware he had been holding his breath. This was worse than anything he could have imagined.

'What happened then?'

'Aman thought he saw me get off the tram but then I disappeared, so he came up Abbey Street looking for me. He said there were three people with me, a woman on either side and a man pushing me. He ran past us and then turned around so he was blocking the path. I could just about make out it was him and I was trying to call out to him but no words came out. But he started talking to me anyway, asking me who my friends were, why I wasn't going to class and that really confused them. The woman said she was my caseworker and that I had become unwell during a meeting and she was taking me to see a doctor.'

She paused and took a breath, it was obviously difficult to relive however matter of fact she was trying to be about it all.

'When I realised they had stopped moving I tried to get my panic button, but I was really floppy and I sort of fell forwards. Aman caught me and activated it. Then he just held on to me so they couldn't take me anywhere. The gardaí came really quickly and the three of them disappeared as soon as they heard the sirens.'

What could he say? It was horrific, worse than horrific.

'It was very different,' she went on. 'More subtle than last time. That's why I think it might be the ones who are looking for you, they didn't hang around to argue when the gardaí showed up.'

'I'm so sorry, Megan,' his voice was cracking.

'It's not your fault, Jay.'

Her tone changed as if she was smiling. 'And I

thought we agreed to stop saying sorry.'

'You're right, we did, sorry.'

'You just said it again!' she laughed

It was impossible to be frivolous, his heart hurt.

'I can't bear to think of people hurting you, because of me. I wish I had been there to help you.'

'It's better you weren't.'

Her tone was sombre again and she didn't need to tell him what that meant – they wouldn't be able to see each other for a while. There was a pain running through his chest as if he had been cut on the inside. It was so hard being apart from her, not being able to see her or hold her even for a moment.

Megan murmured something in the background, Aman was with her, how had he forgotten that? He tried to think of something to say that acknowledged him in a warm and friendly way, but everything he thought of sounded fake.

Megan spoke into the silence. 'Jay?'

She said his name like it was a question and then stopped for a moment as if plucking up the courage to continue.

'This changes things, you know?'

His stomach plummeted, she was going to say they couldn't be in contact any more, that it was no longer safe for them to be friends, she was going to let go of him so she could get on with her life.

'What do you mean?' he forced the words out.

'I don't think we can stay here.'

He could barely hear her over the thudding of his

heart.

'I don't understand,' he faltered, dreading what was next.

'I don't think they are going to give up on trying to take us back, not for a while anyway.' There was anxiety in her voice. 'It's too close, and it's too easy for them to just drive over here, swoop one or both of us off the streets and drive back again.' Her voice changed again. 'I don't think they are going to let what either of us have done lie for a long time.'

She paused and then, sounding determined, added, 'We need to get further away. I don't think Ireland is safe enough for us at the moment.'

His stomach was rolling with a million possibilities. Was she going to leave Ireland with Aman? But she was talking to him as if he was included.

'What do you mean?'

It took work to level his voice.

'I think we should leave Ireland and go to mainland Europe for a while. It won't be so easy to follow us there and they might start to lose interest if we are further away and go quiet for a bit.'

Was he hearing her right? It was hard to know what was real between his pounding heart, his racing thoughts, and the stream of words flowing from her. Could she really be suggesting abandoning this whole new life in Dublin and going somewhere else with him? And how did Aman fit into it? Was she planning for them to go to Europe as a trio? And what would it be like living every day in such close proximity to their love – right now that felt only marginally less hellish than prospect of her and Aman going without him.

'It won't be forever,' she continued, sounding more assured. 'But as soon as you get your documents we should go.'

He didn't know how to respond, it was a million miles from anything he had been expecting.

'Jay?'

'Ah, I don't know what to say. It seems like a huge decision.'

Part of him wanted to add that she had had a massive shock and might feel differently in a week or so, but he was feeling pretty shocked himself and on much less solid ground than she seemed to be.

'I know, but I think it is the right one. I talked with the gardaí and they agreed it might be a useful to get a bit further away for a while – and that was without them knowing anything about your situation. Taking that into account makes it indisputable, or it does to me and Aman, anyway. Will you think about it, at least?'

At last a mention of Aman at last, but no detail about he fitted into it all.

'Of course I will. But are you sure? What about everything you have got going for you over here?'

It was the closest he could bring himself to asking directly about Aman, but there was also the degree programme she had been hoping to start as well as her writing for the *Irish Times* and, of course, her flat.

'I just have to believe that if things are going to work out here then they will when the time is right, but nothing will ever work out if you and I are not safe. If something is meant to be then it will happen.'

A small bubble of hope rose through the wound in his chest. Was she referring to Aman? Perhaps he wasn't going with them after all, perhaps she meant that if he was the one for her then it would work out between them eventually, in the future, and that left room for something else to happen as well, Aman might not be the one after all. He pushed it away, why was he thinking like that?

'You're starting to sound a bit like the Brethren now!' he joked. 'Please don't tell me it's all part of God's plan!'

'It's you that has been invited to high tide prayers and whatever else, not me!'

Megan laughed abruptly and then her tone changed. 'But seriously, Jay, think about it. We can get to Spain and the rest of Europe really easily from here. I'll still be able to access my UBI payments in Europe and you will too once you get your citizenship. We can take the car and the boat. We've crossed borders already and we'll both be legal this time so it will be easy. We can come back when things have settled down again.'

'You seem to have it all figured out already.'

'Well, I've been in hospital all day with not much else to think about once the meds wore off.'

She had been thinking about him and her all day? Another piece of his heart reassembled.

'I will definitely think about it,' he promised. 'It's just a bit of a shock right now.'

Part of him still longed to angle the conversation

back to Aman to get some concrete answers. What did he think about it? After all, he had been at the hospital with her all day and must have been her sounding board. If it was him in Aman's situation he would definitely want just the two of them to go and not have Jay tagging along like a wet rag. Aman might have even tried to persuade her against it, that's most likely what he would have done. But, then again, maybe Aman was a better person than him, the kind of person Megan deserved.

As much as he needed answers, it was impossible to turn the conversation to Aman without asking directly, and he didn't trust himself not to mess it up, especially when he knew Aman was there with her. It would be so much easier to talk in person, but it was going to be a while before they could do that again.

Chapter 45

'Sorry,' Jay said, squirming slightly. He was doing it again, making a dick of himself by trying to get them to like him, to believe him. 'I'll just answer the questions.'

'It's better if you do,' Pádraig affirmed, an almost imperceptible smile softening his mouth.

At least it was gradually becoming less fraught and more routine, and they hadn't asked anything else about Silvie in a long time, but he still hadn't mentioned it to Megan. When they were away from all of this, safely in Spain, just the two of them together, he would ask her properly, but not now.

He sighed, every so often they started asking him similar questions in different ways or, like now, they would throw in a question about something completely off-topic they had asked him previously. He understood why they were doing it, it was designed to trip him up if he was lying to them, but it was exhausting. If only they would just believe him, but anytime he tried to make himself seem genuine he only ended up looking stupid or guilty.

'The demo was organised by the friends and relatives

of the people that died. It wasn't any organisation. We just did it.'

A wobble was rising in his throat, so many of those people had paid such a huge price for what they did. He took a sip of water and glanced around the room to steady himself. It was a significant improvement on the grey room with the furniture bolted to the floor where his first couple of interviews had taken place. Now, they interviewed him in a room with a window that let in daylight – albeit through thickly frosted glass. And there was a sofa as well as the desk with padded ergonomic chairs where they sat. The camera was no more discreet, though, it was fixed in the top corner of the room and trained on him at all times.

'I don't know what happened,' he exhaled. 'Most of them were detained. I don't know if anyone else got away.'

He put his face in his hands, he hadn't done anything to try and help any of them in the aftermath, his only concern had been saving himself and how he might get rid of Megan. Really, he deserved everything that had happened to him since.

'Alright, Jason,' Pádraig sounded uncomfortable, probably afraid that Jay was going to start crying again, he had already shed far too many tears in front of them.

'We'll break for forty minutes, it's close enough to lunchtime.'

A uniformed man appeared and led Jay to the respite room where they fed him. It didn't make sense they wouldn't let him go out at lunch time when he was free to go every evening and return each morning, and no doubt they tracked his every movement on the phone they had given him. He had taken to leaving it at the safehouse when he went to Sandymount, though it was risky, but the amount of time he spent with the Brethren might look suspicious and he didn't relish his chances of convincing them that he went there for no other reason than to distract him from his racing thoughts. Perhaps they worried he might have secreted something away during the interview that he could pass onto the outside world if he was let out midway through the day? But he could just as easily do that in the evening if he wanted to. Either way he wasn't going to ask, he kept his thoughts to himself and tried to stay on the right side of everyone.

A screen displaying a muted news channel with running subtitles mimed to itself on the wall and a couple of sofas squatted beside a low table which was scattered with mostly inane publications. It was comfortable enough, it reminded him a little bit of a doctors' waiting room, aside from the cameras that watched over every millimetre of the space. How many hours of his life must he have spent in there already? He slipped off his shoes and settled himself cross-legged on the sofa and picked up the tray that had been left for him. Chewing cautiously at a wrap with an unidentifiable filling, he thumbed his phone for a distraction.

Occasionally he picked up a Gaelic/English dictionary and tried to learn something, but even when he could remember some of the words he found it almost impossible to understand how they should be pronounced, B's and H's danced in front of his eyes like bubbles that popped in the air as soon as he tried to enunciate them. More recently, he practiced Spanish and sometimes he caught Megan in between classes and they exchanged messages for a while. Other times he did press-ups or sit-ups on the floor, desperately trying to disrupt the deadening impact of sitting and talking for hours and hours on end.

At least they had been positive about him going to Spain with Megan, agreeing it would be wise for him to keep a low profile and a safe distance for a while when he was naturalised as a full citizen. They didn't seem to think he would be a target in the long term, the whole political and economic system in England was far too precarious to use up time and resources chasing him indefinitely. If only they were right and something or someone much more significant turned up so he could fade into a distant irrelevance.

He swallowed, whatever he was eating was cold and bland, nothing like the food Megan or the Brethren made. His heart skipped in anticipation, Megan had invited him for a picnic later and a little voice inside him kept whispering that was something she did with her boyfriend. He fumbled with his phone, with any luck all of this would be over by the beginning of October and he would finally be free to leave with her.

Megan spread the blanket on the ground and began to unpack the picnic bag, she was early, excited to see him and share her news. The Iveagh Gardens wasn't the ideal backdrop for what she had to tell him, it had been restored to its austere Victorian formality and didn't fit her mood at all but at least it was shady. She rearranged the tubs of salads and pies twice more and then settled herself to wait.

Eventually, she saw him turn through the gate and scan the park for her.

She waved, 'Jay, estoy aqui!'

He grinned and trotted towards her, dropping to his knees beside her and elaborately kissing her on both cheeks. 'Hola, que tal?'

'Muy bien gracias,' she grinned. 'Muy, muy bien!' She pulled him into a hug.

He pulled back and looked at her. 'Verdad, que pasa?'

She was going to run out of words soon. 'Tengo unas … muy bien … Ugh! You win!' she laughed.

'Por supuesto!' he grinned.

She punched him lightly on the shoulder. 'Enough!'

'No lo creo,' he shrugged, trying to overlay his delight with a contrived European nonchalance.

'Ah! No me gustas!' she laughed, lifting her hands to playfully push him away.

He raised his hands in mock defence and their palms met. Instinctively their fingers interlaced and they were smiling into each other's eyes. Silence cloaked them and the space between them was shrinking. Jay's expression was changing and her heart was accelerating. Then he dropped her hands like hot coals and sat back on his heels.

He raised his palms in simulated surrender and forced

a laugh. 'You win this time.'

Megan turned to open the tubs of food, trying to ignore the twisting knot in the pit of her belly.

'So, tell me your news,' Jay smiled between mouthfuls.

The fizz of joy returned. 'I've been commissioned to write a book! The *Irish Times* want me to produce a book based on the articles I have been writing. And they are paying me an advance! I'm getting paid to write a book!'

She knew she was gushing but this was one of the best things that had ever happened to her and she wanted to share it with him.

'It solves another problem as well!'

Jay looked confused.

'The car! I've probably got enough to buy us a car, so we don't have to go to Spain in the Skoda. We can get something here, with Irish plates, it will be much safer, and electric as well.'

Jay didn't want to crush her dreams, but when she told him how much her advance amounted to, it was obvious the kind of car they could get, even second hand, would barely accommodate both of them and her chair, let alone anything else they needed to take.

'You're right,' he said as gently as he could. 'A different car would make things much easier and safer, but I don't think it's a good idea Megan.'

'Why not?' she looked perplexed.

He took a deep breath. 'It would still be a struggle to afford the kind of car we would need even if we used up all of your advance,' he sighed. 'And it doesn't seem right to spend all your money on something you won't be able to use yourself, you've already had to postpone starting your degree, you shouldn't keep having things taken off you before you've even started. It's not right.'

Her eyes looked damp and his heart twisted, upsetting her was the last thing he wanted to do. He thought about taking her hand, but after what had already nearly happened it was best not to.

Instead, he tried to reassure her. 'You said yourself we are probably going to need a bit more than our combined UBI payments whilst we are away since we are going to have to pay for accommodation as well as our day-to-day living costs.'

'You said you would be able to work,' she snapped back.

There was no ambiguity in her expression now, she thought he was being selfish, he wanted her money to make his life easy.

'And I will!'

It came out louder than he intended, but he couldn't bear her thinking he was trying to freeload off her – he had depended on her far too much already.

'Of course I will,' he said more quietly but still firmly. 'And you will be able to write, that's the most important thing.'

This time he reached over and squeezed her hand before he could stop himself.

'I'm really happy for you, it's amazing news and you deserve it.'

Her eyes softened and his heart unknotted.

'Thank you,' she smiled. 'I just can't believe it's real, it's like all my dreams are coming true.'

Then her face clouded. 'I'm sorry, I didn't mean—' she stopped.

Sometimes her train of thoughts were as hard to follow as the guys from the department.

She reached over and took his hands in hers, the callouses on her palms gently chafing his skin.

'You know if there is anything I can do, you only have to say the word.'

He shook his head, still not understanding.

'I could contact your family, let them know you are alright?'

Every time he thought of his parents it felt as if his lungs couldn't take in air. What had he done to them? He had destroyed their lives and everything they had worked for. It made him want to scrunch himself into a ball and disappear. He felt Megan's hand move to his knee and looked up, her eyes were so earnest and tender, he closed his lids and breathed in her sweetness.

'I, I—' he opened his eyes and looked away.

Part of him longed to say yes. It would be such a relief to get some kind of message to them. All he had offered was a two-word apology before he had destroyed his phone. He had no idea how they were, what they knew, or if they had been interrogated and accused of conspiring with him. Just a simple message to tell them he loved them and that he was sorry would make such a difference. But what risk was that? What would happen if they received a message from him? And what would they do? Might they report Megan, leading the authorities to her as a trade-off for leniency for him? Did they know he and Megan had come to Dublin together?

'I can't ask you to do that, it's not safe, but thank you.'

He looked away and swallowed, he spent most of his time fighting back tears these days, he was a total wreck.

'I'm sorry,' Megan murmured, she leaned over and pulled him into a hug.

He folded his arms around her, breathing in the scent of her hair and her skin, it was the worst comfort possible.

Dusk was setting in as he walked Megan to the tram stop. He was being clingy, wanting to squeeze out every last moment of his time with her, it was pathetic really, but he couldn't help himself. He wanted to wait with her until her tram arrived, to watch her board and then hold on for the very last glimpse of her red hair as she was drawn away from him along the thin metal tracks.

'I'd better get going,' it was an enormous effort to leave.

'Okay.'

Megan opened her arms, enfolding him in a tight a hug and he leaned in closer, relishing the conviction of her embrace. And there it was again, that feeling, that knowing. Just one small movement from her would transform it from a friendly hug into an intimate embrace. His heart accelerated, was it really happening?

Was this what the moment in the park was leading to? All it would take was one tilt of her head or shift of her body to tell him what he longed for. He kept breathing, his heart pounding against her, willing her body to invite him in. Then he broke away, he had to stop doing this to himself, torturing himself with something that could not be. She was with Aman and, Spain or not, it was obvious they were besotted with each other. And after all the mistakes he had made, after all the things he had thought and felt, well, Megan was hardly going to consider him was she?

'See you soon,' he said, part question, part plea, part statement of truth.

Even if they didn't see each other again until the day they left, that was still relatively soon.

Megan smiled and nodded and he forced himself away. He would walk to Sandymount stomping some of these stupid, pointless feelings out through his feet. Except he didn't really want to, he didn't really want not to love her. Loving Megan felt like what he was meant to do whether or not she ever requited it. And loving her meant there was always that delicious, excruciating slither of hope that one day she might feel just a little bit for him of what he did for her.

Chapter 46

By the time he crossed the driveway to house three he had managed to divert his thoughts to something that was only indirectly about Megan. Had he been too hasty to dismiss her suggestion of using her advance to buy a car? After all, it would make their lives a lot easier.

Peter waylaid him before he reached the door.

'It's all done,' he said, looking pleased with himself.

Jay raised an eyebrow in question, pulling his attention back into the present.

'The engine. Its finished. It will run off regular vegetable oil now; no need to worry about diesel – bio or otherwise.'

Had Peter completely lost his mind, it wasn't really possible to run a car off vegetable oil, was it?

'It's a great car,' Peter continued.

Jay looked at the Skoda, that certainly wasn't how he would describe it.

'Really?' he said trying not to sound too sceptical.

'Yes, it has very low mileage and mechanically it has been very well maintained. The body work is a bit of a mess but there's years of use left in it.'

'Really?' Jay said again.

Perhaps they could go to Spain in it, after all. Except it would make them very conspicuous, driving around in an ancient car with English plates and an exhaust that smelled like fried vegetables.

Aoife appeared from the kitchen and hovered in the background. Seeing her and Peter in close proximity pushed the possibility of them as a couple into his mind. They could be a good match, they were close in age and both of them were kind and down to earth. Had they ever moved in that direction? Except, if it wasn't for where they were, Jay's instincts would have told him that Peter was gay. It wasn't anything obvious, not like the vibes he got from Aoife, but there was something about him, something that made him certain neither Aoife nor any of the female Brethren would ever interest him. Although, why a gay man would join a group who believed same sex relationships were a sin was another question.

Peter was still chatting happily about the Skoda, eulogising about specifications that turned to fog in Jay's mind – perhaps cars were Peter's real love after all.

'I have a contact in Cannonbridge, not far northeast of Portpatrick, who can fix the main problem.'

What problem? A minute ago Peter had been reassuring him the car was in excellent condition.

'He can make up a set of CU plates for the car, either Irish or Scottish.'

Now it made a bit more sense, well in some ways.

'Isn't that a bit risky? Re-registering it is going to

make it very obvious where I am.'

'Oh no,' Peter smiled indulgently. 'No one will ever know about it.'

All sense was lost again, the epitome of life with the Brethren.

Peter must have read his confusion. 'He can create a set of plates and hack them into the system so they show up as legitimate.'

'Are you sure? Isn't that err…' He needed a word other than illegal, 'erm, dangerous?'

'I'm more than sure. He's helped us out before when there have been problems with some of the car registrations.'

Jay tried not to look shocked, were some of their cars stolen? It was hard to imagine any of the white-clad Brethren as car thieves, although nothing about them really surprised him anymore. Even so, how they reconciled car theft, hacking, and fraudulent registration plates with their notions of sin was beyond him. Perhaps they thought their dodgy dealings were all part of God's plan – after all, God's will seemed to align with earthly agendas with convenient regularity. But he kept his mouth shut, it would be stupid to piss Peter off with too many questions, especially when this could solve his and Megan's problems *and* they were helping him without expecting anything in return. Perhaps they thought that was God's will too, another part of the divine mystery unfolding? Whatever they were thinking, he needed to stay on their right side.

A jolt of recognition at his own moral flexibility

arrested his train of thought. Perhaps he was more like them than he cared to admit: as long as the outcome fitted his agenda then he could justify the means. Was that what they saw in him? Were they right? Did everyone know him so much better than he knew himself? And did that mean Megan knew how he felt? And if she did, did it increase or decrease the possibility of her ever reciprocating? And how come, whatever he was thinking about, he always came back to Megan? The thoughts were hammering through his mind like the express train to crazy, he had to stop thinking like this.

Peter was still talking about the car so he arranged his face into a grateful, interested expression.

'We'll do the journey all in one, just before you leave. That way, even if someone does try and put a trace on the new plates you'll be on the boat before it is completed.'

Jay nodded, trying to keep up.

'If we leave early enough in the morning we can get over to Cannonbridge, get the plates sorted and come back overnight in plenty of time for you to drive down to Rosslaire for your boat.'

'I don't think Jay should go to Scotland,' Aoife piped up. 'That's not very safe for him.'

Peter looked at Jay. 'You have Irish ID, don't you?'

Jay nodded again.

'It will be fine, then.'

Peter looked at Aoife, his smile gone. 'I don't see any risk. And we'll need two of us to share the driving.'

Jay forced a smile in agreement, it was the least he

could do.

'You could take someone else to drive,' Aoife persisted.

Her worry was seeping into his veins, but he could hardly refuse to go, it was his car after all.

'I'm sure it will be fine,' he said as confidently as he could.

Peter looked satisfied. 'We'll only be gone for twenty-four hours at the most, we will be perfectly safe.'

Peter looked at Aoife again with an authority in his gaze that he had never directed at Jay, and which completely unravelled any illusion of the two of them together, Peter's desires aside.

'God wants Jay to go to Spain and we have to play our part in making that happen.'

Aoife's face constricted, but she didn't say anything, she just turned and went back into the kitchen. Megan or Silvie would have stayed and argued the point, after all God could just as easily have not wanted Jay to go to Scotland, but Aoife seemed used to being overruled, it was sad she had so little fight in her.

Chapter 47

Megan steered the handcycle out of the Pearse Street gate and turned right in the direction of the Grand Canal Docks, it was only a few days until they left. Still, her heart lifted the moment she spotted him waiting for her on the corner. He was dressed in expensive-looking running vest, shorts, and trainers – remnants of his former life, the luxuries he had taken for granted and would probably never be within his grasp again. He smiled and moved towards her removing his sunglasses as he leant down and kissed her on the cheek and then hugged her. When had he started doing that: kissing her as well as giving her a hug when they met and parted? It had become the norm and she liked it despite the way his beard prickled against her skin, it felt good him being that close to her.

'Come on, then,' she smiled. 'Let's get moving!'

'Right,' he said and pointed down Pearse Street.

They set off along the same route she had taken the first time she had gone to see his strange new life for herself. They kept to the edge of the road, him running on the inside of her, while she adjusted her speed to keep pace with him. It was Sunday morning and the only other signs of life were a smattering of other cyclists and runners. This had been her idea, cycling with Aman had made her realise she could share Jay's runs, and it was important to show him she could do all of the things he could, albeit in a different way. The last thing she wanted was them going to Spain together with him imagining she would be dependent on him like she had been in his flat.

He was fast, she nudged up the power assist so she could easily keep pace. He was breathing too heavily to talk, but every now and then he looked at her and smiled or pointed in the direction of the next road they would take.

Jay smiled across at Megan. Her hair was tied up in a high ponytail on top of her head, the length of it swinging behind her like threads of polished amber. He imagined it falling loose around her bare shoulders and him stroking it over her soft pale skin. He pushed the thoughts away, pounding the pavement with his feet.

He was working hard, running faster than his normal pace. It was stupid, trying to impress her, but he couldn't help it, and running with her was turning out to be much more enjoyable than he had expected. Normally he ran alone, it was his time to straighten out his head and to be by himself. So he had surprised himself with how readily he had accepted her suggestion. It was effortless, they fit together in a way which felt natural, easy. Surely that had to mean something? And there it was again, that nagging hope, always on the prowl for any sign something more than friendship might be possible.

Sweat damped his back and his hair was clinging to the back of his neck. Megan looked unflustered, it was unlikely he would be able to maintain this pace for the whole route, but he pushed himself on.

Megan could feel the familiar heat in her biceps. Her muscles had become more defined from cycling regularly and she loved the feeling of her body powering her along as Jay's feet hit the tarmac beside her. For a moment her heart swelled at his presence, the sense of belonging with him, then she thought of Aman and a shard of pain cut through. It was going to be beyond terrible saying goodbye to him, something very special had begun to grow between them and it was unfathomably cruel that it had to end before they had even had a proper chance. He was beautiful in every way and he stole a little bit more of her heart with each passing day. And yet, at the same time, they had both been weirdly rational about their approaching end: they would stay in touch, but they knew it would be hopeless to try and stay together when they didn't know how long she would be gone and he had no way to be with her. They had talked about it all day in the hospital and then over and over again in the days that followed, talking and having sex. It didn't make sense, they were discussing her leaving, planning the end of their relationship, and then binding their bodies back together again and again. But Aman was her first and would always be, even if they were never together again he would hold that eternal place in her heart.

They turned along Sandymount Strand and the Brethren came into view gathered at the sea defence. Jay raised a hand in greeting as they passed and one or two nodded discretely in acknowledgement, but most remained absorbed in their prayers. At least no-one had a hammer to the sea wall today. Jay indicated to turn right onto Trimleston Avenue, his skin was glistening and he was breathing hard; a different scenario sprung into her mind and her stomach lurched. At least she was already flushed from cycling so it wasn't obvious, but she should absolutely not be thinking like that. She had worked so hard to starve all that ridiculous longing out of existence, certain that when she stopped feeding it with her stupid dreams and fantasies, and when her heart was overflowing with feelings for Aman, it must have surely shrivelled and died. It must be the prospect of leaving Aman which was sending her off kilter.

Jay indicated a couple more turns and they were in the grounds of an old golf club. Much of the land seemed to have been requisitioned for growing food, but other parts had been left as untamed wilderness. The rationale was hard to decipher from its current state as it receded into scrubland. A gentle breeze picked up scattering a fine dust over them and Jay lifted his vest to wipe the haze that clung to his damp skin. Megan averted her eyes, she would not look at him like that.

After the golf club they crossed the Dodder and continued onto Leeson St, they were close to Trinity now and Jay looked fit to burst. Finally, they reached their finishing point just inside the campus. Jay was panting and dripping perspiration, resting his hands onto his knees he looked across at her.

'You haven't even broken into a sweat,' he gasped.

She grinned, 'I thought that was just the warm-up!'

He laughed through lungful's of air.

'I was using e-assist some of the time.'

'That's cheating!' he spluttered in mock indignation, lifting his vest again to wipe his face and neck.

Megan turned, reaching into the bag on the back of her chair for a bottle of water.

'You should do it all over again without the power!' he joked.

'Only if you come with me.'

She took a slug from the bottle and offered it to him.

'No chance,' he smiled, panting and gulping at the water.

'Do you want to come back to mine for breakfast?'

She hadn't planned it, but all of a sudden she didn't want him to go, not just yet.

He looked like he was about to accept but then he said, 'I need a shower, I can't go anywhere like this.'

'You can do that at mine, most of your things are there already.'

Jay didn't need to be asked twice, every moment with Megan was precious, even though they would soon be inseparable. Recently, and without discussing it, they had slipped into being much less vigilant about where they spent time together. Now he had his citizenship and their departure was imminent, it was as if the embrace of safety had reached forward from Spain and wrapped itself around them. Even so, he hadn't told Megan about the drive to Scotland yet, everything had been feeling so good lately he didn't want it disrupted by the Brethren's plan which was sure to make her worried and suspicious.

Megan returned the handcycle and he sweated self-consciously beside her on the tram, diving gratefully into the shower as soon as they arrived at her flat. The smell of cooking enveloped him as soon as he opened the bathroom door, and the moment he sat down she presented him with a breakfast of spelt pancakes stuffed with berries, cashew cream, and sprinkled with coconut. She radiated in his enjoyment of her food, relishing his surprise and delight at the new tastes and textures she offered him. It was a sensual pleasure they could share. And, despite the disparities of their previous lives, she still frequently managed to find things that were completely new to him.

Jay moved her laptop from the table to make space for the tray.

'Are you still planning to take this old thing?' he asked.

He had already hinted she should get something more up-to-date to write her book, but she hadn't seemed interested.

'I had this when I was in Bootle Cares,' she replied. 'It's poetic justice to write the book on it. And Silvie gave it to me, I owe it to her.'

'You're right,' he smiled gently. 'I remember how tightly you held on to it when we drove down from

Larne. Of course you should use it for the book: it has been with you on your whole journey.'

He grinned, 'And then maybe you should put in a museum!'

But Megan remained serious.

'I owe it to you, as well – my freedom.'

She placed her hand over his, if only she would keep it there forever.

'You don't owe me anything,' he said softly.

She held his gaze; he could drown in those eyes. He had to say it, to tell her he loved her, the words were in his mouth ready to spill out and it felt so right. Then the gut-wrenching fear resurfaced, telling her could ruin everything, they were so close to going away together and he could destroy it all if he wasn't careful. He mustn't ruin their special friendship by invading it with his desire. She had told him how sex had been used against her before, and he would rather die than do anything that made her feel like that again. The truth was he had to settle for what they had and keep his feelings in check.

He placed his other hand over hers for a moment and then lifted it away.

'Really,' he said. 'You are never in debt to me.'

He looked down and busied himself with eating, hoping she didn't notice the tears close behind his eyes.

Chapter 48

Change of plan, the message read. *I'll be over in a couple of hours.*

Megan frowned, that was cutting it really tight and they shouldn't be changing the plans again at this late stage. She should have been more insistent about going to Scotland with them or, better still, Jay not going at all, either way she wouldn't have let them start gambling with time like this. What were they thinking?

What's happening? she messaged, not bothering to dress up her annoyance with niceties.

It's a surprise!

His light heartedness was even more irking.

Tell me.

I'll show you in a bit. I'll come over at ten.

He obviously wasn't going to be drawn, and it wasn't even nine o'clock yet. Sighing the irritation out of her chest she turned and picked up her gym bag, at least she could go and work off some of her annoyance until he finally told her what he was doing.

It was ten-thirty when he messaged again. *I'm outside. Come down.*

He was waiting by the main entrance as she exited the block, the beard was gone.

'Come here.'

He indicated for her to follow him across the road, reaching out, almost as if he was going to take her hand, but then he pointed in the direction of the parking bay.

'Come and look. This is ours! Well,' he corrected himself, 'Actually, it's yours.'

She followed him across the road and he stopped, grinning, beside a white van with a colourful BGW logo painted on the side. She looked from Jay to the van and back again, not sure which surprised her most, him or the God-wagon he was clearly delighted with. He looked so much lighter than he had done in a long time, partly because the beard had gone, taking a few years off him, and his hair had grown quickly, too. He tucked it behind his ear, causing a little pulse in her heart. She liked him much better like that – although she wasn't supposed to like him in that way at all. Anyway, it wasn't just how he looked, there was something else as well, a shift in his energy. His frown was gone and there was a puppy-like quality to his anticipation of her response.

'What's going on, where is the Skoda?'

'Peter's on his way to Scotland with it to get the plates swapped. They've given us this instead.'

'What are you talking about?'

'The van. It's ours, well, it's registered in your name. They did a straight swap with the Skoda. Peter is really enamoured with it for some reason, something to do with the engine and being self-sufficient in vegetable oil.' He shrugged. 'It seems to me like we got a really good deal, it's only a few years old and it's electric so it's going to be much easier than trying to find fuel.'

He moved to the back and opened the doors.

'And there's loads of space for your chair and everything we need to take with us. We might even be able to camp in it if we need to.'

It was pristine, whatever else about the Brethren, they certainly knew how to look after things – not like whoever had previously owned the Skoda.

'Really? This is not some kind of joke?'

'Of course not,' he reached out and touched her cheek, his expression suddenly serious. 'You know I wouldn't joke about something as important as this.'

The air thickened between them.

He took his hand away but imprint of his fingers tingled on her skin. Tears rose behind her eyes and she looked away. But it was too late, he had noticed, and he wrapped her up in a warm hug.

'Are you alright?' he asked into her hair.

She nodded against his shoulder, his body was firm and comforting.

'Yes, I'm sorry,' she pulled herself away, wiping her face with her hands.

'I didn't mean to cry,' she smiled apologetically. 'I don't even know why I am crying.'

'You don't have to say sorry,' he smiled tenderly at her. 'Let's go inside and talk.'

Talking was the last thing she needed right now, and she definitely didn't want the added confusion of him being all caring and attentive, it was easier when she was annoyed with him.

She led him inside the flat, steering the conversation back towards their plans while she made coffee. But after they had double- and triple-checked their bags and the route to Rosslaire, there was nothing else to do. Just the two of them in the flat together made her acutely aware of Jay's presence, as if the dial had been turned up on her senses.

'Let's go out,' she suggested. 'One last drive around Dublin.'

It was impossible not to notice people glancing at the van as they drove, their expressions somewhere between pity and contempt. Parking up seemed much less inviting when they were attracting that kind of attention and Jay must have felt it too be because he began to head back towards the sea defence where the van would be in home territory. The road was quiet and Jay pulled over and looked at her.

'Do you want to try driving?'

Uncertainty crept under her skin, he wouldn't mock her, would he? She studied him, it was like the first time Aman had asked her if she wanted to cycle.

'It's really easy,' he reassured her. 'It's mostly hand controls and if you use both feet together on the pedals you should have enough power to do it.'

A warmth spread in the pit of her belly, she had never imagined he paid much attention to what she might be capable of. Most of her life she had been underestimated, especially by him, but it felt like he could really see her now. And it mattered, especially in the open wound of having said goodbye to Aman.

'Go on,' Jay encouraged. 'You should try.'

A thrill of anticipation pushed the other feelings away. 'Alright, I will!'

Jay checked behind him and jumped out of the van and ran round to the passenger door while she moved herself across onto the driver's seat.

When he was inside with the door closed she held his eyes. 'Are you sure? We might both be going to Spain in wheelchairs after this!'

He laughed. 'It's fine, there's no-one around and you're not going to do any damage so long as you steer away from the sea wall – although, if you do knock a chunk out of it the Brethren will probably canonise you!'

They were smiling into each other's eyes again, and there was something pulling taught between them, but Jay quickly looked away and began describing the controls to her.

When she was confident she understood what everything did, she pushed the gear stick into drive, released the parking brake, and pressed down on the accelerator with both her feet. The van inched forward. Channelling everything she had in her legs she pressed a little harder and the van moved smoothly along the road. A giggle of delight bubbled from her chest, she glanced over at Jay, he was smiling at her with an expression she couldn't quite read. Was it pride? Or was that what she was feeling? It was so much to absorb, she was in Ireland, driving a van that apparently she owned with Jay beside her smiling and encouraging her onwards. Her heart was broken and yet there was a small but unmistakeable stirring inside her.

When she had driven as far as the faded roundabout her legs were full of tremors and weren't going to hold out much longer. She turned a messy circle and headed back in the direction they had come. Thankfully the old petrol station was in sight and she drew the van to a halt on the weed infested tarmac. By the time she had double checked the parking brake and made sure the engine was off, her legs were shaking uncontrollably.

Rubbing her thighs to quiet the jittering, she turned to Jay. 'That was wild, and you are completely mad!'

He beamed at her, he seemed illuminated from the inside by something that he wasn't sharing.

'I knew you could do it!'

He leant over and kissed her cheek and then jumped out of the van and ran round to take driver's seat.

As he pulled out onto the road she glanced across at him. She was going to have to be very vigilant around him, the more he touched her, the more he reignited those old feelings. How could it be happening again? They were so close to going away together and her heart was broken for Aman. Was it possible to love more than one person at the same time? And if he tried to kiss her again was she strong enough to resist him? But she must for all of their sakes: hers, Silvie, his. She would not let herself succumb to being some kind of pathetic substitute for her dead sister. It would be hard, but she would make herself. She had lived through so much already she was strong enough not to give in – they would go to Spain as friends and it would stay that way.

Jay took an unfamiliar route back to her flat, trundling slowly along Ailesbury road so they could take in what had once been the most expensive street in Dublin. Huge, ornate houses that were once embassies and diplomat's residences had been requisitioned for the post-melt world and converted into multi-occupancy dwellings to accommodate the quays and Rings End residents when their homes had been submerged – in a few more years they might be moving westwards again.

At the next junction, he turned onto Stillorgan road and then through Ranelagh and onto the canal past the tram line. She had not even been living here six months and yet her life was unrecognisable, nothing she or Silvie could have dreamt up came anywhere near this. Her block came into view and Jay turned right over the canal. She committed every detail to memory, holding onto every last moment in Dublin, the place that had changed her life forever.

Chapter 49

Jay lingered for as long as he could at Megan's flat, rechecking their bags and talking through their plans for the millionth time. But it was obvious he had to leave, there was no reason for him to be there, and Megan must be spending her last night in Dublin with Aman. Despite how much he hated the thought of it, he had to get out of the way. He meandered back through the city, revisiting their first journey through the hospital and onto James' street. But it was too difficult to try and reconcile how much his life had changed since then.

He skirted Trinity and the reconstructed Quays and then followed the remaining flank of Ringsend back to the familiar territory along the sea defence. At least he would spend his last night with the Brethren rather than alone in the safe house with his mind in freefall. Then, in the morning, he would drop off the keys before he collected Megan, that way Aman should be well and truly gone and he wouldn't have to witness the hellscape of their last goodbye.

The Martello Tower came into view and the familiar warm cloak of home spread around him. A small, leaden cloud hung low over the white painted houses, very low. Not a cloud, a plume of smoke: a plume of grey rising from a bright crackle of orange, rolling upwards into the sky. Instinctively, he jammed his foot on the accelerator, his mind fighting what his eyes told him.

There was someone running up the middle of the road towards him, white clothes turned grey with soot, arms waving, face distorted with ash and fear. It was Aoife. He slammed on the brakes and jumped out of the van. She ran straight into him, her arms extended, pushing him back into the van.

'Go! You've got to go!' she panted. 'They got Peter with the car just after the bridge. He told them he left you in Belfast but they're here looking for you.'

Jay struggled for words, Peter had lied for him.

'The fire?' he managed to stutter.

'We're all okay,' Aoife was a little calmer now. 'Help is coming.'

Did she mean real help? Surely they were not depending on divine intervention to put out a fire, especially not in this arid heat. Their eyes locked, only a thin rim of green was visible around the distended orbs of her pupils. She was still catching her breath.

She laid a palm against his cheek.

'Go,' she said more softly now. 'You were not meant for us.'

Her eyes misted and she blinked hard, but a tear escaped, forming a track in the dirt on her cheek. She wiped her face with the back of her hand and looked away.

Jay reached out and took her hand and she turned back to him.

'Thank you,' he said and leant forward and kissed her forehead.

She smiled with such sadness that his own eyes prickled with tears.

'You need to go,' she repeated, the urgency returning to her voice.

She held the door whilst he climbed into the van and then closed it quietly behind him. 'Goodbye, Jay, God bless you.'

He turned the van around and Aoife jogged back up the road towards the burning houses.

He was still shaking when he parked the van under some trees in Phoenix Park. Part of him wanted to go back and help. But what could he do? They needed a fire engine, water. He skimmed his phone for local news. Finally he found something: fire crews had been called to a blaze in Sandymount. At least they had got some help, at least the world was still decent enough for that.

He messaged Megan and waited, but nothing came back. Her phone was probably the last thing on her mind right now. All the energy drained from his body and he leaned forward, resting his arms on the steering wheel and laying his head against them. A shard of pain split the centre of his chest. He took a deep breath and a crescendo of tears unleashed from the pit of his being and he sobbed until he had nothing left inside.

Dusk was drawing in when he finally opened his eyes. If no-one had found him by now it was safe enough to leave the van here for the night. He wiped his face in his hands and checked himself in the rear-view mirror, he looked less of a wreck than he felt. Locking the van he checked his phone again but there was still nothing from Megan. Trudging slowly through the park in the direction of the safe house, his body was full of lead. Perhaps he had finally reached his limit, perhaps this was the sum of what he could endure and keep going, perhaps he really couldn't take anymore. He stopped. Was this it? Did he really have nothing left? After everything he had seen and everything he knew?

No, he took a deep breath and forced himself into a sprint, pelting through the darkening landscape as if he could outrun the burning houses, Aoife's eyes, Megan in Aman's arms, his forsaken family, and the molten cauldron of pain and hope and loss that churned relentlessly inside him.

Chapter 50

With the keys returned he was now officially homeless again, it was a small comfort that at least he wasn't also stateless again this time. He climbed into the van picking up his phone to message Megan, he still hadn't heard back from her since yesterday and it was impossible not to worry. Even if she was with Aman, surely she would have looked at her phone at least once in the last sixteen hours? It might be better to call her, instead. He pressed his fingers to the screen and was answered by a feint buzzing in the back of the van – spinning round he could see her phone lit up and vibrating on the floor by the wheel arch. He dropped the call and clambered into the back and picked it up: *Eight new messages.* All his? His thumb hovered, she might not have changed the password since he set it up. He swallowed and then gently tossed the phone onto the passenger seat, he wasn't going to start their time together like that.

Megan pressed the door release and flew into the corridor, flinging her arms around him as soon as he emerged from the lift.

'I was so worried about you, I saw the news this morning and I couldn't find—'

'This?' Jay offered her phone.

Megan smiled and untangled herself from his waist so he could lean down and hug her properly. She held him tight and then took his hand and led him to the flat. It was only when she let go to open the door she realised how natural it felt to move along with him like that, how much he had attuned to her, falling into step at her side as easily as Aman. It made her want to take his hand again, but she pointed him towards the sofa and went to boil the kettle.

'What happened? Was anyone hurt?'

'I don't know, I don't think so.'

He looked shaken, she moved over and touched his arm, when he looked up at her his eyes were damp.

'I just saw the fire and Aoife running up the road. She told me Peter had been caught and they were looking for me.' He swallowed. 'I think they were trying to burn me out of the house.'

She leaned forward and held him for a moment.

'We just need to go.'

His voice was flat, fearful, but he was right, they should leave. She switched off the kettle and unplugged the last few electricals in the flat, circling around checking everything one more time while Jay took the bags to the van. This was it, goodbye to the new life she had barely begun, she was leaving and had no idea when she would be back. Fear threaded through her veins, accelerating her heart. Was she afraid that by leaving her home so soon she might lose it? But it wasn't that, she had an indefinite tenancy and her rent allowance would continue even in her absence. Perhaps it was leaving Aman, but the worst of that was done, they had said their last goodbyes two days before. Maybe it was what had happened to Peter. It didn't feel right they could leave the country whilst Peter paid the price for their escape. Yet it was too late, he was already paying for it. The buzzer sounded. Jay must be getting impatient, was it something to do with him? Perhaps his fear was contagious.

Breathing slowly and focusing she locked the flat and zipped the keys in the pouch under her wheelchair. What might the world be like the next time she was home?

Jay put her wheelchair in the back of the van in silence and then turned the van around to head southwards out of the city, avoiding the coast road until they were well beyond the Sandymount and city limits. Megan twisted in her seat, craning around for a last view of her block and then the familiar landmarks of Dublin as they faded into the distance.

Jay stepped out into the sunlight and looked around the service station forecourt, Megan was nowhere in sight. He walked over to the van in case she had miraculously got herself inside even though it was locked and he had the keys. No sign of her. He went back into the building and checked the shop and the café, nothing. How could he have lost her in such a small place? Surely he hadn't been queueing for coffees for that long? Most likely she was in the bathroom. A little self-conscious he hovered in the corridor by the toilets. The door to the disabled toilet eased open and relief began to spread through his body. But a young man with dark skin and a bright orange shirt wheeled out; not Megan.

Where was she? He felt sick, he shouldn't have left her for a second, they could still try and take her. As quickly as possible without drawing attention to himself, he trotted back to the van. What was he planning to do? A high-speed chase back to Dublin? That was hardly likely, he didn't even know who he was supposed to be chasing.

A splash of hot liquid stung the back of his hand and he slowed down. Reaching the van, he rested the cardboard cup tray on the bonnet of the van and then something caught his attention moving along the far side. Megan; he almost collapsed with relief.

She looked up and smiled, her expression gradually fading as his anxiety registered. She opened her mouth but he spoke first.

'I couldn't find you,' he gasped. 'I thought—'

He stopped, she was doing something to the side of the van.

'What are you doing?'

He moved towards her, as dizzy now with relief as he had been with fear a few second before.

'I know it looks shit,' she said holding up a can of mismatched spray paint and nodding in the direction of a garage across the service road, 'But this was the best I could get.'

She studied him. 'Are you alright?'

He took a deep breath. 'Yes, I just got a bit of a fright when I couldn't find you.'

Part of him wanted to add she shouldn't do anything without telling him first, that he must know where she was at all times, except it would make him sound like her jailor not her friend.

'Sorry,' she gave him a conciliatory smile. 'I wasn't thinking.'

Maybe he was overreacting, he was still skittish after the fire. Was it really only twenty-four hours since he had been light with anticipation, presenting the van to her like an unexpected gift?

Megan moved over and rubbed his back. 'You should have come to mine last night, you shouldn't have been on your own.'

'I wasn't sure if—' he looked at her and couldn't finish the sentence, all he wanted was to wrap his arms around her and never let go.

She was watching him, wating for the end of the sentence.

'It doesn't matter,' he said and smiled and changed the subject. 'I still have no idea what you are doing.'

She looked back at the splotch of grey she had spray painted.

'Well I had to do something, there is absolutely no way we are going to Spain with *Brethren of God's Will* on the side of the van!'

Jay sighed. 'I guess you're right.'

He hadn't even thought about it, it was amazing how

quickly he had got used to their weird ways. A stab of pain jarred him — they were going to have a lot of difficulty maintaining any of their ways now.

'I hope they didn't think we would be spreading the word for them in Europe!' Megan's voice was much lighter than he felt. Whatever their motivation for swapping the van for the car, The Brethren had as good as saved his and Megan's lives. He owed them, they both did.

Megan moved round to the other side of the van and Jay watched as she transformed the multi-coloured logo into another grey blob.

She looked up at him, sensing his mood. 'They didn't really expect us to keep their logos on the van, did they?'

'I honestly don't know.'

'But I guess as far as they are concerned whatever happens is God's will.'

It sounded like a joke as he said it, but for the first time he could feel how comforting it might be to see the world like that, to imagine that everything, including what happened to Peter and the fire were not catastrophic disasters which threatened their very existence, but evidence of a much greater wisdom at work — a divinely orchestrated plan unfolding. He sighed again, glad they had something to sustain them.

Megan continued spraying. 'God moves in mysterious ways, or something like that?'

She shook her head and frowned, as if chasing away a memory.

'Well, not on the side of our van he doesn't!' her

expression lightening.

Jay watched as she completed the grey splodge and replaced the lid on the spray can. The urge to kiss her was suddenly overpowering.

'Here,' he said to distract himself, picking up the carboard container and offering her a coffee. 'Do you want one of these?'

She put the spray can on her lap and took one of the cups in her hands, her fingers grazing his skin and lighting fireworks inside him. Could she feel it too?

He forced his mind away. 'We need to get going in the next fifteen minutes and no more stops if we are going to get to the port in good time. So if there is anything you need, you should get it now.'

Megan took a sip of her coffee, her neon eyes peering up at him over the rim. For a moment he was sure he could see something there, feelings for him he wasn't just wishing into existence, but then she blinked and it was gone.

'Right,' she said handing him back the cup and the can of spray paint. 'I'll just go to the toilet and grab a couple of things, and you can check that there's no more signs of God or any of his brethren anywhere on the van.'

Watching her wheel across the foyer until the doors of the service station swallowed her up, it felt like his whole body was screaming at her to come back, as if every time she moved away from him she ripped another piece of his heart out of his body. He wanted to touch her so much it hurt, but he had to stop, he couldn't keep thinking about her like that. He had messed up with her in so many ways and he could ruin everything if he told her how he felt and what he wanted. But another part of him was so crazy with it that he knew it couldn't all be for nothing, he couldn't feel like this for no reason. Perhaps, in time, she might feel differently, in a few weeks or months she might find her way to liking him, or maybe he would have gotten over this madness by then. And, at least for now, they were friends – and at least Aman was not there with them.

Chapter 51

As soon as they reached the outskirts of Enniscorthy, the traffic ground to a halt. Only one lane was passible and an endless tail of vehicles inched forwards from the other direction. Some of it looked like port traffic, the ferry must have been docked for a while already. Megan glanced across at Jay, he smiled at her but it didn't mask the worry in his eyes. Was he fearing the same thing and just like her not daring to name it – that it was some kind of roadblock to detain them? Was that even possible? Could the people from England that wanted him, or her, come over here and stop up a whole road? They probably could for a while, until the gardaí were alerted and put an end to it. After all, they had already taken Peter and he was Irish, and they had tried to burn Jay out of the houses.

Time sped up on the dashboard clock but they remained gridlocked, check-in at Rosslaire was already open and the van was slowly filling with tension. Their plans were slowly unravelling. They should have travelled down the previous day, they could have found somewhere to stay or even slept in the van if they had to.

It had been stupid to stay in Dublin, messing around with the van, giddy as if they were going on holiday rather than escaping from the state that hated them both. That might have been their last stupid mistake. She looked across at Jay again, he was visibly worried. He noticed her watching him and reached out and squeezed her hand.

'It's all right,' he said, clearly trying to sound more assured than he looked. 'We'll be alright.'

Ten minutes before the ferry was due to depart, Jay tucked the van into the wheelchair parking bay on the car deck and switched off the engine.

He placed his hand over hers and locked eyes. 'We made it; we did it.'

She was sure the space between them was shrinking. She forced herself to turn away, shocked by the power of her response, by how much she wanted him. It was as if it had never gone away. But she was not going to give in to it, she wouldn't let him see her wanting him, she would stay strong.

Jay removed his hand from hers.

'Come on,' she said trying to sound light. 'Let's get our bags and get on board.'

Jay lifted her chair from the back of the van and brought it alongside the passenger door, picking up the two small holdalls they had packed for the boat and locking the van with a flick of the fob.

They weaved their way through the throng of other passengers until they found a door with the number that matched the key they had been given at check-in.

Opening the door, Megan couldn't restrain a burst of laughter. Their cabin was described as wheelchair accessible, but it seemed to have been designed with everything only a few centimetres wider than her chair. She could just pass between the two single beds that took up most of the room and when she slid open the door to the bathroom she laughed again. Her chair fit into it with just enough space to turn ninety degrees to her left to reach the shower seat or right to reach the toilet.

'Palatial,' she declared. 'Almost as good as Bootle Cares!'

Jay threw the bags on the beds and stood behind her, his hand grazed the back of her neck and came to rest on her shoulder, raising goosebumps where he touched her skin. It took effort to repress a shiver of delight and she hoped he couldn't feel her body responding to him. She could feel his breath moving through his body and the scent of his skin and cologne wrapped around her until she felt lightheaded. It had never occurred to her that being with him was going to be this hard, it was only their first day together and yet, here she was, desperately trying to extinguish these silly feelings like they had never gone away. Jay didn't remove his hand and she could feel the heat from her body devouring the space between them.

'Let's go on deck and say goodbye to Ireland,' she said to break the spell.

Turning to move she added, 'I think I'm going to have to go reverse out, there's no way I can turn a full circle in here.'

Jay hopped onto the bed behind him out of her way. 'After you,' he smiled.

They took the lift to the deck and Jay pushed open the heavy door and the wind whipped them, lashing salt and damp across their faces. They moved over to the railing on the starboard side, peering down as the ropes tethering the ferry to the dock were being wound in.

'This is it,' Megan said, but her words were stolen by the wind.

The last of the ropes clunked into the side of the boat and a plume of black rose from the funnel. The water churned beneath them and the boat began to move away from its birth. Jay perched on the life vest store and took her hand as they watched Ireland shrinking very slowly into the distance.

'Megan,' he said eventually, turning so he was facing her and reaching out to touch her cheek.

'No,' she said with all the resolve she had, dropping his hand and pushing back from him.

He leaned forward and took a lock of her hair. 'Please let me te—'

'No,' she said again, turning herself away and wheeling up the deck away from him. Not again. Not now.

A blast of wind caught her and rushed her forward. She shrieked and then laughed despite herself. As the next blast approached she lifted her hands from her wheel rims and let the gust take her almost the full length of the deck. It was like flying, she felt wild and free and exhilarated. She spun around, the moment between them forgotten, her eyes sparking against the wind that pulled her hair in every direction. Jay trotted towards her and she automatically opened her arms for a hug.

Jay could feel his heart breaking. She was so beautiful, she radiated something that worked on him like a drug. He had never felt like this about anyone before, not even Silvie. It was obvious she didn't want him but he couldn't stop himself loving her, he simply couldn't control it. He leaned down into her hug and buried his face in her hair.

'I want you,' he whispered.

Suddenly she was rigid and pushing him away. Her eyes were wet, he didn't know if it was the wind or if she was crying.

'No!' she almost screamed at him. 'No. I am worth something for myself, not just because I remind you of Silvie.' She was definitely crying now. 'You want her not me, and I am worth more than that even if you don't think so!'

Jay sunk to his knees in front of her, longing to bury his face in her thighs.

'Oh God, Megan, that was a different lifetime. Please—'

He felt her about to turn away again so he placed his hand on her wheel rim.

'Please, Megan, just listen to me.'

Another blast of wind caught them, almost throwing him into her lap.

'Megan, I love you. I love you for you.'

It was out now, he had said it.

'Yes, I loved your sister and nothing will alter that, but it feels such a long time ago. Everything has changed since then. *I* have changed since then. This is not about her or anyone else, it's about you. I love you and it's killing me to be so close to you and not to be able to be with you.'

He swallowed hard. 'Please, Megan, just give me a chance.'

He watched her carefully, preparing for his heart to be finally and completely torn apart forever. He couldn't help himself when he was around her, and now he might have ruined everything: he had told her the truth and there was no going back. He swallowed again, not wanting to add his own tears to the mess.

Megan's expression was softening, she was still crying but she was smiling, too. She reached out and touched his face, drawing him closer. He leaned towards her, his body replying to hers before his mind could catch up. As their lips touched the wind turned and whipped her hair across her face and into their mouths. Megan pulled back laughing, her eyes wedded to his. She swept her hair over her head so that it was billowing behind her, then she reached forward, holding his cheek and bringing his mouth to hers, running her fingers through his hair. The boat swayed lightly over the cresting waves as he slid his hands around her waist. Gulls cawed overhead and the wind whipped spray across the deck, sending the other passengers scurrying to the warmth indoors, but he could stay there forever.

Eventually, Megan gently pulled away from him and,

hand outstretched, led him back indoors towards their cabin.

Acknowledgements

First of all, thank you to SRL Publishing without whom *Overspill* would never have travelled beyond my laptop. Thank you to Jo and Nana whose insightful comments on the first draft enabled me to dig deeper and tell the story I imagined. Thank you also to Rose who tirelessly fed back on later drafts until the manuscript was finally ready for the world.

Special love and thanks to Precious and Lovely who have zero interest in this book, but who grew up whilst I was writing it and who are now firmly established as the (feline) heads of household and who never fail to remind me how much better humans must be.

Much love and appreciation to Matt, and Jo again, for friendship and for proving every day that not only is the alternative possible, but it's also very beautiful. It's an absolute privilege to be a part of the Owl and the Lizard community and to see a little part of the ecosystem thriving under your care.

Thank you to everyone at Wheels For Wellbeing for striving to make the world a better place for disabled people and for showing what is possible when disabled people lead the way.

Love and thanks to Trace, whose zest for Liverpool and for life was unrivalled, who brought love into my life, and then left us all far too soon. Heartfelt thanks to Julie for accompanying me with steadfast love, patience, empathy, and humour. Blessings and gratitude to Orlaith, Brid, and Catherine for unwavering enthusiasm for all of my endeavours. Whole-hearted (and bodied) thanks to Mal for surprising me with love and being the best playmate I could have ever wished for.

Finally, thank you to Octavia Butler, Malorie Blackman, and all the other minoritised women writers who have persisted against the odds and gifted the world with the most powerful, prescient, and lifechanging story-telling.

SRL Publishing don't just publish books, we also do our best in keeping this world sustainable. In the UK alone, millions of books are destroyed each year, unsold and unread, due to overproduction and bigger profit margins.

Our business model is inherently sustainable by only printing what we sell. While this means our cost price is much higher, it means we have minimum waste and zero returns. We made a public promise in 2020 to never overprint our books for the sake of profit.

We give back to our planet by calculating the number of trees used for our products so we can then replace them. We also calculate our carbon emissions and support projects which reduce CO2. These same projects also support the United Nations Sustainable Development Goals.

The way we operate means we knowingly waive our profit margins for the sake of the environment. Every book sold via the SRL website plants at least one tree.

To find out more, please visit
www.srlpublishing.co.uk/responsibility